HELL WALKS

A Kaiju Novel

David Dunwoody

ONE

"I've never seen a dead one," Caitlin whispered.

"Me neither," Frank replied. His voice was barely even a whisper, but it carried clear as a trumpet across the vacuum which seemed to have enveloped the group. Was anyone even breathing? Frank sure as hell wasn't, not that he always had a choice. His lungs felt particularly weak in this, April's damp precursor to dawn. There had been little rain lately but the grass was slick with dew and the air moved like oil over bare flesh. It made Frank feel sick. Sicker.

Caitlin was knelt behind a slab of concrete, which had probably once been part of a blast wall. It lay embedded in the earth at a diagonal angle, as if it had been thrown into the air and then dropped, which was very possible, but that had been long ago. Moss stained its surface and gathered inside gaping lightning-bolt cracks.

Frank was about to speak to that, but Caitlin's sister beat him to it. "That wall's not safe. Come over here," Autumn said, beckoning. Her voice was a protective hiss and a bit louder than any of them would have preferred. Frank heard someone that was crouched behind him sigh – probably Dodger, who, if he didn't have a sarcastic comment for everything, made sure at least he was heard. For her part, Caitlin didn't so much as make a face at her older sister. Instead, she moved away from the concrete slab and joined Autumn in the relative shadow of a skeletonized car. Looked like it had been a compact, the kind Frank had once driven to an advertising agency where he wrote dubious copy about fat-free snacks. His mouth watered a bit at the thought of chocolate. God, how long had it been since chocolate was a thing?

"You ever see a dead one?" Caitlin asked Chia.

The old man's face creased in a sort of wincing smile and he shook damp wisps of gray from his forehead. "Never have, sweetheart. Heard of them. Seen pictures, but we always steered clear of the real McCoy." Chia sounded regretful that they'd taken a different course of action this time, but their hand had been forced by...

Well, no sense breaking it down now, Frank thought. There were eight men and women huddled behind a line of blistered dead cars, waiting for dawn to break so that they could welcome the nightmare sight of a dead giant. *"Them's the facts, deputy. Now y'all just settle down. Pretend you're in a pew on a Sunday. Hell, maybe today* is *Sunday."*

After hearing Chia's words, Caitlin seemed a little less eager to see the real McCoy. There was once a time when the nineteen-year-old would likely have had her face in a smartphone and dissociated herself from the terrible tension and wonder that gripped them all. Hell, Frank would have too. As much as he'd always criticized the way that phones seemed to isolate everyone from one another, he'd more often than not preferred that little bubble of seclusion, especially in a waiting room, an elevator, bus, or Thanksgiving. That infrastructure, as far as he knew, was gone now. The only news and information came either from direct experience, or from the reports of other nomads they passed in the dark. Those reports were about as trustworthy as Frank's ad copy. *If a microwave cheeseburger that will help whip you into bikini shape sounds too good to be true, just stop thinking!*

He supposed he'd been a professional liar back then. The stakes were different now. There wasn't such a thing as a little fib anymore. There weren't even fairy tales. There were only awful realities. The dragons were here now.

The edge of the sky on the eastern horizon bled a dark blue ichor. Dawn would be here before they knew it. From that point, the plan was to identify the location of the rumored fallen monster and give a generous berth as they continued east. From then on? South, maybe. South was usually good. Especially considering they were currently in the Midwest, where nearly any direction was good so long as it led away. This was Missouri, to be specific – Frank was pretty sure the pile of rubble they sat in at present had once been the city of Independence. To think they'd ventured this far into the hottest of hot zones, and all based on what someone had dared call a simple fib. However, this was no time for ruminating. The blue was spreading across the sky and soon they would see.

Frank sat on his butt in the road and glanced past Chia, their de facto leader, to the group's two newest additions. It was too soon yet to tell whether these would become permanent members or just drift away. Frank suspected the former. The kid, a seventeen-year-old called Duckie, was clearly disabled. There was nothing about his appearance that suggested it – he was only as disheveled and frail as the rest of them – but it had been his blaring exuberance when he'd run at them yelling, *"We seen a Little One that's dead! It's right up there and it's dead!"*

This had been the previous evening. The kid had emerged from a crumbling auto dealership just as the group was walking past it, and God how he'd been hollering. It was as if it were the greatest thing in the world that a Little One lay just a few miles ahead.

Quebra was the only armed member of the group and he'd drawn a bead on the kid immediately. The kid was frozen, face slackening, bewildered, and perhaps dismayed at the reaction. The rest of the group, Frank included, had just stared.

"You're a little too excited, son," Quebra had said in his flat tone of authority. His stance rigid, he'd followed Duckie in his sights as the kid wavered from side to side, face ashen.

"You sick?" Quebra called. It seemed the only reasonable explanation for running blind at the group of strangers, for yelling at the top of one's lungs. Kid had to be infected.

Duckie had said, "Yes," almost shamefully, hands falling at his sides.

At that moment, Quebra was training an AR-15 on the kid. Frank remembered watching Quebra's tensed forearms, the only part of him not swathed in camouflage. He remembered wondering if the soldier was just going to shoot the kid right then and there, all business, no mercy, and if that wouldn't have been the right thing.

Then a woman's voice had called from the auto dealership. She'd stepped through a shattered display window and shouted shrilly, "He's not sick, not like that!" She was middle-aged and frizzy gray hair (they all had at least a little) fanned out around her head. She held her arms out pleadingly and walked toward the street.

"We're not sick," she'd said, more softly. She pulled up the sleeves of her ratty cardigan sweater and pushed the hair back from her neck. "Duckie," she called, "pull up your shirt and show them. Very slowly." To Quebra she added, "He's unarmed. He's a child."

Quebra had not moved in all that time and did not reply then. His silence said it all. *Doesn't matter if he's a kid. If he's armed or infected, that's what matters.* Not that Frank believed Quebra to be a cold man. He was just a man who did the things no one else could bring themselves to do, things that had to be done.

Duckie, with an almost comical slowness, as if he were mocking the woman's command, had peeled his navy blue sweatshirt up from his waist. He'd pulled it up past his pecs and then, at the woman's direction, had turned in a slow circle to show his bare torso, front and back. He was clear of sores. Quebra had lowered the rifle a millimeter.

"He's mentally disabled," the woman had said. There hadn't been any exasperation in her voice – no tone of *How could you not know? How dare you?* – but Frank had heard a certain weariness, the weariness of someone who has made a firm and loving commitment and who is being exhausted by it. He remembered thinking she must be his mother.

O'Brien, as it had turned out, was Duckie's Special Education teacher, or had once been. She had explained that Duckie's family was dead, as was hers, and she'd been shepherding him across the Midwest ever since. She'd gone from an educator to a full-time caretaker, and Frank supposed it was because neither she nor Duckie had anyone else left. He hoped there wasn't anything weird going on between the two, though that thought seemed ridiculous now in the early hours of dawn, as he watched O'Brien sponge dirt from Duckie's face with a spit-moistened sleeve.

After accepting O'Brien and Duckie, the group had rested up inside the auto dealership until dark and then had resumed their trek on a path which allegedly contained a dead giant. They had moved with painstaking slowness, stopping often, and so it was only now that they sat in this car-choked stretch of road next to ruined blast walls, and waited to see the creature – the Little One, as Duckie and so many others called them. Duckie, however, did it with no trace of irony. He did it because, in spite of the fact that the Little Ones were some three hundred feet tall, there was simply a much bigger one standing to the north. *Them's the facts.*

There they sat as the sun played chicken with the night sky. Frank, an ad man with bad lungs and joints that screamed whenever he shifted. Chiapperino, an old fart originally from Queens who exhibited an almost superhuman patience and incredible empathy with people – and who had said nothing during Quebra's confrontation with Duckie. Duckie himself, who was a nice kid even if a little loud sometimes. He had to be reminded frequently that there were human monsters of which one must be wary. O'Brien was every bit the part of a surrogate mother. She looked to be about Frank's age, forty-ish, though weathered as they all were.

Caitlin and her sister Autumn were also recent additions to the group. Caitlin's long hair was startlingly dark, maybe because it was unwashed, although it seemed healthy. That was why it caught Frank's eye so often. The girl was attractive to be sure, but Frank's mind, even in its most idiotic recesses, no longer processed the sight of a girl in that way. Those idle, often ugly thoughts which seemed to crop up regularly in a man's brain regardless of circumstance, had been retired when the shit hit the fan and deeper instincts took charge. Autumn was pretty too, and her hair seemed smooth and clean, even if it had to have been at least a month since they'd had enough clean water to wash anything. Autumn's hair was red. Somewhere along the way, while traveling alone with her orphan sister, Autumn had taken the time to break into some Walgreen's and apply scarlet hair dye. She looked maybe thirty, "Cate" being her kid sister. Frank only really thought of her in reference to Caitlin, because Autumn had been careful so far not to exude a lick of personality. She was fiercely guarded. Though Caitlin was more outgoing, Autumn kept her on a short leash and the tension in it was apparent on rare occasion.

Then there was Quebra, who was always good for a joke unless he'd been "activated." That was what Chia called it when Quebra's training kicked in and he went rigid. Frank had found the comparison akin to a hunting dog but had said nothing. When he wasn't activated, Quebra and Chia could sit around a fire for a solid hour and trade one-liners until everyone was struggling to keep from laughing at the tops of their lungs. That was good, if a little unsafe, because Frank was certain that if they didn't all laugh once in a while, they never could have gotten this far. Quebra, their trained killer, knew that perhaps better than anyone did.

The final member of their octet was Ethan Dodgman. Dodger, he preferred to be called. Twenty-six, the son of a governor and the nephew of a U.S. Senator, and wealthy. These were the things Dodger wanted everyone to know about him, things that no longer mattered in the real world. Frank had no reason to doubt any of Dodger's claims, but like everyone else, he didn't give a shit either. The only compelling part of Dodger's story was that he'd been cast out of his family's state-of-the-art doomsday shelter when he'd drawn the short straw. *"I'm sorry son, we just don't have enough for all twelve of us, but you're young. You'll have a better go of it out there than your old man will. America needs your old man, son. They need him down here in the war room."* Frank imagined Dodger's father had delivered this icy farewell from behind a tumbler of scotch. A mad aristocrat who believed that the American government still existed and that there was a seat of power with his name on it. Then again, Dodger also seemed to believe these things. Even though he'd been out here in the shit for a good three years - had watched civil unrest become civil war, and then civil nothing - he still talked like Mr. Class President gunning for an internship with a Congressman.

They were waiting to see a dead giant. *Them's the facts.*

#

When it was light enough for Quebra to use his binoculars, he stood with his elbows on the roof of a stripped sedan and took a look.

"There it is," he breathed, and his whole body tensed. "It's right there, compadres."

Dodger rose immediately to his feet. "Let's have a look."

Without removing the binoculars from his eyes, Quebra said, "Go ahead."

They each stood and approached Quebra's back slowly, as if he could shield them if the thing suddenly became undead and spotted their position. Frank had never, ever heard of such a thing, even in the craziest ramblings of fellow nomads, but he half-expected it just the same. His knees creaked and groaned as he left his seat in the road and stood beside the soldier.

Lord God, it was only a hundred yards away. The great, fearsome head lay in a crater of asphalt in a fast-food parking lot. It was *right there.*

Frank had never been this close, and as the sun proper finally rose, he saw the so-called Little One in such gruesome, startling detail that he nearly jumped. It was like realizing one had been sleepwalking, just as one's hands reached for the orange-hot oven range. Similarly, he saw Dodger and Autumn jerk away. The latter clamped a hand on Caitlin's elbow.

The Little One's head was long, narrow, the entire thing beak-shaped, and made up on sharp, offensive angles. It was like a giant pair of jagged pliers, only these pliers were made of a smooth, bone-like matter, a sort of armor, or an exoskeleton, Frank supposed. He'd seen them before on TV back when there was TV. He'd seen photos back when there was photography. Some people called them bone giants, but now, this close, he saw that the creature's substance resembled petrified wood more than bone. There were subtle grains running along the sharp snout, a snout which ended in grasping hooks. The mouth was closed, but Frank had seen footage of the open maw. Rather than opening into top and bottom halves, it split into four splaying mandibles that clawed at the air like the fingers of a hungry hand. In the palm of that hand, Frank had glimpsed the great wet wound that was the actual throat. They had eaten people. That was fact. It didn't seem that they needed to. They didn't seem to subsist on anything other than wanton destruction. Long, barbed arms with clubby fists plowed into vehicles and buildings. Frank had seen the film. Their curiously bowed legs rammed straight into bridges as if the structures had no right to be there – and the bridges would disintegrate, throwing cars, cables, and people. That was what they did, the Little Ones, when they were alive. This thing was completely unmoving and the blood-red orb of its eye was covered by what looked like a sheet of bone. It looked dead as dead could possibly be, what Frank could see of it anyway. Beyond its shoulders, the rest of the body was hidden behind a strip mall blackened by old fire.

"How long is it?" Caitlin asked. She was talking to Chia.

He said, "Never got any bigger than a few hundred feet, not as far as I know." Three hundred feet, though – that was fifty men, an office tower, the end of the goddamn world if it stepped on you. It was marvelous to behold for all the terror it inspired. To think of the moment when this beast had collapsed here. How the earth must have quaked, how any unbroken windows in the vicinity must have shattered, how junked cars must have jumped and blast walls crumbled. When a Little One moved with will and intent, it was worse, of that Frank was sure. He never wanted to glimpse another of these things alive again, not after the last one.

"If that's a Little One," Caitlin asked, "how big is the big one?"

In moments like these, it seemed everyone turned to Frank. He wanted to tell them he was a copy guy, not a poet, certainly not a journalist, but they wanted to hear him tell it. Even though he'd only ever seen it on the news – just like the rest of the group, so far as he knew – he was considered to be the resident wordsmith. Caitlin followed the others' gazes to him and her questioning eyes threw glints of sunrise at him. He turned from her for a moment, clearing his throat, and then spoke.

"It's – did you ever go on an airplane, Cate?"

"When I was a baby," she replied. "I don't remember." At nineteen, she would have been born right after all this started. Wouldn't have been long after that when commercial airlines began closing up shop. Frank thought for a few seconds. "Well, airplanes, the kind you and me would travel on, used to get up to about thirty, thirty-five thousand feet. Up there in the clouds, if you can imagine. You would fly above the clouds sometimes and stare down at them from your window seat. It was really kind of fantastic." It had been. The sky had belonged to Man then and far above it, the exosphere with its unthinkable litter of satellites and junk, but this was about the Big One who stood now in Chicago, dormant for years. What *dormant* meant was anyone's guess. Most knew to leave it at that, lest their recurring nightmares got worse.

"The Big One," Frank said, "stands about seven miles tall. That's around thirty-seven thousand feet. Its head is literally in the clouds." Caitlin didn't acknowledge the turn of phrase and Frank went on. "The highest peak in the world is Mount Everest. The Big One has it beat by eight thousand feet. They never did figure out how something that big and that heavy managed to walk at all."

"Most people don't call it the Big One," Quebra said, his eyes still in the binoculars. "They call it the Dragon and things like that. Doesn't really look like one though, especially now. Hard to make out any features on anything that big. It always was just like a giant mountain."

"I prefer the German *Hölle geht*," Chia said quietly. *"Hell Walks."* He looked at the others and said, "Very theatrical – Biblical, I guess - but I've ever seen some Biblical shit, it's that thing."

The Beast, some others called it, and there were other variations based upon language and religion but Chia was right, *Hell Walks* pretty much summed it up. Except it didn't walk anymore, and if there was a God, it never would again.

Unless He'd sent it, of course.

Autumn pointed at the Little One lying in the parking lot. "We saw one once. Not quite this close, but..." she trailed off and held Caitlin close. She'd almost said something personal, had almost given away some backstory.

Caitlin did. "I remember. I didn't get to see it because I was under a bunch of crap in the back of a van, but it was when we were in Tornado Alley. I saw the tornadoes, three of 'em chasing us, before my head got shoved under a bunch of luggage." She glanced sideways at Autumn to indicate that her big sister had done the shoving. "We grew up there. They say the storms got worse and worse and worse because of the monsters. That's how Mom and Dad died."

"Caitlin," Autumn said sharply.

"It is, and we were trying to outrun these three tornadoes with the Gunderson family and their van, and Autumn saw a Little One behind the storms and pushed me down before I could see. She said she saw it clear as day and it was *running*."

Frank didn't say anything, just watched the air between the two sisters, but Duckie spoke up. "It ranned away from the twisters? That's what tornadoes are. Twisters."

"Right," Caitlin said, her eyes distant, "but no, it was running after us."

"They target people," Quebra said. "We learned that early on. That's why they've stuck mostly to the cities, even ones like this that've been flattened. Because new people always show up."

"People like us," Chia grunted, "but we were tricked. Otherwise, we would've never come here."

"Then you would never have saved Duckie and me," O'Brien said. No one said anything to that.

"You did save us," she went on, "and we'd like to go with you. I know we don't seem like anything other than dead weight, but we'll both work hard. Duckie's a helluva lot stronger than he looks."

"I am," Duckie agreed. "Helluva."

"Well," Chia said, "we don't exactly put it to a vote or anything, but I guess we ought to make it official. Anyone got any problem with these two nice folks?"

Dodger's silence was deafening. As if he carried even half his own weight, but at least he did the decent thing now and kept his stupid spoiled mouth shut.

It was as if the Little One lying dead across the thoroughfare had lost all its novelty. Funny how a genuine human moment could do that, thought Frank.

It occurred to him then that, even though they were downwind of the corpse, there was no smell of rot. There wasn't really any distinctive odor at all. He tapped Quebra's shoulder.

"Yeah, boss," Quebra muttered.

"Any way to be absolutely – I mean two hundred percent – sure that thing's dead?"

"It's been there for a week at least," said O'Brien.

Dodger shoved his hands in his slacks and began pacing. "Yeah. Maybe we ought to fall back. Plus, there's the sickness. Wouldn't want anyone to get infected."

"We're not touching it, Dodgman," Quebra said.

"Who knows what it's touched?" Dodger snapped. "You know the infection comes from those things! What if it bled or spat or shit all over the place when it died?"

"Okay, okay," said Chia. "The man's got a point. I think we've seen enough. Let's count our blessings and move along."

There was a low, rumbling sound, like a fart, and Duckie laughed. Frank's eyes fell upon the Little One and for a second he was sure, two hundred percent sure that it had shifted in the rubble. O'Brien pinched Duckie to silence him and they all stared at the giant.

Little Ones had been felled by multiple missile strikes. That was a long time ago. Frank had never seen anything less work. This seemingly unblemished creature...had it just died of old age? Could such a miracle be possible that all this was going to come to an end? Due to age, stress? Or maybe this one had caught the goddamn common cold just like *The War of the Worlds.*

Maybe it wasn't dead.

Maybe it had moved.

Everyone had stopped breathing again, Frank noticed. His lungs screamed and he let out a too-loud gasp. Quebra shot a glare at him.

Quebra's eyes quickly changed and he pointed the binoculars over Frank's shoulder. "Shit."

TWO

Quebra, in a very casual motion that carried him two steps forward, parted the group and swung the assault rifle upward. He barked "Mills!" and let off two rounds.

Caitlin jumped. Duckie clapped his hands over his ears. Frank turned, following Quebra's line of fire to a parking garage across the street next to the shell of a hospital. It took a second but Frank saw the silhouette perched on top of the structure. From here and in the early morning light it was hard for Frank to identify the figure as Mills, but he trusted Quebra, and moreover, wasn't surprised in the least.

They'd met Mills less than a month ago, not long after Autumn and Caitlin. Mills had told them she once worked for the CDC and that there was a treasure trove of vaccines, antibiotics, and medical supplies in a bunker outside Kansas City, and they'd believed her, and came here. That was the long and short of it. They'd believed her because there couldn't possibly be, not to anyone's reasoning, a malicious reason for such a yarn. Why venture toward Illinois and Hell Walks, toward a large city that was likely still a target for Little Ones? Why make up a story about medicine when there was nothing to be gained in terms of shelter or goods? It would be suicidal to do such a thing, to lead six people down that primrose path and then admit at the last that it was just a fib.

They hadn't known Mills. If anything, it had served as a cold, raw, real lesson about those human monsters. Mills had lied to them because she was out of her mind and because, in her words, she'd been bored.

When she'd told them the truth, standing on a blistered freeway at the KC limits, she'd said it very matter-of-factly. There hadn't even been so much as a villainous smile. She'd just said, "I should probably tell you I never worked for the CDC."

Mills was middle-aged and...well, normal looking. Frank was sure that assessing her in such a way betrayed some dumb prejudice in himself, but the fact was he'd accepted her as a normal person who couldn't possibly be a psychopath. They all had. It was more than just wanting to believe her story. It was the belief that a fortysomething white woman just couldn't be a homicidal loon. Lesson learned.

It wasn't that anyone had been sick, at least not in the traditional sense. There hadn't been a desperate need to reach the mythical CDC stockpile. Frank's condition was a genetic disorder of the connective tissue and some of the group didn't even know about it. As for the rest, they seemed healthy. Had to be a hearty bunch in order to have made it this far. They were a good group, solid, and even if their most ambitious agenda was merely to see the next sunrise, they had a sense of purpose in a purposeless world.

And Mills, she'd been bored, and she'd fibbed. She'd told them she was amazed, they actually followed her all the way to fucking KC and then she'd tried to stab Chia with a sliver of rock when he approached her.

Quebra had taken that same AR-15 and laid the butt upside her head. When she awakened, Mills had found herself bound with some frayed rope from the soldier's pack.

Chia had been the one to address her. "We talked," he'd begun, speaking in the same simple terms Mills herself employed. "We're leaving you here like this. We're leaving you alive because we aren't like you, but we're leaving you bound. And..." His expression had darkened, Frank remembered, the creases of his face growing deeper. It had been hard for Chia to say any of it, but at last he'd finished. "Whoever comes across you, or whoever you come across, they'll know what you are. You won't hurt anyone again the way you hurt us."

Mills had stared curiously at him, and then asked, "What do you mean? What, did you brand me?" Then she'd twitched. The thought of being branded must have piqued her senses and she'd felt the stinging in her back. People in this world always hurt somewhere on their person, all of the time, but she'd identified a new pain and now she was on her knees, thrashing her bound arms and tracing semicircles in the dirt with her toes. "What did you do? *WHAT DOES IT SAY?*"

Quebra had carved "LIAR" into her back with his knife.

The soldier had knelt next to her then, that same blade poking into the skin behind her jawbone, and she'd shut up. He'd told her, "You wanted to play with us. Now we're playing."

They'd left her there, and it had been a long walk before the stream of hoarse curses faded into nothing.

Only a few days ago they'd done this. Frank had actually started to forget about her. Quebra clearly hadn't – he'd doubled his hours on night watch, sometimes sitting up from dusk until dawn without anyone to relieve him, and he'd also taught Autumn to use the different guns he kept on himself. Though Quebra was trusted with his little arsenal, he'd shown Chia, Frank and now Autumn to shoot. Dodger's pleas to join the club were always ignored.

Dodger, in fact, had joined the group not long after Autumn and Caitlin and right before Mills. There seemed to be periods like that, when a few people either died or appeared at the same time. This past month had been a particularly busy one, though, and it looked as if the fun wasn't over.

Atop the parking structure, Mills thrust her free arms into the air. Then she ducked behind the roof's concrete lip.

Quebra's two-round burst had been a warning shot, but now he was carefully trailing her and he said sideways to Chia, "What do you think, boss?"

"She's not going to leave us alone," Autumn said from behind him.

"Who is she? What did she do?" O'Brien asked.

"She's trouble," Chia said quietly, "bad trouble, and we gave her her chance."

"She's the one who tricked us into coming out here," Frank said to O'Brien. "You're right, we wouldn't have found you if we hadn't, but she's nuts. Like really nuts. She'll get us all killed."

Quebra nodded in agreement. Frank knew he'd wanted to kill Mills all along, but he'd deferred to Chia and his sense of mercy. That was all over now.

"Think she's alone? Still unarmed?" Frank asked the soldier.

"Let's hope so," Quebra said. His eyes narrowed. "She's not up there anymore." He began panning the rifle over the entire parking garage. "Bitch just wanted to let us know she was still out there. Should have just done her. Fuck."

Frank felt sick now and he wished the same. Being actively stalked by Mills was going to become their whole world until they dealt with her. Should have just left her dead on the freeway. Not that Frank himself had the cojones to do it, then or now, but then again...they couldn't go on with Mills' specter in every shadow of every building. The emotion caught in Frank's knotted stomach turned from fear to anger. He looked toward Chia to see if the old man's heart had turned in the same way and saw only grief.

"Don't blame yourself," Frank said quickly.

"Can't blame anyone else," Chia grumbled.

"Well," said Dodger, eyeing the parking structure, "I suggest we find some high ground of our own." It was either that or run, and it felt as if the unspoken consensus was to stay and resolve this before leaving town. As if in confirmation, Chia nodded.

"I'm going to scout the building west of the hospital," Quebra said. He hefted the considerable weight of his pack off his back and into his arms. Fishing out two pistols, he handed one to Chia and one to Frank.

Frank felt the uneasy weight of the gun and glanced at Autumn. "Any chance you'd want to play lookout?"

"Not today," she said. Frank grimaced and stuck the gun in his waistband.

He looked back at the Little One, whose spectacle had once again been eclipsed by human drama. It was still there, still lying in the same crater of asphalt, eyes closed, but they did need to get away from it, dead or no. It was ironic, he supposed – though he wasn't entirely certain he was using the word correctly – that a lie about a cache of medicine had led them to this fallen beast which carried a horrifying and incurable disease. It was a disease foreign to the planet Earth, a bacterial infection from some other planet or dimension or wherever the hell the giants had come from. It manifested itself first as big red sores the size of saucers. The skin became taut, hard, and painful. Then sores split into bleeding mouths and eventually – if the victim lived long enough, so Frank had heard – the mouths became wretched dry sockets and death would soon follow. Frank had seen first and second-stage infected, but not these final Swiss-cheesed horrors, who were said to lose their minds, and who wouldn't?

The group sat in the street in the shadows of the skeleton cars. Moving to the sidewalk and using the cars as cover against Mills would mean moving closer to the Little One. Watching Quebra slip down the road and vanish, Frank said, "How about in the cars?" He gestured at a few vehicles down, at a long Chevy van. "We could all fit in that one."

"Check it out," Chia said. He looked crestfallen, was still debating himself mentally over the decision to let Mills live. Frank gave him a pat on the shoulder as he stepped by.

The van was clear, free of debris and waste, and the side door opened with a little effort and a metallic groan. Frank ushered the others inside.

All the windows were gone, of course, and there was likely nothing under the hood – not that such a thing mattered when gasoline was only a memory – and it was colder in the van than it had been outside. Caitlin shivered against Autumn. "It'll warm up," Autumn said. "We've got heat of our own. Anybody know any good jokes?"

Dodger cocked his head toward the Little One. "Ha." He tilted his head the other way, presumably in the direction of Madwoman Mills, and added, "Hee."

"Pretend we're your constituents, why don't you," said Chia. "Make us feel good, Dodger."

The younger man fell silent and sullen. He'd never have constituents. His own kin had thrown him to the wolves. Chia's line had probably come across harsher than he'd meant, but no one appeared to give a shit because Dodger was quiet.

"Are you all friends?" Duckie asked. He'd been quiet, too, for so long he'd almost faded into the background.

Frank, seated in the driver's seat next to Chia, glanced back. "I guess it's as good a term as any. You need friends nowadays."

"Doctor O--" Duckie seemed to catch himself and clenched his fists. "Miss O'Brien is my best friend."

O'Brien smiled. "I've been trying to get Duckie to dispense with the formalities. He knows he can even call me Mary if he wants."

"Not until you call me Greg," Duckie replied.

"But I thought you liked Duckie more."

"I do." Duckie smiled. He was missing a fair amount of teeth. Frank's tongue explored the empty slots in his own mouth. There were only a few but it probably wouldn't be long before he was gumming crushed berries to get by.

"So how long have you all been traveling together?" O'Brien asked.

Chia sat up and thought. "Well, it's only been four or five weeks, I suppose, since the girls and Dodger joined up." He clapped Frank on the arm. "We've been riding together going on four years."

It was more like three and a half, but Frank didn't say anything. May as well have been a decade. Figures didn't matter if the company was good.

Frank angled his thumb at Chia, who kept watch out the shattered windshield while Frank spoke. "We met up right after the collapse. When the government fell and everything went to shit."

"Had my wife and boy along then," Chia added in a practiced absentness. "Josie and Bryan. They're gone now."

Duckie looked confused at that. He glanced at O'Brien, who gave him a knowing look, and he understood. Beside them in the middle seat, Dodger stared out the window in boredom.

"We met Quebra...it was over a year ago, wasn't it? Him and Kotz." Chia looked at Frank, who gave a half-shrug half-nod. Chia continued. "Kotz...poor SOB. Stepped in an old beaver trap and lost his foot, got sick. We never knew if the trap was left over from some legitimate pre-collapse business or if crazies put it there."

Quebra had delivered the mercy bullet to his fellow serviceman. Frank remembered that he had been unable to watch but that Chia had forced himself. Chia had said he needed to learn to be brutal. The old man was still in need of lessons, it seemed, but Frank didn't mind that one bit.

"So we know Mary was a teacher, and Duckie, you were a student," Frank said. "Caitlin, you too. Autumn, what did you do before all this? I mean, for a living," he added at the last, so as not to seem too intrusive.

"Cashier," was all she said. Good enough for the question, Frank figured.

"How about you, Dodge?" Frank asked.

"School," Dodger said, "and worked in good old Dad's office. Did a little computer work for the Senator now and then. I was a computer prodigy." Frank wondered if Dodger had been privy to any inside baseball about Hell Walks and the Little Ones. Dodger didn't elaborate, however, and Frank turned to Chia.

"Chia here's a jack of all trades. Like a Swiss army knife."

"That's code for 'retired and restless.'" Chia grinned a little. "I always said I'd work 'til I die, and well, I guess I'm still at it, aren't I? Living itself is a chore these days."

"How about you, Frank?" Autumn asked. He thought she was angry about having been put on the spot, but she appeared genuinely curious.

"I wrote copy for an ad agency," he said. "Magazine stuff mostly, mostly food. Exciting, I know. I was as thrilled as you all look, but it was decent money."

"Did you have anyone?" Autumn asked.

He studied her face in the dark of the van. *Was* she trying to get him back, to let him know not to pry when it came to her and her sister? He couldn't tell, but he wasn't going to give anyone the satisfaction of clamming up, wasn't going to let them imagine his tragedy as something other than exactly what it was.

"I was divorced – no kids – but I was seeing somebody when everything went to hell. She was hit by a car. The sort of civil unrest we'd all been living and ignoring had turned to war, and...I don't even see how you call it war, but that's what they called it. I guess technically that we're still in it. There doesn't seem to be any clearly defined sides, after all. Not since the government went kaput. It's just people giving up.

"Anyway, it was panic in the streets – there was a sketchy report that one of the Little Ones was headed our way – and we were crossing a street, she stumbled, and this truck just ran right over her. That's it."

Thunder grumbled from some distance. The van's occupants looked out their glassless windows to see which direction it had come from. Staring into the newborn sun, Frank felt a dull ache in his chest. It became a tightness that radiated through his joints. *Shit. Come on man. It's just rain, don't get stressed.* He always felt as if moisture and precipitation exacerbated his condition, but no doctor had ever corroborated that. It was all in his head, and he needed to calm down and look away from the sun—

#

Back before the shit hit the fan and dreams stopped mattering, Frank used to have fantastic dreams. He wrote most of them down and had entertained waking dreams of someday being a writer, a real writer, quitting the ad job and extracting novels from his voluminous, tattered dream journal. He never had. For this morning's dream he had not even a pen nor paper to jot down its details, but Frank would remember them, always, because the dream nearly got him killed.

#

He was standing on a cobbled path at the bottom of a hill. The hill was a foothill and the path continued up the mountain beyond, only the carefully placed stones soon have way to a winding dirt trail, he saw, and the mountain itself vanished up into a tower of mist that made him think of one thing. Hell Walks. Hell Walks today, the inert artificial mountain sitting in – on, rather – the east side of Chicago which bordered Lake Michigan.

Yet, Frank was walking up the path – hurrying, in fact, to get past the cobblestones and onto the raw earth of the trail. As his feet struck the dirt, there was a woman before him.

He assumed she was woman. Her back was to him, a considerable back, long, lean, and wreathed with what looked like reddish-brown vines. Her skin was a pale gray that looked icy to the touch. The vines gathered in bunches about her hips, encasing her buttocks and then becoming disentangled and flowing like water down and about her long cool legs. The back of her head was similarly wreathed in arterial-looking plant matter, although there were thorns here and there. She was a woman, a Gray Woman, and when she spoke, he knew that her lips did not move.

Who are you? she asked. Her voice had the reproachful quality of a schoolmarm who'd just found a boy mucking about in the hall.

"Mucking about," Frank thought. "I've never said *that*." Then he realized he'd been speaking aloud.

This time he knew her lips moved. She said, "Where are you from?"

Having no better answer, Frank said, "Connecticut. Originally."

The woman began moving slowly up the trail. The vines around her legs swish-swished back and forth like a beaded curtain. Frank found himself following her. At some point, he noticed his feet were bare, but the dirt path with its uneven surface and pebbles did not hurt him. He renewed his focus on the Gray Woman and soon, wisps of mist were curling about her dress. They were going high. Frank became afraid.

"Should we be doing this?" he asked.

"You don't have to do it," came the reply.

Frank continued following her.

Now the mist was a cloying fog and it made Frank feel claustrophobic. It made him feel the way he did when he had real bad episodes. It had been a long time, but he still remembered the tightness in his lungs and heart, and the thought that he was going to die, that his elastic arteries were at last going to split open and drown him in his own blood. That memory drew his eyes to the vines encircling the Gray Woman, a woman who stood at least eight feet tall. She was a giant to be sure, but she meant him no harm. Frank relaxed and pulled himself through the fog after her. If he lost sight of her, he'd have no point of reference and walk right off this mountain.

The fog took on an ethereal glow as it caught sunbeams. At last it began to break up. They were at a craggy, jutting point about halfway up the mountain. Frank craned his neck to try and glimpse the peak, but at that height, things were shrouded in dense clouds.

"Don't worry about that now," the Gray Woman said. She stepped off the edge of the jutting point and onto a swaying rope bridge which was just suddenly there. Frank followed still. The ropes were frayed and pulled taut, and the bridge's wooden planks didn't seem to be fastened to the ropes by any means, just resting there in a bed of knots. Yet, each held firm beneath Frank's feet.

"Why am I here?" he asked the back of the striding Gray Woman. The bridge took a smooth right turn – utterly impossible – then sloped upward, leading them toward another mountain.

"We're close now," was all the Woman said.

They reached the end of the bridge and the new mountain. There was a cave-like opening before them. Without turning to face him, the Gray Woman mounted the ledge before the cave and stepped aside to allow Frank entrance.

He went in. He didn't try to glance at her face when he passed her, for it was understood that he would only see the back of her, no matter what angle he came from.

The interior of the cave was red rock and it was warmly lit by some unseen source. Frank walked its narrow corridor and at last, the tunnel opened into a room.

The room had shelves carved from the rock wall itself, and upon them rested enormous books. Each volume looked older and more ornate than the one before. Each dwarfed Frank's hands when he began to reach out and he'd pull them back. He was afraid to touch the books because whatever truth lay between their gilded covers was going to hurt.

Then he saw the book with the gleaming metal cover. Its surface showed a relief of a dragon in repose. This time he couldn't stop himself. He picked it up from its place on the shelf, a place where it had sat undisturbed for perhaps millennia – maybe as long as the Gray Woman had walked that mountain path – and when Frank held it, he found that it was feather light in his hands. He took hold of the front cover and lifted it back.

The first page was black and smooth, a fibrous paper thicker than what he was used to. Frank reached to take its corner and peel it away.

It happened all in an instant – the paper tearing and twisting and knotting itself, four segments ripping away from the center and folding back and becoming the four mandibles of a screaming Little One, those splayed pincers capable of snapping a city bus in half, and the book lunged at Frank.

He let go of it as soon as he recognized the horror, but somehow, the book was still coming at him, defying gravity, and now from the pitted red hole at the center of the flailing mandibles came the scream, the scream of the giant in all its hideous glory. It came at him.

"Frank! Frank!" It was, absurdly, his own voice that he heard, and it was coming from his mouth. There was no one else here to wake him up.

Wake? This was a dream, after all. "WAKE UP FRANK!" he screamed at himself as the book's covers beat like wings and the mandibles snapped at his cheeks.

"WAKE UP, FRANK!" Chia hollered, slapping Frank again. His uneven fingernails nipped at the flesh of Frank's cheeks.

Frank sat up in the driver's seat of a dead van and coughed. His lungs cried out and he slammed a fist into the steering wheel. "Fuck! I was--"

"We gotta go!" Chia cried, leaning over Frank to throw open the door. Frank glanced outside and saw the others were already there, and running.

"Mills!" he coughed.

"It ain't fucking Mills!" Chia barked. He pushed Frank out the door, and by some grace, not his own, Frank found his footing and began to stumble. God, his knees hurt, and his ankles too. As he hobbled away from the van, he turned to ensure that Chia was following and—

There. *RIGHT THERE, RIGHT FUCKING THERE.*

Guess it was just sleeping.

The Little One rose into the air, debris falling from its bony shoulders, and as it turned its beak from side to side, there was a ratcheting sound. Then it looked down at them and its beak flew apart in that four-pronged shriek.

Frank's ears sang misery and he expected his heart to explode, but then Chia had his arm and goddamn, could the old man move. Frank looked ahead at the others racing down the street. Autumn, Caitlin, Dodger, Duckie, O'Brien. No Quebra. He must have still been scouting. Well, he'd know by now.

That reminded Frank that he had a gun and he pulled free of Chia to fish it from his pants. He stared stupidly at the thing. The ground quaked under his feet and for a half-second. He wasn't standing on anything.

He looked back. The Little One was advancing. It roared again.

Chia yelled Frank's name. He began running as best he could on his shitty legs. It made sense that he was at the rear of the pack. He was the wounded antelope. The monster would take him first and maybe that was all right, if it saved the others. Frank thought all of this in a very distant voice as he limped along. He should give Chia the gun though, if this was to be his end. No sense feeding good ammo to the Little Fucker.

It isn't little at all. Caitlin's a smart kid.

He almost laughed but he had no breath. The ground shook again and he was nearly spilled onto his face. Chia slapped at his arm. "Frank! What are you doing, Frank!"

"My knees," Frank gasped, then, "my breath."

Without hesitation, Chia stopped in his tracks, whipped up his pistol, and squeezed off a volley of shots at the beast.

The roar that followed couldn't have been more than one of annoyance – the things were bulletproof except in their throats – their eyes couldn't even be injured, couldn't be cracked or so much as blinded by directed-energy attacks. Chia had only pissed the giant off and Frank told him as much in a strangled wheeze.

"It's already pissed!" Chia shouted, but his eyes agreed. The others were a few hundred yards away, next to the hospital, and Frank saw that Caitlin and Autumn, or one or the other, had stopped. They were struggling against one another. Frank couldn't tell who had tried to run back to him and Chia and who was resisting. He could have taken a wild guess, but there was no reason to resent it. He, and maybe Chia now too, were dead men.

Frank's teeth vibrated and he heard the blistering crunch as the Little One stomped on the van. He turned again to face it. "Chia, man, go."

"Hell no! You crazy!" Chia shook Frank's shoulder so hard Frank thought his arm was going to fall out. "You're not done, Frank! *Move!*"

The Little One seemed to look right at Frank then, its emotionless red bird's-eye stopping mid-roll. Somewhere in the crimson sea of the eyeball, Frank glimpsed a sharp little pupil. Then it was gone again and the thing's open beak swung down at him. Just like a dream he'd once had, Frank thought, and was content with that thought being his last.

Thunder crashed, much closer now. The rattle of automatic fire put it to sorry shame. The roar of the Little One when ragged chunks flew from its open throat was hands-down the winner of the contest.

Quebra. Wasting good bullets trying to save Frank. Well shit. Frank began to run again. The Little One raged forward but it passed right by Chia and Frank, its cataclysmic footfalls toppling them both as it flattened a line of cars on its way toward the source of the AR-15.

Frank shoved himself to a standing position and readied to fire at the back of the thing, but Chia slapped his pistol down. "Quebra's drawing it off us! Let him!"

The Little One, in fact, bypassed Autumn and Caitlin as well, who at this point, had agreed upon running and were on the hospital's shattered threshold. The others must have already gone in. Frank hoped, so that no one had been pulverized into the asphalt. The craters in the Little One's wake were the size of vans and crushed bodies wouldn't even be recognizable in their pits.

The ground was still shaking but Frank's bones had settled. The Little One was beyond the hospital – Quebra had said he was scouting out the building just past the medical center. He had to be on the roof. That he'd hit the Little One's maw from that range was incredible. Maybe his weapon was modified, although Frank didn't know guns. Maybe Quebra was just a hero. Either way, he was fucked now.

Frank could see Quebra's silhouette on the roof. He could hear the continuing gunfire. The Little One was going to smash him like an insect. Frank had not watched the mercy killing of Quebra's brother-in-arms, Kotz, just as he had refused to participate in the necessary amputation of Kotz's foot. When Chia's family had been crushed by a falling wall, there hadn't been much to see in the seconds before dust and hailing debris had filled Frank's vision. He was going to see Quebra get batted off that low roof like a mosquito and he deserved to see it because it was his fault. Frank stood still in the middle of the street and watched in helpless agony.

Then Mills ran into the street across from that building – on *their* side of the street, opposite the parking garage – and she threw something the size of a loaf of bread at the Little One's legs. There was a flash, which for a moment, Frank thought was the sun glinting off the Little One, but the sun didn't do that, and besides, the sky was dark gray now. The storm was here, and so Frank thought the boom that followed the flash was thunder overhead. All those errors flitted through his head in the space of a second, then another, and the more present part of his mind said, *Bomb.*

The Little One let out a shriek that tore the air. It stepped – no, staggered – sideways and looked down at the dissipating ball of fire on its thigh. Then it looked at Mills.

She was screaming, God was she ever screaming, just standing there and screaming. Whether it was mindless terror of mindless defiance, Frank didn't know. All he knew was that the Little One wasted no time in reaching down with one fearsome claw and squeezing her until she popped.

Chia dragged Frank toward the parking structure from whence Mills had earlier taunted them. Frank caught a glimpse of Quebra before walls of concrete interrupted his line of sight. The soldier was rappelling down the side of the building, a low building but still several stories high. God willing, he'd be on the ground before the Little One remembered him and looked back from the ruin of a woman who'd thrown a bomb at its legs. The bomb – IED maybe? Could Mills do that? Who knew? Mills was a complete stranger, a liar, a psychopath, and the bomb had probably been meant for the humans, but she'd used it on the Little One.

She was crazy. Or maybe she was crazy and trying to redeem herself. Dead now. You saw her head pop out from the top of its fist. Stop overthinking things, Frank. Overthinking is for writers and dreamers and this world no longer suits either.

They were on the ground floor of the empty parking garage and the ceiling vibrated noisily as the Little One started stomping again. Rebar sticking from various wounds in the structure rattled and gave off a hum like a cloud of angry hornets. Chia led Frank to the darkest, most inaccessible – also most inescapable – corner and they knelt there.

Frank remembered to breathe. Remembering didn't make the act any easier. His chest felt like it was caught in a vise.

They saw, through the open entrance, the Little One's right foot. It was covered in soot and Frank thought, maybe even cracked, but the bomb had gone off up higher along its leg. *Wishful thinking, Frank. Overthinking.*

"Shut the fuck up," Frank muttered. Chia looked questioningly at him. "Brain," Frank said in explanation, and that seemed to cover it. In the middle of a crisis like this, a trauma, everything unfolding in either slow-motion molasses or dizzying hyper-speed, Frank imagined everyone's mind contained some wild argument. His argument was between instinct and imagination. Frank believed both could be lifesavers, but it was true that the former probably took precedence when a giant monster was chasing you. Maybe.

The Little One's foot was gone and both the sound and tremor of its steps were fading. Rain began pattering the street outside.

"It's still looking for us, has to be," said Chia. "It'll come back and smash every building on this block. We've gotta get to the others."

"Maybe it'll just go," Frank said.

"Josie and Bryan were afterthoughts," Chia said, and he was mad now. "It didn't have to do that. It didn't know they were behind that wall."

Frank just nodded. "Okay, Chia."

He was breathing better now, not that anyone had asked. He and Chia made their way back to the street and peered out in the direction the Little One had gone. There was no sign of it, but that didn't mean Chia might be right.

Thank God for the storm darkening the city. Frank felt much more comfortable moving through shadows and rain as they hustled to the hospital. As they came upon it, someone called, "Over here!"

It was Autumn. She was under the corrugated steel roof of the ER's drop-off area, and she beckoned to them. They ran to her and then they were inside the dark, smelly remains of the hospital.

The rain drummed maddeningly outside. Autumn brought them to a triage room which was devoid of supplies – even the cabinet doors were gone – and there they found all the others, Quebra included. He looked more than a little winded.

"Hey," Frank said, "thanks."

Quebra nodded and beat his fist against his chest. "I need water."

"There's lots outside," Duckie noted.

Quebra coughed out a laugh. "You're damn right." He started to get up and Autumn stopped him.

"Sit," she ordered. "O'Brien, will you help me find something to collect rainwater in? Then we'll go out there. Duckie too."

Frank and Chia both slouched to the floor. Dodger leaned in to them. "That bitch."

Frank thought he meant Autumn and started reaching for his neck when he realized Dodger was talking about Mills.

"Bitch," the young man repeated. "She was going to blow us up. She threw it at the monster. Idiot."

"For better or worse, she saved some of us. Maybe all of us," Chia replied.

"You didn't know she'd do that. You left her alive and she could've *killed* all of us."

Chia leaned in, consuming the space between himself and Dodger. Their foreheads rested against one another and Chia spoke in a soft, gravely whisper. "We all left her alive. You could have killed her, Mister Hindsight, Mister Foresight. Maybe you didn't think we'd allow it, but you didn't even bring it up. Not then on the freeway. Only after she's already dead do you have anything smart to say and I'll tell you something, it ain't smart. It's stupid." Chia sat back and used his sleeve to wipe sweat from his brow.

Dodger stayed in place, unbelieving. He looked at Frank.

"What?" Frank asked mildly.

Dodger sat back in the dark and said nothing.

#

The rain broke a few hours later. The water that had fallen from the sky had a rubbery, ashy aftertaste, but it was good. Autumn, O'Brien and Duckie had filled every available receptacle with it. Frank got to scrub the crud from his hair and sponge off the filthiest areas of his body. He wasn't clean by any means when the water ran out, but he felt renewed.

He and Quebra went out into the sun. They didn't find much of Mills. There was a shoe which Frank thought contained a foot, but it was just the shoe. Quebra poked at a red mass and said it was a leg. Then there was her head. Her purple, staring head, just lying there in the gutter.

"Let's bury her," Frank said.

"Why?" Caitlin asked from his back.

He turned to see her looking curiously at the severed head. Autumn was in the hospital's front entryway but made no move to retrieve her sister.

"She wanted to kill us, right?" Caitlin said. "I mean, even if she didn't, she told all those lies before. She was evil."

"Evil." Frank turned the word over in his mind while Quebra unfolded the compact shovel from his pack. "Maybe. I don't know."

Finally he told Caitlin, "It's not about her. Life has value. I can't just leave her like that. Look at her." By her he meant Mills' head, and Caitlin stared at it for a few silent moments.

Then she looked at Frank. "Do you really believe that? Or is this some sort of lesson?"

He smiled. "God, are you cynical."

"I'm nineteen."

Of course, nineteen-year-olds thought they knew everything. They'd figured out that the world was bullshit, there was no Santa Claus, their parents had done underage drinking, and that everything between here and the North Pole was shades of gray. The world now, the world after Hell Walks, and the collapse, had to harden a teen's naïve cynicism even more.

"I get it," Frank said. "I do, but – well, maybe this is a lesson, yes. A lesson that if you aren't still holding onto any of those silly rose-colored values about life, then you don't have shit. Because we don't have money anymore, do we? Or things. All we have is today and even that's a maybe. So we bury Mills and we ponder what it all means and we..."

"Have something to do?" the girl said.

That was the right answer. *A reason to go on living* was not, and that was what Frank had almost said. There was something to be said for a healthy sense of cynicism.

He nodded at her. "Will you help Quebra?"

She did. The entire group stood around the tiny grave as Quebra patted it down with his shovel, and then they had a moment of silence because no one could think of anything good to say.

Then Dodger spit on the grave, and the lesson was cancelled, and they moved on.

THREE

Mills had probably barely filled half of the Little One's fist. Hell, the building Quebra had sniped it from only came up to its knee. Yes, it had made a point of scooping her up so that her head still stuck out, so that it would pop off. Frank was sure of that. Why was the world being punished? He supposed there were ten thousand different religious explanations, but most of the major clubs had blown themselves off the map a long time ago – now there were only cults, some of whom claimed to represent Christ, Allah, or Buddha, but all of whom had seemed like raving lunatics in Frank's estimation. These were among the crazy nomad groups he and Chia had crossed paths with in their travels. Lacking the grace and accoutrements of the fallen churches, these guys and gals came across as mere street preachers. Frank supposed that the early prophets were perceived much the same way. Except those dudes could part seas. That was the difference. Frank would have saddled up with any group whose leader could turn water to wine. He just had yet to see it.

Forgetting them and their fool's explanations, why was the world being punished? Because it was and that was for damn sure. Frank was an atheist, but it was plain as day that this was some cruel shit.

"Let's talk about your episode back there," Chia said to him, breaking his dismal reverie. "Back in the van."

"I passed out," Frank said. "It's my cardiovascular system. You know what's going on with me." Yet, there was the fact that he'd had a very vivid dream. A very strange one, and the fact was that in hindsight, Frank felt like he'd been awake the entire time. A hallucination brought on by...what? Lack of oxygen? Enough to make him see the Gray Woman but not enough to make him lose consciousness?

"Look," he told Chia, keeping his voice down. They were walking at the rear of the group, and some of them had already heard Frank say these words, but he still always said them with caution. "Chia, if I become a liability, you know I just want you to leave me."

"And you know I won't."

"So we both die. What good does that do?" So they'd be ground into one another beneath a Little One's broad, flat feet. No one would be able to tell they'd once been two separate men.

"I know, Frank. I know I do some senseless shit like trying to save your ass, but I heard that little speech you gave the kid. About the value of life?"

"I didn't mean mine," Frank snapped.

"I wear rose-colored glasses, Frankie. They turn blood spatter to oil stains. They turn a sunset to a painting by one of the masters. They turn your shitty life into something with meaning."

"I hate you," Frank said out of the corner of his mouth in an attempt to suppress his smile.

"I know," Chia said, and walked ahead. Terms of endearment these days came off sounding like nothing of the sort, but they'd perhaps never been more sincere.

"So, in what direction are we headed in, ultimately?" O'Brien asked. "Anyone have anyplace specific in mind?"

Quebra looked to Chia. "Back the way we came? Before Mills?"

"There's nothing back there," Chia shrugged.

"Nothing any other way either."

"Hell Walks is northeast," Frank said, not entirely sure of why. He added, "Five hundred miles. Or clicks. Is that what a click is, Quebra?"

Quebra didn't answer. He was staring strangely at Frank. Then he said, "Hell Walks is five hundred miles northeast. And...?"

"I don't know," Frank said. "When the Little Ones came out of it, they fanned out. Just thought maybe it'd be safer up that way, nearer to the point they radiated from."

Quebra batted his eyes and wiped a slick of sweat from his face. It occurred to Frank he might volunteer to carry the soldier's pack, but somehow he suspected that right now, Quebra wouldn't go for that.

"Hell Walks hasn't moved in how long, since the collapse?" Quebra asked.

"Right."

"Frank, what makes you think it won't wake up and start moving tomorrow?" Quebra raised his voice. "May I remind you that just a few hours ago we saw a 'dormant' Little One get up and squash Mills? It almost squashed you, friend. You okay?"

Quebra thought Frank was cracking up after the morning's encounter. Nice. Could he blame the man though?

"It was just a thought," Frank said at last. "I thought we were throwing out ideas."

"Sane ideas," Dodger said. "I say we go southwest. The opposite direction. Baja's always nice."

"Does it matter?" asked Autumn.

"Yes, it matters," Dodger retorted. "Some ways are known to be a really bad idea. Others have promise. At least they have the promise of not being Chicago. *Got it?"*

"Why don't you ever talk that way to me, Dodgman?" Quebra cooed, rifle resting on his shoulder. Dodger scowled but clammed up.

"Fuck you, Dodger," Autumn said.

That lit him up again. "Oh *really?"* Dodger cried. "You all want me gone? You want to exile me? Wouldn't be a first for the boy. I can handle myself just fine. I try to help you."

"You don't do shit," Chia grumbled, "and we've talked about this before. Don't escalate it."

Frank sat on the shoulder of the road and plucked a small canteen from his belt. It was a little plastic red number with a faded ninja stenciled on it, some kids' camping toy. He took a swig of rainwater and closed his eyes.

Eighteen years ago, it had been when the world ended. Eighteen years and it was still ending.

It had begun with freak superstorms across the globe. They didn't even have time to name all of them, at least not to Frank's recollection. Scientists were more concerned with the storms' unnatural movements. They defied natural law itself, sweeping northward, each leaving terrible devastation in its path. He remembered there had been twenty-seven in all, and many had satellite hurricanes and tornadoes that laid waste to city and countryside alike. Everywhere became a potential disaster zone. Governments were on full alert and it didn't take long before they started pointing fingers. The religions too. As capitals fell and winds and waves raged, accusations of everything from sin to secret technology to aliens were lobbed. Everyone found a convenient way to blame their archnemeses. Meanwhile, the storms raged, throwing planes and buildings alike before converging in the Arctic just north of Greenland.

They met right above Lucker Deep, a deep-sea trench in the Eurasian Basin whose bottom was three and a half miles below sea level. There were deeper trenches in the world, but this one, since the Earth is not a perfect sphere, was closer to the planet's core than any other. That had always been an interesting factoid in Frank's mind, even if it still didn't make any sense.

The storms had piled into what was termed an "ultrastorm," a monolith of howling winds and snow that rose nearly to the exosphere. Satellites were thrown off course and communications worldwide began breaking down. Bad for governments and churches on the verge of war. Bad for uneasy populations on the brink of what they called "civil unrest."

The ultrastorm was estimated to be four hundred miles tall, which again defied nature. The preachers said this was proof that the scientists had always been wrong. The scientists begged for time to make sense of it, for world leaders to keep their fingers off their buttons.

The storm didn't listen to anyone. For one hellish month, it raged and people stayed home with their families and watched it on the TV, the tablet, and the phone until signals began to cut out. There was still some coverage available on the day the storm abated. In fact, once the clouds had broken up a lot of telecom services were restored, albeit temporarily. In that day, as the Arctic grew calm and a blue sky began to bleed through the tower of white, some people felt better. Like things were going to be okay now. Like we'd soon have answers and then we could build a thing or pass a resolution to prevent it from happening again and then everyone could go back to life as usual.

Then we saw what was behind the clouds.

Seven miles tall, its body covered in what looked like plates of obsidian rock or metal. It looked like an armored lizard from a children's book about prehistoric life, only this thing was not from Earth. Everyone knew that without asking. It was standing in Lucker Deep and so at first the world only saw half of it. Then it started to climb out.

The tsunamis were immediate and unlike anything in recorded history. There was no time to prepare, even as a viewer on the other side of the globe, for the apocalyptic tidal waves. Within an hour of the storm's end, cities were underwater. Hundreds of thousands of people were dead in the first minutes and there was only more to come.

Hell Walks. It lumbered across the Arctic floor, each footfall triggering earthquakes that resonated across the Northern Hemisphere. It moved ponderously slow, taking days to extract itself from the Deep. Each day it was taller and taller until its head, an undefinable thing shaped like a cosmic arrowhead, was lost in the normal clouds.

It stood as high as the Earth's troposphere and every little move it made ratcheted up the death toll. Hundreds of thousands were quickly millions. It reached Greenland and came ashore. The country was gone – gone, all dead – in days. Ultimately, it would take the monster fourteen years to reach Chicago, and every long day in that interim was its own Armageddon.

It was so massive and moved so slow that many claimed it simply wasn't possible that it existed. They pointed right at it on monitors and said it was a hologram masking a weather machine built by the U.S., China, or both. In the case of Israel and Iran, it remained unclear as to who launched their nukes first. It's only known that no one intervened on either's behalf. North Korea nuked itself. Russia pointed their weapons at everyone and asked to be left alone.

The U.S. and Canada, meanwhile, had a problem to deal with. Hell Walks was coming. Missile strikes and recon drones had all failed due to the thing's enormous electromagnetic field. There were malfunctioned warheads scattered across the Arctic floor. Very few were confirmed to have hit anything. The coal-black exterior of Hell Walks showed no signs of damage.

A coalition of fifty-two countries agreed on a new plan – this time, to send soldiers out to the thing, *onto* the thing, to bore into it and plant charges. Their hope was that they could loosen or cast off one of the monster's plates and reveal something vulnerable beneath. They got half of what they wanted.

Of the broadcasts made by the soldiers who ascended the right leg of Hell Walks, very few were discernable. Their radios went out of service quickly. The most well-remembered quote, said to be from a Brit named John Carlson, was, *"God, it's so hot – like lava for blood – we're all finished."*

It was weeks before anything happened, and though there were grainy satellite images of the men climbing in the groves and cracks in the monster – one picture of them sleeping fitfully on the lip of a plate that made the cover of every remaining periodical – their mission was deemed a lost cause. The robotic drill did manage to get under the edge of a craggy knee-plate and did bore into something softer underneath. If the soldiers managed to transmit any information to the coalition, the transmissions were never released. All that was known was that the men began frantically rappelling down and then leaping to their deaths.

When the Little Ones first came out, they had wings. They had launched straight out from Hell Walks and as Frank had said, fanned out in every direction. They moved far more quickly than their – mother? *Mothership?* No one knew. Planes were scrambled and missiles were fired.

This all took place a full seven years after Hell Walks had first appeared on Earth. Some people – most people, to be truthful, including Frank – were still trying to live semi-normal lives. Eastern Canada was mostly abandoned, yes, with much of the northern U.S. also reduced to ghost cities. There were days when the main headline wasn't the slow, certain progress of Hell Walks, but the annoyance and cost of refugees and overcrowding.

A few of the Little Ones were dropped as they flew across the globe. Dozens more reached their destinations, major cities worldwide, and their weird bony wings were shed and they began their work.

It would still be another seven years before the United States government, along with most others, fell. Seven years with monsters rampaging through some cities and people trudging to their jobs in others. Seven more years of talking heads being gainfully employed. They actually made movies during this era. Most were bright, loud comic romps meant to lift people's spirits, the Three Stooges on LSD. One of the largest studios in the world started producing and distributing pornography. There were documentaries too, of course, with scientists and sages who claimed they could end the nightmare if people would just listen to them. No one did, and they were lying anyway.

The final American Presidential election took place just before Washington was struck by a pair of Little Ones, effectively ending government. A new President, a fella named McAvoy, did get elected in a voter turnout that was rather pitiful even for the U.S. McAvoy was crazy and so were most of the voters. Thankfully, he was never inaugurated. Although hell, he could have America now if he wanted it.

It was around that same time that Hell Walks stepped out of Lake Michigan and onto a large portion of Chicago, and stopped. The mad storms and tremors that had accompanied its every twitch stopped too. Hell Walks hadn't moved since. Its head was still in the clouds, its body standing erect, but it hadn't moved. It still made no sense how it had been able to haul itself along in the first place, let alone how it stood straight like this. It was as physically impossible as the storms had been. The answer could have been magic fairies for all it mattered now. The civilized world was bye-bye and the Little Ones were continuing to hunt for scraps.

Three and a half years later, Frank screwed the cap back on his kids' canteen and hung it from a belt loop on his jeans. He stood and stretched his arms, trying to rid his joints of their miserable ache. Made it worse. He sighed. "We decide anything yet?"

"I like the Gulf Coast better than the West," Quebra said.

"Why not Florida? If it's still there," Chia said. He snapped his fingers. "How about the Keys? Can you imagine, if we could find a boat and then an island?"

"I'm sure a lot of people have thought the same thing," said Autumn. "We thought it, once."

"Yeah, but most people probably don't make it," Chia said. He realized a second too late that Autumn and Caitlin's parents were probably among that number, and his face fell.

"An island," said Caitlin. "I don't care where it is as long as it's warm. An *island*."

Dodger was pacing in silence, probably imagining himself as mayor of said island, a life all leis and booze and tanned boobs. Or maybe that was Frank's fantasy. He was, after all, the one thinking it, and thinking about having a woman made him think of Nan. Shit.

He'd had his worst episode four years ago, and back then Nan had been alive and they'd shared an apartment. Frank's doctor, an incredible man who had continued to see patients until his office was blown up by some maniac with an RPG, had told Frank it might be time to start making "arrangements."

Final arrangements, he meant. Frank had a bad heart valve and it wasn't likely he could get it replaced anytime soon. So he'd gone home and told Nan that he was going to die.

She'd sat with him on the couch and watched his face. She'd been waiting for him to cry, he knew, but he hadn't, and she'd finally asked, "What are we going to do?" Nan with her frizzy brown hair and her sweet shining eyes and her fucking feckless optimism. Always *doing. What are we going to do?*

"We?" Frank has asked dryly.

"What are *you* going to do, then?"

"I don't know what you mean." He had, it was just that it made him angry. "You mean quit working and abandon this place and go backpacking? You mean die beautifully in some Greek fishing village at sunset with cats all over the fucking place? Nancy, I don't have a *plan*. I'm going to die, that's what I'm going to do."

"Frank--"

"No. Just don't. You can't know, and you don't have a plan either, by the way."

"Okay," she'd said, and turned from him. "You're angry. I understand."

"How can you understand if I don't?" he'd yelled. It had reverberated around the mostly-empty apartment. She'd jumped at it. He'd immediately felt like shit.

He'd heard her sniffling and said, "You're crying."

Without turning Nan had replied, "For you. Not me."

"You should be crying for you. You're the one who has to go to my funeral and shit." The obstinate, infantile way in which he'd muttered *shit* made Frank stop. He'd started to laugh.

She'd turned then. "How are you laughing?"

"I'm sorry," he'd wheezed, and broken down. He'd cried in her arms for a long time, maybe until dark.

He had lived with that bad valve and was still alive today after an encounter with a Little One. Nan was dead because of some asshole in his delivery truck. So maybe yes, Frank was a little shaken today, a little weird, a little too carefree about the direction northeast.

"I like islands," he said simply.

FOUR

They were four days out from Independence, Missouri before they saw another human being. He was dead, lying next to a spent campfire in a grove of trees. Quebra was the one who first spotted him and he immediately raised a fist to stop the others. Duckie, who had grown less talkative as the plodding monotony of each day's progress had set in, stood on tiptoe to see what had frozen the soldier.

Quebra glanced back and pressed a finger to his lips, then crept forward. Frank still had his pistol and drew it, letting it hang at his side. He rested his shoulder against a tree's rough hide and waited for the next order.

They'd found bodies before and it was standard procedure for Quebra to check it out. First, he'd want to make sure it wasn't some sort of trap or, if not, that his presence didn't spook any companions they might may have had. Then Quebra would want to know how the man had died – murder, misadventure, or malady. If the man were infected, Quebra would come right back. No sense in rooting through the guy's stuff for supplies if he'd been sick.

Quebra came right back.

"Guy was alone. He's got a gun and some vegetables next to him." So no one had been with him when he died, and this group was likely the first to have come across his remains. Dodger said as much aloud, adding, "You get the gun?"

"Guy was infected," said Quebra. "Bad. Holes all over."

The description alone made Frank shudder.

"Damn." Dodger kicked at some underbrush. "Could have used another gun."

"We have enough guns," Quebra replied. "I've got a weird feeling."

"What about?" Frank asked. The group had drawn together now and he spoke in a whisper.

"He was infected but it looks like he was pretty clean otherwise. He's got a vest and all the pockets look like they're full of supplies." Quebra looked back at the body, hidden partially from view by tall grass. Frank could see a clothed leg and the top of a bare arm, though no sores. "I think he was sent away from a group."

Exiled due to the infection...but Quebra's implication was that the man had been cast out only recently, given enough supplies that when he died he left many of them behind. *Holes all over.* Final stage infection. That *was* weird. Unless...

"You think we're talking a whole infected group?" It was Autumn who spoke now. "They kept him around an awfully long time from the sounds of it. They're all sick too."

"Sent him off to die by himself. Maybe it was even his request," Quebra said. "It looks like he's been dead only a day or two. Up until then, I think he was part of a decent-sized, well-stocked group."

Dodger shivered. "We gotta get out of here."

"Hold on," Caitlin said. "What if they had just...I don't know, quarantined him? Then let him go when he got holes? Maybe they're not all sick."

"Could be," Quebra said, "but we ought not to take any chances. I'm going to scout ahead just a bit and see if I can guess which direction they were going. Then we go another direction."

There were likely to be many such bumps, detours, and delays between here and Fantasy Island. Some of the people standing here now might be dead themselves by the time the group reached the ocean. Frank knew there was a better-than-average chance he would be one of them. His knees ached terribly. By his age, a lot of the people with his same condition were in wheelchairs, or graves. His chest tightened at the mere thought and he gasped to catch his breath.

Quebra went into the trees surrounding the dead man's camp. "We gotta bury him too," Duckie said.

"No, we can't," said Chia. "He was sick. Very contagious. We can't touch him."

"Messed up," Caitlin said. "Mills got a funeral, but not him."

"We can give him everything we gave her," said Frank, "except a burial. Hell, maybe we'll have more to say about this guy. We can make up stories."

"That doesn't sound right." Autumn's eyes were on the dead man and they were glistening. She clamped her mouth shut tight after she spoke. She was trying not to cry – and probably it had little, if anything, to do with the man beside the cold campfire. Her parents, maybe, or some traveling companion who'd come down with the infection.

Frank was silent too. He was thinking about the one he'd lost and about that stupid little argument he'd had with her after he saw the doctor. How none of it mattered now, and how he should be holding onto the good memories, not the bad, but it had always been his tendency to preserve moments of embarrassment, anger, and hurt in their original pristine condition. Nan wouldn't have wanted that for him, but she wouldn't have wanted any of this.

That argument, though, ate at him more than anything else. Even if he had cried afterwards, and she had comforted him, and then they'd laughed together, he still held onto the argument. He'd felt so bitter and it was almost like he was lashing out at her for *not* having a possibly-terminal illness. It made him think of his earlier marriage and how that sort of thing had done them in. He and his wife had been best friends, and great lovers, but they'd always turned on one another in times of stress, had brought out the claws and bared the teeth when they should have been leaning on each other. Life, loss and dysfunction had all continued even while Hell Walks was traversing North America and causing tremors that were recorded as far south as Mexico. Frank and his wife had been discussing – no, debating – the terms of a trial separation when the Little Ones came pouring out of Hell Walks like living blood. The Little Ones and the infection that had killed this man.

Frank supposed it was human nature to focus on petty shit even when the world as coming to an end. Before Hell Walks, there had been countries where bombings, shelling's, and gassings were the order of the day, and the people there still went to work and cooked dinner and bought shit they didn't need. It was enough to make a man misanthropic, and maybe Frank was just that, even while he preached on the value of life. He just wanted Caitlin's generation - if they were somehow to endure through all this, if there was in fact an end to this state the world was in – to be better.

Quebra returned and reported no signs that a large group had ever been in the vicinity. He figured the man had been exiled from the group far away and had walked some miles before settling here to wait it out.

"We were talking," Frank said, "and thought we ought to do something for the guy before we go. A moment of silence, something."

"We should burn him," said Dodger.

Quebra shook his head at that. "Whole forest would go up. Besides, I don't want to attract anyone's attention." He wasn't just talking about the dead man's former friends, he was talking about Little Ones. The one that had pulped Mills was out there, still a threat even after four days' walking. There had been a couple of times during the protracted off-road hike that Frank had thought he felt a slight quaking beneath his feet, but no one else had and he'd put it down to his bad knees.

"Let's just go," Dodger said. "This is retarded."

"Excuse me," O'Brien snapped, then softened her tone. "Please don't say that."

Dodger's face reddened but he wasn't about to apologize. "Did I use the word wrong?" he said. "This is dumb. Let's get away from that corpse."

Duckie didn't appear to have taken offense at the word, but he stood protectively beside O'Brien and stared hard at Dodger. Dodger rolled his eyes. "Would someone speak up here? Can we agree there's no need to hold a memorial service? I do not like being this close to that *shit.*" As he said the last word he stabbed his finger at the dead man. "Retard is a medical term, by the way. Words like idiot and moron were too before people got all sensitive about it. That isn't what matters now."

"Then drop it," said Chia. "We'll go."

"All I'm saying," Dodger persisted, "is that if you don't want a medical term to be co-opted as some sort of slur, then come up with a word that doesn't sound *hilarious.*"

"Jesus, Dodger, shut the fuck up." Frank was exasperated and he didn't bother trying to talk the man down. "You'll fight about any goddamned thing unless it's something that actually matters. You would have made one hell of a Senator, kid."

"Ha ha," Dodger retorted. "Never heard that before." Frank had already turned and was walking away. Dodger would rant on and on until Quebra gave him the high sign. He was scared of Quebra, a man who could and had fought the important battles. He probably saw Frank as some pencil-pushing yuppie worm. So be it.

As he walked, Frank thought about Dodger's family and his own exile. He tried to feel sorry for Dodger. It didn't work.

They'd keep him around for the same reason they had buried Mills' head, because of something Frank had said in a speech to Caitlin, something he'd nearly forgotten already.

#

Didn't help tension any when Frank began to notice Dodger noticing Caitlin.

They were furtive, sideways looks, but Dodger wasn't as subtle as he believed and Frank had taken notice of it, of Dodger's eyes following the girl's hips as he loitered about at the rear of the group. One night, a couple of days after the dead man, Frank and Chia were picking berries and Frank brought it up.

"Well, what do you want to do?" Chia asked as he knelt to uproot a small plant. "We knew from the word go that Dodger was going to be a general nuisance. We knew – even if no one said it – that having a pretty girl like that was going to be a problem sooner or later."

"How do you mean?" Frank demanded, but he thought he did know.

"You and I may be gentlemen, Frank – Quebra too, and the kid, Duckie, doesn't seem to know girls even exist – but Cate was always going to be trouble down the line, with or without Dodger." Chia brushed his hands on his knees and said, "Let me rephrase that. It's not her that's the trouble, it's the fact that sooner or later, she's bound to draw the unwanted attention of some pigshit. Whether it's our boy Dodger or some red-eyed nomads, it's going to happen."

Frank sighed. "So I don't get it. What are you saying?"

"I'll say two things. One, she's a tough kid. As tough as her big sister, I think, though less experienced. Two, we're around her at all times. All of us, including Autumn. Especially Autumn. So, when and if something happens, I think the odds are in the girl's favor."

"You're saying it *will* happen. Sooner or later she's going to be in trouble."

"I don't like it, Frank, but I see it. I acknowledge it." Chia's creased face peered up at that of his friend. "Josie and I, we raised Bryan right. He was a young man if ever there was one. You know that most guys out here in this wasteland are playing Lord of the Flies. They're scared, they're mad. Nothing worse than a little boy in the body of a full-grown man."

Nothing scarier, Frank silently agreed. Even the Little Ones – well, they were animals, at least that was how humanity perceived them. So there was no thought of attempting to reason with them. By contrast, one could, and would, try to reason with a madman, and when the madman's empty eyes smiled, when one found oneself looking into a face that was at once both human and inhuman, that was terrifying.

Chia agreed that they would both keep an eye on Dodger but that he was unlikely to try anything, and so, on life went. It was a day later when the group encountered the man in the road.

They stuck mostly to off-road travel, but several fallen trees – completely covered in moss, probably the long-ago work of a Little One – had forced them to get onto the highway. A few hundred yards ahead, a man in a suit had stepped out onto the road.

"Excuse me! Hello!" the man called, waving.

"I'll be butched," Quebra said, bringing up his rifle.

"He's wearing a three-piece suit," Autumn said. Her perplexity was matched in the faces of those around her. Frank noted that the suit was filthy and rumpled, but the man's hair was immaculate. It was sandy brown and the sideburns were frosted with gray. He did his best to smooth his blue suit while waving.

"That's fine," he called to Quebra, as if giving him permission to aim the rifle. "That's okay, don't blame ya. I'd just like to talk with you from right here."

"I don't know if we want to talk," Quebra called. Chia came to stand beside him.

"Well that's okay too, but let me just tell you," said the man in the suit, "that there are four snipers surrounding us." His hands each produced two fingers and pointed into the trees along either side of the road. He looked like a flight attendant identifying the exits. "Now that's not a threat," he added quickly. "They're for my safety and yours too."

Chia leaned in to Quebra and muttered, "Let's hear him out. May as well assume he's telling the truth."

Quebra nodded. The rifle was still trained on the man. The soldier said, "So what is this?"

The man smiled. It was a broken smile, several key teeth missing, but he still knew how to work what was left. Frank suddenly had the feeling that this guy was either a cult leader or a...well, probably a cult leader.

"My name's Jack Robbins," the man said. "I and my friends in the trees, we represent a small community about half a mile from here. We hang out along the roadside and try to catch – excuse me, wrong choice of words – try to meet with other survivors. We're trying to grow our community. We're a self-sustaining group. We have a farm."

This was a pretty elaborate setup. If these guys were nothing more than highwaymen, Frank thought, they were overdoing it.

Without making a move toward Chia, Frank whispered to him through gritted teeth. "Cult. Cannibals."

Chia didn't look back, just nodded. He spoke then to the man in the blue suit. "So you're after supplies?"

"Oh no," said Jack Robbins with that same infomercial smile, "we have plenty. Of course, we welcome whatever you bring to the table, but what we're looking to do is build the community. As I said, we have a farm, fortifications, and limited medical resources, but they're there. I'm inviting you to visit and consider joining up. This is about taking America back."

Dodger stepped past Frank and joined Chia beside Quebra. "You say Jack Robbins?" He called. "DNC?"

Frank was about to hiss at Dodger to shut up but the smile of the man in the suit broadened. "That's right, sir. I represent Bill McAvoy."

"I'm Ethan Dodgman," Dodger replied. "Chris Dodgman was my uncle."

"You Governor Dodgman's boy?" Robbins called back. "How is he? Is he okay?"

Dodger replied with a quick no that the governor had tragically perished in a plane crash. Which was, of course, a lie; Governor Dodgman had been the one to show his son the door after the family had drawn straws, but everyone knew well enough to let that go.

"You mentioned McAvoy," Dodger said once condolences had been offered and accepted. "Is he with you? At your camp?"

"Yes he is," said Robbins. "The President runs things for us and he does a damn fine job."

"Not the President," said Autumn. She grimaced. Probably hadn't meant to say it so loudly but it was true. McAvoy had been elected, yes, and the sitting President had been killed when D.C. fell, but McAvoy had never been sworn in.

Robbins raised his hands palms-out in a gesture that said, *I'll give you that one, but hear me out.* "With his predecessor dead and the Vice President missing in action, we consider Bill McAvoy to be America's commander-in-chief. He wasn't able to be inaugurated, but he did win the vote. We go by the voice of the people."

He laughed. It sounded forced. "You can call him President-Elect if you like, he won't take offense. The point is, he's our leader. He's the one who sent us out here to recruit."

Frank was still thinking cannibals, but the fact was that Robbins didn't look that well-fed. His face was sallow and the reason the suit was so rumpled was because of how thin he was. Maybe in another life that suit had fit him like a glove, a custom job paid for by the McAvoy campaign, but now all he had was his hair(piece?) and his smile.

Chia whispered something to Quebra. Robbins called to the soldier. "What's your name, son?"

"PFC Sean Quebra," came the reply.

"I'll bet you've had a lot to do with the health and safety of this little crew you've got," Robbins said. "I'm sure the President would thank you if he were here. We have a number of active and retired military in our community. The four snipers out there – who, again, aren't meant to threaten – are all Marines. We have a very strong security presence back in town. That's what we call it, by the way. Too big to be a camp."

Dodger took point again. "It's been a long time since we've run across anyone so civilized, Jack. You understand why we'd be a little thrown by your kind offer, but I do nonetheless apologize."

Christ, this was Dodger's wet dream. Frank looked down so that no one would register his eye-roll.

"Of course!" Robbins said, and this time the laugh that followed was a little warmer. "Listen. If you wish to continue unhindered, my men and I will back off right now. You're free to go. If you'd like to see the town and meet President McAvoy, you're most welcome to do so, and even then there's no obligation to stay."

"I have a question," Chia said. "A few days ago we came across a dead man. He was infected. He had a lot of gear and supplies."

"You're asking if I know the man?" Robbins nodded. "A few days out, you say. Judging by the direction you're coming from, I'd guess that was Sergeant Ryan Reimer. He took sick unexpectedly and asked to leave. It wasn't easy for any of us, but the sergeant was determined to prevent anyone else from becoming infected. We were happy to give him the provisions he wanted. He was a very good man."

Robbins clapped his hands together. "I'd like to become better acquainted with you all, but we should probably move off the road. You aren't going to be asked to surrender your guns or anything else. What do you think?"

Dodger looked from Quebra to Chia to Frank. His eyes were pleading.

"We need to talk about this," Autumn said.

Caitlin nodded in agreement. O'Brien stood protectively in front of Duckie. Dodger sighed loudly.

Jack Robbins raised his hands again in mock surrender. "Take your time," he said, "but not too much. I'm getting off the road." He stepped to the shoulder and then into the trees.

"This could be another Mills," Autumn said. "How do we know there's a 'town', and how do we know there are snipers?"

"I was erring on the side of caution," Quebra said. "If there are snipers, it's survival to stop and listen. If not, if he's just a lone nut, no need to rush him."

"My point is that Mills *was* a lone nut," Autumn said.

"Jack Robbins isn't a nut. He's one of the most influential conservative Democrats in the nation," Dodger said.

"That doesn't mean a goddamned thing anymore," Autumn shot back. "No one gives a shit, just like we don't give a shit about your pedigree." She took a half-step toward Caitlin. Frank realized she'd noticed Dodger watching Caitlin too. Of course she had. She'd probably noticed it long before anyone else. She just hadn't said anything until now, and now it was as good as a hard right to Dodger's teeth.

The young man pursed his lips and glared at Autumn. "You listen."

"Easy, Dodge," Chia said. "We're being watched, remember? Do snipers read lips?"

"All of you listen," Dodger growled. He was completely undeterred, even as Quebra fixed him with his steely gaze. "You may not care about law and order anymore but these people clearly do. We're talking Bill McAvoy here. Everybody catch that? It's not about right, left, red, or blue. These people are trying to hack it just like us. Survival in numbers. Success in numbers. This has got to be a once-in-a-lifetime opportunity."

"You don't know that any more than I know what I believe," Autumn replied. She was trying to match the measured intensity of Dodger's tone but was faltering all the same. She was losing the debate.

"Chia," Dodger implored. "I know it sounds too good to be true, but hey, there are still good people out there. Right? Don't we all believe that? Isn't there a chance this is legit?"

"And if it isn't?" Chia asked. "Are we to hold you accountable?"

"If we don't like their setup, we're free to move on." Dodger shrugged as if the idea were too simple to question. "They don't want our guns or anything else. If it's a no-go, we go."

"What if they're lying?" Caitlin said. "That's what Autumn meant. Not, 'what if the town is lame.' She meant 'what if the town is bullshit.'"

Dodger turned to Caitlin and nodded. "I get it. So we ask ourselves, is it worth the risk of taking a look? I think it is. With Quebra in the lead, with my rapport with Robbins, I think it's well worth the risk. If someone wants to hold me accountable, fine." He raised his hands in a gesture mirroring Robbins. "If it all goes south you can leave me behind. I won't follow you like Mills. You can be rid of me."

He really believes in this Robbins character, Frank thought.

Quebra elbowed Chia. "We've gotta make a call."

Chia looked into the faces of each member of the group, his expression calm. He said, "Anyone against this? Against just checking it out?"

"If Robbins is with us," Quebra said, "walking with us, then I'll feel a lot better about it." In other words, if Robbins were available as a hostage. Frank gave a shallow nod at that.

O'Brien crossed her arms. "I really don't know about this, but Duckie and I can't make it on our own. I guess we're coming."

"To the farm?" Duckie asked. O'Brien nodded.

"So that's it," Autumn said.

"It sounds like we're going," Chia said. "That doesn't mean you have to come with us – in fact, maybe some of us can go and the rest can hang back until we return. If we're not back by dark, hoof it out of here. How's that?"

"That's up to Jack Robbins," Dodger said. He turned and called into the trees. "Jack?"

Robbins stepped out again. "Mister Dodgman?"

"How would you feel if some of us stayed behind for the first visit? I'd be happy to come, of course, but some of us are still feeling overly cautious. It's a learned behavior, you know."

"Understandable," said Robbins. "I'm a relative stranger to most of you. Well, I can't leave anyone behind to guard those who remain, but if half of you would be willing to come then I suppose we could make a return trip later on."

Half. Dodger glanced at the others. "So me, Quebra, who else?"

"Why does Quebra have to go?" O'Brien demanded.

"I should go," Quebra said.

O'Brien and Duckie were obviously not going to be separated, and Frank supposed the same went for Autumn and Caitlin. He didn't like the idea of leaving that quartet behind. Fuck it if that made him look like a male chauvinist. There just wasn't enough hardened experience between the four.

"Autumn," he said, "how about you and Cate?"

Her countenance went from surprise to anger to something he couldn't identify. "Why us?"

"I want to stay with the kid." Frank motioned toward Duckie. "My knees are shit anyway, heart too. I'd hold the group back if things went bad."

"What's wrong with your heart?" O'Brien asked.

"Hauer-Griggs Syndrome," Frank said. "It's genetic. I'm well past my life expectancy."

"You're volunteering me to stay behind too, I notice," said Chia.

"Unless Autumn's willing to leave Cate."

"You know what?" Autumn said to Frank. "I am. Happy to. Sorry if that fucks things up for you but I think Caitlin should stay."

Caitlin began to object and her sister cut her off. "You don't know who or what is out there. At least here, you'll have people you know, and Frank, if he doesn't drop dead, will be able to protect you."

That stung. Frank lowered his eyes.

"I'm not helpless," Caitlin argued.

"Then you can stay here," Autumn said. "You can live half a day without me. Right?"

Caitlin realized Autumn had talked her into a corner. If she insisted on staying with her big sister, it betrayed her fear, and that would come back to bite her somewhere down the line.

"I'll be fine," Caitlin muttered. "Just fine. It might be nice. Good luck." She walked to the shoulder of the road and sat cross-legged in the grass.

"We'll come back for you," Dodger said in his best Prince Charming voice.

Frank wondered if Autumn was going to use this opportunity away from Caitlin to confront Dodger. He'd have to wait until dusk for the gory details. *Poor choice of words, Frank.*

"So me, Quebra, Autumn, Chia." Dodger nodded. "That's good. All right, let's go over and talk to Robbins, and we'll go."

"I guess so," Quebra said. He dropped his pack from his shoulder and fished through it. Producing a second magazine for Frank's pistol, he handed the clip over and said, "If you hear my rifle, it went bad."

Frank nodded. He was scared now. His heart ached from the stress and he tried his best to hide his shortness of breath.

Autumn saw it. "You'll be fine," she said.

"Is that an apology?" he wheezed.

Her face darkened again. "You first," she said, and then followed Dodger down the road. He saw the sisters exchange a wounded but caring glance. He hoped they'd see each other again soon.

#

Based on the sun's position, Frank figured it was late afternoon, four o'clock maybe. Sitting in the shadow of a leaning tree, he used a penknife to loose pebbles from the treads of his boots.

"Does anyone like games?" Duckie asked. He was sitting in front of a pile of twigs which he'd been trying to make into a house. Now he scattered them with a sigh.

"What kind of games?" Caitlin asked.

Duckie brightened. "Xbox."

"I only ever played computer games," Caitlin said, "but there were some of the same games as Xbox. *Black Ops.*"

"Yeah." Duckie smiled. *"Zombies."*

"I liked that one." Caitlin picked at her shoelaces. "We played a lot of board games too. Mostly those. Autumn worked at a thrift shop. We played old-school stuff."

"Maybe even O'Brien and I have heard of those," Frank said. "Like what?"

"Hungry Hungry Hippos," Caitlin said. "It was okay. I liked it because she did. We actually brought it with us when we left the house – after Mom and Dad died – but we ended up having to use it for kindling."

Frank thought that was odd but didn't say anything. Even in an urban environment there was plenty of stuff lying around that one could burn for warmth. Maybe they'd burned it to try and let go of the past. Never worked.

"My favorite is Chinese checkers," Duckie said.

"We played that every day at the – at school," O'Brien said. "At lunch, right Duck?"

"Public school?" Frank asked.

"No, it was a private institution. Duckie lived there."

"I miss my mom and dad all the time," Duckie said, looking again to Caitlin. "I missed them back then too."

"They didn't visit," O'Brien explained.

"Did you have friends?" Caitlin asked Duckie.

"Sometimes," he said, gathering the twigs again. "Sometimes no one liked me but other times, yes."

"Well, you've got some friends now," Caitlin said.

"When are we going to the farm, you think?" Duckie asked her.

"When my sister gets back. Soon I hope."

Duckie busied himself with the twigs. Frank caught O'Brien's eye and smiled at her. Things felt oddly pleasant as early evening crept in and the shadows grew long.

#

The others came back just as the sun disappeared behind the trees. They looked okay. Dodger was grinning. They were accompanied by two men in fatigues, both bearing rifles.

"Let's go home," Dodger said with a genial wave.

FIVE

As Frank walked, he tried to gauge the pain levels throughout his body. The trek into the woods was proving much longer and more arduous than he'd anticipated. There were trees which had been intentionally brought down atop one another to dissuade outsiders, and carefully-obscured trenches which were required to reach the town. The soldiers escorting them pointed out pits covered by branches and vegetation, traps that could only be identified if one knew which flowers to look for. All of these measures were intended to keep out those who weren't invited. No such measures existed for the Little Ones.

"They never come this deep into the woods," one of the soldiers said. "They stick to the roads and the cities. Sure, they might go off-road once in a while if they see someone, but we're as far from their eyes as is humanly possible." The man grinned through a reddish beard. "Adaptation."

Frank went back to cataloguing the growing aches in his joints. His knees and ankles, of course, were bad. The tightness in his chest was his lungs, heart, or both. Sometimes he couldn't tell. All of his connective tissue was weak, too elastic. Lately, he wondered if his brain wasn't headed in the same direction. He thought back to the waking dream in the van, the one that had almost gotten him stomped. The Gray Woman and the book that had unleashed...it was almost as if his opening the book in the dream had roused the Little One lying in that parking lot.

It was at this point in Frank's thinking that a voice usually chimed in gently to remind him that such ideas were crazy. No voice came this time. Instead he thought, *you're talking elasticity of the mind, not the brain. Not Hauer-Griggs. You think the sheath enclosing your unconscious has softened to a permeable veil? You think you saw something from* outside?

Then Frank dismissed it. No, his dream hadn't stirred the Little One, it was the other way around. When the thing began stirring, he'd heard it in his subconscious and incorporated it into the dream. As for the Gray Woman, well, not everything in a dream had to have some real-world counterpart.

There was a log wall coming up and an armed guard peered over it. The soldiers accompanying Frank's group waved silently. Trees overhead rustled and Frank spotted men in sniper nests. This place certainly seemed like the real deal. It had already received Quebra and Chia's endorsement. Autumn had spent most of the walk describing it to Caitlin. She said there were all sorts of structures, everything from simple lean-tos to small cabins. She'd seen cows, goats, and chickens, and she said she'd shaken hands with Bill McAvoy. Who was still not the President but who had risen in her opinion to a man worthy of trust.

One of the things Caitlin had said in Autumn's absence was that they originally were from north Texas, McAvoy's old stomping grounds. Though that region was part of Tornado Alley, Frank hadn't caught any hint of an accent in either girl's voice. Still, he was inclined to believe Caitlin. After all, he didn't think he had an accent either, but who knew how a Connecticut native sounded to two Texans.

A gate swung open and the group was ushered in. Frank heard the distant bleating of a goat and wondered if they might eat meat tonight. He couldn't remember the last time he'd dined on anything better than squirrel and his mouth practically filled with water.

Within the walls of the town, much of the tree canopy had been cleared away to allow natural light in. The faintest indications of the night sky were bleeding through the weathered day. Azure had darkened to indigo and the black of space was ever more present. Along the path the group walked, which was flanked by wooden walls, men and women were lighting torches and mounting them in metal clips. The torches' glowing heads sat inside crude sheet-metal housings with glass faces. They reminded Frank of Victorian streetlamps and there was a certain charm in that. This all seemed idyllic compared to the outside, and as it stood, Frank hadn't even really seen any of the town yet.

The path opened up into a large clearing dotted by picnic tables and small shacks. The "facilities" were easily identified by the crescent moons cut into their doors. Another, slightly larger shack looked to be an equipment shed. Torches were being handed out from its open door. Frank saw young teens helping in the effort and wondered at how such a place could exist mere miles from the road and urban ruin.

One of their armed escorts, the red-bearded man who called himself Attic, invited them to sit at a picnic table. "Supper'll be along soon. Stew, probably. Just sit tight and we'll get to ya. The President will be along in his time."

Despite the clearing's size, its tables only accommodated a few dozen people, and Frank supposed there had to be other areas throughout the town where people gathered to eat. "Do people own property here?" he asked Attic.

"Everyone who works has a home," said Attic. "There are nicer places a bit deeper in the woods. This is sort of a receiving area for new folks. You'll get a hot and a cot tonight, and tomorrow they'll figure out where to put you to work."

"If we stay," Autumn said. Though she'd seemed more optimistic about the place after her first visit, she still had her guard up. Caitlin rolled her eyes.

Quebra said, "We got to see more of the town than this. I guess you'll see it tomorrow, Frank. The forest was settled a year after the collapse. Lots of work has gone into it."

"Does it feel like home?" Frank asked him.

"As much as anything can," Quebra said. "Tell you what, it feels safe."

"You still having second thoughts?" Dodger asked Autumn. "After everything? C'mon. You think there's somewhere better than this down the road?"

"I want to know as much as I can before I'm forced to make a decision," she replied. "We got a nice little tour, we got to meet McAvoy, and everyone put their best foot forward. I'd just like a little time to see how things run day-to-day."

"Seems fair," said Chia. "Robbins promised there'd be no pressure."

Attic, standing next to the table, said nothing. He was watching the stars come out, but he had to be listening. Was he to report all this to his superiors later on?

Dodger sighed. "Well hey, you guys do whatever you want. My mind's made up. We aren't tied to one another anymore."

"We never were," Autumn said. "We accepted each other. Remember that."

"I don't have anything against you," Dodger said, looking now at Caitlin. "I like you. I hope you'll stay." His stare lingered a second too long and Caitlin looked down. Frank's skin crawled.

"I don't think we'll be neighbors," Autumn said. "I think you'll be busy with Robbins and his crew. Maybe you'll be the new highway ambassador."

Again, Frank wondered if Autumn had spoken to Dodger about Caitlin. If not, it looked like they were having the conversation now. It was one part innuendo and one part dirty looks. Dodger narrowed his eyes at Autumn and said to her, "It wouldn't hurt to have a friend like me in a place like this. Maybe you still believe that the world out there is the real one, but this is the place. Out there, we're part of the food chain. Out there, we're reduced to cavemen who shit where we eat."

People were bringing stacked bowls and steaming pots into the clearing. The smell of the stew, of cooked meat and vegetables, hit Frank's nostrils and he forgot all about the spat going on at his table.

"That smells like real goddamned food," Chia breathed.

Frank hadn't realized how hungry and tight his stomach was until it began to mewl. Caitlin turned at the sound and laughed. "Me too," she said to his gut.

"Thank God I still have teeth," Quebra said. He nudged Duckie. "You hungry man?"

"Always." Duckie was focused on the activity at the tables where people were being served. His mouth hung agape with longing.

Dodger offered Autumn a conciliatory smile. "We'll sleep on it."

"Stay the fuck away from my sister," Autumn said. Well, there it was.

Caitlin stared into her lap again. Dodger's smile stayed fixed in place. He turned from Autumn to await his bowl of stew.

#

Frank had two helpings. It was more than his eyes could believe, and as it turned out, more than his stomach could take. After eating, he moved from the table to a grassy patch beneath a tall tree. There he laid back and waited for the ache in his belly to subside. God, but it was worth it.

He stargazed for a while and then drifted off to sleep. It must have only been a few minutes. When his eyes opened again, Caitlin was nearby, her feet bare, standing in the cool grass and staring at nothing. He shifted and she looked over at him.

"I can't believe she said that," she muttered.

"What?" Frank asked, but he knew. Instead of waiting for her answer he said, "You don't like the guy, do you?"

"No," Caitlin said quickly, "but that's not the point. I'm tired of being protected, and I know what you're going to say, I should feel lucky. I don't. Not when I'm being protected from shit that doesn't need it."

"You lost your parents. She doesn't want to lose you."

"To *what?*" Caitlin exclaimed, dropping her voice to a whisper. "She doesn't want a Little One to eat me, I get that. She doesn't want me to get murdered or raped. Like I don't know what's out there. Like I'm too stupid to get that men are...well, not all men."

"I hear ya."

"She's not that much older than me. What the hell does she think *she* knows?"

"It's not about knowing, I don't think," Frank said. "Not necessarily. It's just about caring. Your parents didn't know everything either, but they'd act like they did if they thought it would keep you safe. Right?" He sat up. "I had parents once, too."

"Did you ever want kids?" she asked.

"No. I wouldn't know how to deal with that shit." It came out before he had time to think about it, and he stammered in search of an apology, but she laughed appreciatively.

"I don't think I want kids either," she said. "Even if things get better. Even if the monsters go away."

"It's not for everyone." Frank got to his feet. "I can't speak for Autumn, but I don't think she's trying to be your mom, and I don't think she thinks you're stupid. She's just doing what any of us would do if we had a little sister. Including you."

"You don't know me," Caitlin said.

"I know you're a good person," he said. "I'm sure of that."

She shrugged, accepting the compliment. She was chewing on some thought, he could tell, and finally she asked, "So was Mills evil?"

He started to answer right away but realized he didn't know. So, he said it. "I don't know. I don't know if evil is a real thing. I guess it is, right, if good is. I guess a psychopath is evil but..."

"But what?"

"I don't know that she had a choice in being who she was. I think goodness is a choice. It's almost more against our nature." Frank looked at Caitlin. "Does that even make sense? Because I'm not sure that I get it."

"I think so," she said. "Like animals. They aren't really good or evil, right? They're just animals, but we're different somehow."

"A little different," he said.

"Are the Little Ones evil?" She pulled her hair back and tied it. "I know you don't know for sure, but what do you think? Is Hell Walks evil?"

"We seem to think so. Look at what we named it."

"Maybe it didn't know what it was doing."

"Maybe." Maybe the monsters were just giant animals, but they were still actively seeking to destroy humanity, and so it didn't matter whether they got off on it or not. They'd reduced humans to frightened lesser beasts, to prey. Man was a simple animal again and so maybe questions of good and evil didn't mean so much anymore.

He kept those last thoughts to himself, instead, telling her, "We'll probably never know their motives. You just keep an eye on those guys like Dodger. They're not hard to figure out."

"I know, and I will."

"Just for the record, your sister's not the only one watching your back."

Caitlin smiled. "It's just a good person thing, I guess?"

"I guess so."

"Well, just don't get in my way." Her smiled broadened and then she walked off. It was Frank's turn to laugh, but he knew she was dead serious.

#

McAvoy came by torchlight. He sat on the edge of the picnic table and shook hands, waiting for everyone to return so he could address them as a group.

He looked healthy – robust, even – and his smile was genuine. He wasn't wearing a suit, having opted for jeans and the dress shirt with rolled-up sleeves. Frank knew it was a political look, but it still worked. He had the Texas accent and spoke in a happy drawl.

"Well, I sure hope you'll all consider becoming citizens of our little burg," he told them. "Can you believe we still haven't named it? We've debated it – New Washington, Freetown, and the like - but we can't all agree on one and it seems unnecessary to squabble over it. After all, we get along just fine without a name."

"How many people live here?" O'Brien asked.

"One hundred twenty-two," said McAvoy, "including four births this year. There have actually been more attempts at starting families, but you can imagine the mortality rate is perilous. Still, we do what we can with the resources we've been able to gather."

Frank wanted to ask why anyone would even think of starting a family, but he didn't. *The old American Dream, I guess. Effort and determination always pay off. If you want it enough, it works out.*

"Tonight you just relax. Tomorrow you'll get a better look at the town," McAvoy told the group. "By the way, if you're the praying kind, we hold a sort of non-denominational service every Saturday and Sunday. Tomorrow's Saturday."

So, this was Friday. Frank hadn't known the day or date in quite some time. It seemed utterly trivial but fascinating at the same time. These folks kept a calendar? If that didn't imply hope, what did?

Attic gave Frank the option of bunking with a few of the town guards or sleeping in a hammock outside. He went for the latter, saying he wanted to stargaze a bit more.

"You know how to handle a gun?" Attic asked him.

"Handgun, sure."

"You ever use one?"

"Not on a person, if that's what you mean."

Attic nodded and left Frank to settle in. A few minutes later, as Frank lay swaying in silence, Jack Robbins emerged from the dark.

"Hi, Frank. I wanted to mention something to you. I've talked to the others as well – the other men – I thought it might be better to do it this way, privately, so as not to upset the ladies."

Frank's brow furrowed. "Huh?"

Robbins leaned against the tree to which the foot of the hammock was tethered. "There's a group to the east. A good distance from here, and they don't know where we're located, but we know about them. We've been doing some recon out that way and just happened to spot these people."

"Okay..."

"This isn't a threatening sort of situation. They appear to be American military – at least that's how they dress. Plus, they're extremely well-armed. We've been watching them for some time, just to be cautious, but we're at the point where we're thinking about approaching them. Asking them to join us here."

Frank nodded somewhat hesitantly. He'd just gotten here, hadn't even made up his mind about staying, and it sounded like Robbins was getting ready to ask a favor.

He was. "We want to send a good-sized group to meet with them but we can't send every man, you understand. We need guards and workers. We need some of the most experienced guys to remain behind and do their jobs."

"You want *me* to go?"

"This is just a thought," Robbins said. "I'm just spitballing, seeing if there might be any interest from your crew. PFC Quebra sounds amenable. Dodgman too. I'll be visiting with Chia right after you. It's just something to think about. You'd be traveling with good men, armed men, but as I said, we can't send all of our veterans."

Frank nodded again. "Okay. Thanks. I'll think about it."

He lay alone but couldn't focus on the starscape. These people were welcoming and accepting in a way that almost seemed foreign. What Robbins had asked implied a great deal of trust – maybe faith was the better word, seeing as Robbins didn't know Frank at all. He certainly didn't know Dodger.

He was beginning to feel uneasy and tried to quell his anxiety. So they were decent people trying to make things work out here. A bit of cynicism was a rational response, but why be afraid? *Wait until there's a reason, then you can lose it.*

His chest was tight and he gripped his ribs in a panic, trying to draw in a deeper breath. He wheezed, coughed and…

Was in a long, dim room with a dirt floor and windows along the ceiling. A basement of some sort, the walls concrete but both the floor and ceiling seemingly made from earth. He could see thick trees with barren, winding limbs rising from the floor. Frank went to one of the high windows and gripped the windowsill, trying to pull himself up and get a look outside. It was no good. His arms ached terribly. All he could see from this angle was a flat gray sky.

The Gray Woman…was she here? He turned and examined the room. As his eyes grew used to the dimness, he saw a half-dozen knee-high mounds of dirt on the floor. They rose to tapered peaks, into which were sunk holes. They looked like giant anthills. He hoped he was wrong about that.

The trees' corkscrewing limbs rose up to the ceiling and vanished right into it. If Frank were to look at the room upside-down, he might perceive the branches as roots growing out of the ceiling. The anthills would be stalactites. The idea made Frank dizzy and he slumped against the walls, hands slapping the concrete to stop him from falling over.

This doesn't feel like a dream. I'm not asleep.

It was all too real, too crisp at the edges, his perception too sharp. It was not a dream and yet there was no way out of it. He was trapped in this waking vision – hallucination? – and with a rush of fear, he wondered if he had been transported away from the hammock, the town, and even the stars, to some awful other place.

In answer to his question, one of the anthills shuddered. Granules ran down its sloping sides and a white claw groped out of the hole.

Frank stood numbly and watched as a miniature Little One made its way out of the hole and shambled down to the floor. It couldn't be more than six inches tall. He could trample the thing into the dirt and the impulse to do just that seized him. He took a step toward it. It turned toward him and its beak split into those four lashing mandibles. It let out a shrill croak.

Frank stopped short. He didn't want to lose any toes to that mouth. The Little One turned its head from side to side, making more wretched sounds. Frank knew it was calling others from the other earthen mounds, and as wary as he felt, he didn't quite feel scared. It was almost like watching a puppet show. For the first time, he was able to examine a Little One from overhead and studied the shape of its head and the knobby curve of its spine. To think that, in real life, it would take fifty Franks to match the height of one of these monsters. More of them were coming out from the hills. He walked around the room, giving the Little Ones a wide berth, but moving only with caution, not fear. They made their tiny roars and seemed to be communicating with one another.

Frank felt like Hell Walks standing over its offspring. Were they offspring? Or pilots? After all, Hell Walks stood inert in Chicago with an ice cap encasing its head. Perhaps there was no one at the controls. Or maybe the Little Ones were parasites who had hollowed out their host just as these scale replicas had hollowed the earth beneath Frank's feet.

The Little Ones spoke in gravely cries, paying no mind to Frank. It was they who appeared confused and frightened now, and why not? They were ensnared in his mind, weren't they?

The monster that had emerged first from the ground, now turned and stared directly at Frank. It took him back to the moment in Independence when the towering Little One had seemed to stare at him. Intuitively, he knew this was the same one that looked up at him now.

"What do you want?" he asked. His words came out at a volume like thunder, barely discernable, the trees around him rattling and the Little Ones scattering with shrieks.

All except for the one who watched him.

#

Quebra's voice, at first, sounded just as overmodulated and garbled. "Frank," he repeated, shaking the man's shoulder.

Frank sat up and nearly fell from the hammock. "Jesus. Sorry, I was asleep."

"Didn't look like it," Chia said. "You all right, bud?"

"I just..." Frank wanted a moment to think, to sort out the vision and what it meant. Because it meant *something*. He was sure of that, but the others wanted to talk.

"Robbins come and see you?" Chia asked.

"Yeah," Frank said, "told me about the other group. I don't know. I'm a little out of it."

"Well look," said Quebra, "I've already decided to stay and I think this welcoming committee assignment would be a good way to start building some cred. I vote we do it."

"You know my vote," said Dodger from behind them. He stepped between Quebra and Chia and scrutinized Frank. "Is it your condition? You ought not to go if you're feeling sour."

Frank knew Dodger had no real concern for his well-being. He just didn't want someone dropping dead during his first big mission for the President-Elect. Frank, truthfully, didn't want to go. Not on the mission, anyway. No, he wanted to go east all right, but north as well. Toward Hell Walks. Ambassadorships and islands in the sun were gone from his mind. He thought now that the Gray Woman might represent – might in fact *be* – Hell Walks. She'd just given him a bird's-eye view of the Little Ones and possibly some insight into their nature – if only he could have the time to analyze everything he'd seen.

As to the question of *why* Hell Walks would send waking dreams to any human, he believed he'd only find out if he went to it. To her. Perhaps this meant an end to the apocalypse was in sight. After all, if this was a trap, it didn't seem very efficient. What sense did it make to lure one man to Chicago just to step on him?

Perhaps he wasn't the only one beginning this pilgrimage. Still, he was pretty sure that no one in his own group had experienced these same visions.

No one else has the elasticity.

The experience of standing tall over a pack of frightened Little Ones had emboldened him. Whether it was intended that way or not, it had given him a sense of purpose and even power. He wanted to go to Chicago with or without the others. He decided he wouldn't tell them every detail, but he'd make his point.

"I don't know about staying," he said. "In fact, I think I want to keep moving."

"The Keys are a long ways away, boss," Quebra said. "Especially alone."

"Well now, who said the rest of us are all staying?" said Chia. "We really need to talk this over and I think we should involve the others."

"What, Autumn?" Dodger spat. "And Duckie, yeah we definitely need to consult with him." He stood toe-to-toe with Chia. "McAvoy is asking this of us. The man's been very generous thus far. I don't think it would be polite to turn this down."

"They said we're free to choose," Chia replied tersely, "and free to go if we like."

Quebra shuffled his boots. "I don't know, boss."

Chia looked at him. "Don't know what?"

"How much could it hurt just to stay a while?" Quebra asked. "If you don't want to hang a shingle here, all right, but stay just a bit. Go on this assignment. Help the rest of us get in good with the new boss."

"You think you'll be penalized if we light out tomorrow?" Chia scowled. "That doesn't sound like the Bill McAvoy everyone's been trying to sell me."

"All I'm saying, is that there's no need to rush out of here," Quebra snapped. "What don't you like about the place, Chia? The food? The shelter? The kind people? What's the problem?"

Frank stood. "Whoa, guys. Take it easy." His chest felt tight again.

"Listen to Quebra," said Dodger. He was still standing between the soldier and Chia, and now it looked like he was the only thing keeping them out of each other's face. Chia was bright red, angrier than Frank had ever seen him. Even when he'd lost his family the old man had held it together as best he could.

Frank said, "Chia, I mean, we don't actually have to leave right away, but," he added, looking at Quebra, "I don't think we all need to go on this mission."

"So you're going to wait until Dodge and I head out, and then you'll cut and run." Quebra nodded rapidly, glowering at Frank. "That'll be nice to come home to."

"Home," Chia snorted.

"You gonna take the others? Gather them up and bolt like you're fleeing some death camp?" Quebra stabbed a finger first at Frank, then at Chia. "You don't think that's going to be a problem?"

"Are you running for office, too?" Chia barked. Dodger pressed a finger to his lips.

"Quebra," Frank sat back in the hammock, "there's nothing to suggest that it would make trouble for you if we left. Unless Robbins was lying that is. Do you think he's lying?"

"Frank," Quebra said. The word hung alone in the air for a moment while the soldier drew a deep breath. "I like you, man, but shut the fuck up."

Jesus, Frank had never seen either Quebra or Chia this bent out of shape. It seemed like a non-issue, but...Dodger. It was probably Dodger's exaggerations that had made this issue polarizing. Frank stared hard at him.

"We trust the people here," Dodger said, staring right back. "I, for one, would like to understand why you people don't."

"It isn't even about that," Chia snapped. "It's about whether or not we really have a choice. I haven't said yet that I'm not staying, and you two are up my ass."

"Well, I'm going," Frank said, "but I can wait."

"Tomorrow, we're all going to have this conversation again. All eight of us," Chia said, "and we're going to be civil about it."

"You're not in charge anymore," Dodger said. "Let the others make up their own minds."

"Only after they have all the facts," Chia shot back. "I don't like that they were left out of this."

"Because McAvoy doesn't want to send them on the mission!" Quebra hissed. "Do you really think he told *everyone else* in town except those four?"

"I don't like being split up so soon," Chia argued.

Dodger clapped his hands together. "Because you don't trust the town. Just like I thought. That's what this is. You need to stop thinking like a homeless survivalist. We've got a good thing going here."

"Don't tell me how to think, you little prick." Chia planted his finger in the middle of Dodger's chest. "You only made it this far because we carried your weight. Your own goddamned family couldn't wait to feed you to the monsters. I trust my instincts a hell of a lot more than I do you."

Dodger lunged, but Quebra, anticipating it, caught his arms and wrenched him back. *"Stop it,"* he breathed into the young man's ear. "We'll all be back on the road if we're caught acting like this."

Dodger glared at Chia, saying nothing. Chia, having seemingly regained his senses, turned and walked away. It was the last time Frank would see him alive.

"We'll sort it out tomorrow, then," Quebra muttered. "In the light of day."

Dodger still said nothing. He simply pulled free of Quebra and headed in the direction opposite of Chia.

Quebra glanced sideways at Frank. With a shrug, he headed after Dodger.

Frank was now free to meditate on the vision he'd had, but he couldn't stop replaying the argument in his mind. Finding the town should have felt liberating, but everyone was coming apart at the seams. It would be good to leave this place, he thought, and if he were indeed alone when he did, perhaps that was for the best.

SIX

Quebra shook Frank awake again. His hand was hot and slick with sweat. Frank sat up in the sunlight and blinked sleep away.

"Come on," Quebra said, "it's Chia."

Chia was lying in the narrow space between a pair of one-room cabins. It was in the nicer part of the town, though Frank took little detail in as he was ushered along. It was only when he saw the old man's body that everything came into terrible focus.

Attic and Jack Robbins stood at the mouth of the narrow alleyway. They parted when Quebra and Frank arrived. A small crowd was gathered there and the smell of their unwashed skin – they'd bathed more recently than Frank, no doubt, but this many standing together was a wall of body odor - choked him. He wheeled away, doubling over, and tried not to retch. Robbins called for the people to disperse.

Frank stood, wiping spittle from his mouth. He saw Autumn and Caitlin sitting in front of the cabin on the left. Autumn's eyes were red and swollen. Caitlin stared at the ground, twisting strands of hair between her fingers.

Frank looked back at Chia and his gorge rose again. He grunted and spat in the grass. "Who found him?"

"Benji," Attic said, "one of the night guards. His shift was just ending when dawn rolled around and he saw the body."

"No one's touched him, right?" Quebra asked.

"We had to get in there and check his pulse, but nothing beyond that," said Attic.

"How long before you came and got me?" Quebra demanded. Frank supposed Quebra had come to fetch him first before asking any questions. The soldier was badly shaken and wanted backup. Frank stood with him. He wondered if Quebra had grabbed Autumn, too, or if she'd merely overheard the news.

"It couldn't have been more than twenty minutes between the discovery of the body and when we woke you," said Robbins. "Now as near as we can tell, there aren't any signs of injury. We'll need to get him out of there, though, to have a better look."

Quebra helped Attic with it. He got Chia under the arms, Attic taking the legs, and they slowly brought Chia into the morning light. Autumn got up and walked quickly into the nearby trees.

Frank shut his eyes to the scene and focused on his labored breathing. He could hear murmurs from the trees and the squawking of chickens. A gentle wind rustled the leaves overhead. He opened his eyes and looked down at his dead friend. He saw the mottled lines on Chia's throat immediately.

Quebra did, too, and knelt over Chia's head. He probed at the man's neck and said, "Ligatures." He pulled up Chia's sleeves to examine the arms.

"You mean rope?" Attic asked. He looked at Robbins.

"Wrists are clean." Quebra moved to check Chia's ankles, pulling off his boots. A foul smell struck Frank and he realized Chia must have voided his bowels when he died. He wheeled away again and this time, just as his eyes locked with Caitlin's, the previous night's dinner came up. There wasn't much. Just a few dark, soggy chunks and a rush of hot bile. His eyes tearing, he fell on his knees and groaned at the pain that followed.

"He was strangled," he heard Quebra say from some great mental distance.

Frank cleared his throat and spat. "Where's Dodger?" He looked at Quebra. *"Where's Dodger?"*

"I don't know." Quebra looked to Robbins, who raised his empty palms.

"Find him," Frank said. "He did this."

"Hold on," said Robbins. "Are we sure what those marks on his neck are?"

"He didn't die in that little alley," Frank growled. "Someone put him there."

"Who lives in these cabins?" Quebra asked. "Did anyone hear anything?"

Of course no one had. Chia had been dead long before he was stuffed in there. It had happened while the town slept. Strangled with a rope, likely from behind. The act of a coward.

"Find Dodgman," Robbins told Attic, who set off straight away. Frank wanted to go with him but he knew he'd only make matters worse by attacking Dodger. No, he'd have his chance once the worm confessed. "What do you do with murderers?" he asked Robbins.

"We've never had a murder before," Robbins replied.

Bill McAvoy rounded the corner of the cabin on the right and stopped. He stared at Chia, and then looked into the eyes of everyone else there. He shoved his hands into the pockets of his jeans.

"Lord have mercy," he breathed. Robbins began to speak but McAvoy waved him off. He stood over Chia and he saw the marks on the man's throat.

McAvoy let out a long sigh. He asked Quebra, "Who would do this? Who came into my town and did this?"

Quebra didn't answer. Anger flushed Frank's face as he stood and said, "It was Dodger. Ethan Dodgman. They fought last night. Quebra and I were there."

"Fought?" McAvoy exclaimed. "Over what? What would lead to this?"

"Some of us were thinking about leaving," Frank said.

McAvoy's eyes fell back to Chia. He didn't speak for several moments.

"He wanted to leave," said the President-Elect. That was all.

A sharp cry from behind Frank made him and the others jump. Frank looked back and saw Duckie. The boy began screaming as O'Brien, unable to take her eyes off the body, tried absently to restrain him. She eventually wrestled him down a dirt path and out of sight.

"He was only thinking about leaving," Frank murmured. "I'm the only one whose mind is made up." *You're alive, which proves it wasn't about that. Dodger hated Chia because Chia put him in his place. Chia reminded Dodger that, even now, here in the town, he's still a powerless little prick. Dodger's trying to reinvent himself and Chia stood in his way.*

"I don't know," said Quebra.

"Don't know what?" asked Frank, incredulous.

"Could Dodger have the nerve to do this?"

"How much do you think it took to ambush an old man from behind?" Frank snapped. "Jesus, Quebra. If not him, then who?"

"I sent Attic to find Dodgman," Robbins told McAvoy, who nodded. Surely they wanted to believe it was one of the newcomers who'd done it. It made more sense. Dodger made perfect sense. Why was Quebra hesitating to finger him? Was this somehow about staying in the town's good graces?

"Quebra," Frank insisted, "Dodger's always been trouble, and a coward, and you saw him try to attack Chia last night."

"Why didn't you tell a guard about it?" said Robbins.

Frank waited for Quebra to answer that one. The soldier just scratched the stubble on his cheeks.

"Are you planning to leave as well, soldier?" McAvoy asked him.

Quebra shook his head. "No sir. Like Frank said, he was the only one who had made his mind up. I don't believe Chia had decided yet."

"Do you think he and Dodger talked later?" Frank asked. "That he told Dodger he was set on leaving? Maybe that's what happened."

Caitlin was still seated next to the cabin. Frank asked her, "Have you seen him since dinner? Dodger?"

She shook her head. "You're leaving?" She looked scared.

"No one's leaving until this is sorted out," McAvoy said. "Especially not with the information you have. Jack told you all about the group to the east. This is a very sensitive time."

"My friend is dead," Frank said through his teeth. "I know it's sensitive."

"What group?" Caitlin asked, and Frank shot her a silencing glare. He didn't want her getting sucked into this mess. It was bad enough that she'd seen Chia. Not to mention Frank practically heaving at her feet.

"Miss, unless you know something about this, you'd better go," said Robbins. "This is a crime scene."

Caitlin stood on shaky legs. "Frank, are you really leaving?"

"I said *no one* is leaving," barked McAvoy, and in the echo of his declaration, Frank heard *not now and not ever*.

A few cries sounded from far away. Then more.

Everyone looked to the sound. There was nothing to be seen among the dense forest, no one on the dirt street. It was when Frank glanced up through the tops of the trees that he saw black wisps curling lazily in the air.

"Fire?" McAvoy gasped. He turned to Robbins. "We're not doing a burn today. What is that?"

"I don't know." Robbins just stared at the smoke. A thick belch of it rolled skyward and he added, "Shit."

More screams now. Caitlin began walking down the path. She broke into a run. *"Autumn!"* she hollered.

Frank grabbed Quebra by the shoulder. "We've gotta get everybody. Get outta here."

McAvoy didn't argue with him. He was focused on the darkening sky and saying, "How could there be that much smoke? How could it..."

He raced down the path after Caitlin. Robbins paced back and forth before Chia's body, wringing his hands. "We've got a fire here. Got to clear out." He began heading off, though not toward the smoke, as Cate and McAvoy had. He hustled into the trees and toward the other cabins that made up the neighborhood. His home was probably there, and he was going to grab his shit and run for the hills.

Quebra and Frank went down the path after McAvoy and it wasn't long before there were shouts and frantic cries coming from all sides. Frank could smell the smoke now. It was thick with the rich smell of burning trees, then it was hot, too, and his chest tightened.

He and Quebra came into a clearing where a throng of men were frantically filling buckets from a man-made well. The sky above was dark gray and Frank knew their efforts were for naught. He wanted to tell them to forget it, to get their families and run away from the fire, but he could see that they were determined to fight for their home. They weren't going to listen to some bellowing stranger. Instead of addressing them, he yelled Caitlin and Autumn's names.

"I've gotta get my pack," Quebra exclaimed. "You stay around here! Keep them here if you find them!" and he ran off.

A rippling wave of heat struck Frank. At the edge of the clearing, between the branches, he saw the first licks of flame. However it had begun, the fire was spreading at a terrifying rate. Soon he'd be surrounded by it. The air was growing cloudy and he felt like he was going to suffocate. *Keep it together. You can't die like this. You won't. Hell Walks won't allow it.*

People streaked out of the fiery trees and across the clearing. Some carried bags, others children. A gunshot rang out from the woods. Then another. Between that, the screams of those in flight and the stubborn cries of the men at the well, Frank could barely hear himself as he shouted for Autumn and Caitlin. He shouted for Duckie and O'Brien, too. It was all carried away in ever-increasing waves of heat and smoke. The fire crackled at the edge of the clearing.

Then the forest was shaken by a tremendous roar, and Frank knew what people were shooting at. The shooting stopped very soon after that.

#

Frank had given his pistol back to Quebra when they'd entered the town. Not that it mattered. As the ground jittered under Frank's feet, as his feet momentarily left it and he toppled back, he knew that Man possessed no defense against what was om the other side of those burning trees. The only possible answer lay in Chicago, whether it was Frank's to know or not.

The monster's arrival must have started the blaze. He could hear its footfalls now, each accompanied by the brittle snapping of tree limbs and the frightful fracturing of trunks. Frank's vision swam both from the smoke and the way his bones rattled with every impact. Clouds of acrid smoke and dancing embers shot out from the trees at the edge of the clearing. The men at the well ceased their efforts and scattered.

High above, through the canopy McAvoy's men had trimmed back, Frank saw the beak of the Little One. God, the beast had to be five times taller than the tallest tree. To it, Frank – if it could see Frank down here – must have looked like a plastic Army man. Its entire head was in full view now and swung downward, eyes questing from side to side. It was searching for victims.

Fire spread across what remained of the canopy and smoke filled Frank's view. He stumbled toward the rear of the clearing, calling again for Autumn and Caitlin. It was O'Brien who found him. She caught his arm and spun him to face her.

Her face was streaked with soot and sweat. "Duckie!" she coughed. "I can't--" She broke into a violent coughing fit. Frank steeled his own lungs, refraining from breathing as he pushed her away from the advancing flames. The fire was the Little One's herald, announcing its terrible arrival, and for itself the fire had choking smoke as its messenger. The heat at Frank's back was painful and he pushed O'Brien harder through the trees.

"I can't find Duckie!" she managed to say. "He might be back there!"

"If he's back there--" But Frank couldn't say it. Branches creaked and complained overhead as the Little One's footsteps drew closer. Frank was thrown again off his feet and his shoulder crashed hard against a tree. He fell on his face. Gray and black swirled about him. There was no escaping the smoke. The fire was right on their heels. They were dead.

O'Brien pulled him along, all the while fighting to scream Duckie's name. Frank tried to join her but his lungs were rebelling now, as were his knees and ankles. She was practically dragging him like a corpse. That made him see Chia's face above those ligature marks and he sagged.

"Go," he croaked. "I can't do it."

O'Brien's bloodshot eyes were wide with panic. "Not you too!"

"Okay!" someone shouted. It occurred to Frank that he hadn't heard any other voices since the clearing. He wondered if that was because everyone was gone – dead or otherwise departed – or if his smoky tunnel vision was complemented by diminished hearing. He supposed he wasn't getting oxygen to his brain. The thought seemed to make sense, though the words didn't. He heard that "Okay!" again and figured that meant it was time to black out.

Instead, Autumn and Caitlin took him by either arm and hauled him to his feet. His toes dragged limp through the undergrowth and it felt as if they were moving at incredible speed. He felt like he was flying just above the ground, away from the heat and, yes, even the smoke. Gray gave way to green and he saw the sun through the leafy eaves overhead.

"Can you stand? Frank!" Autumn yelled in his ear.

"I don't know. Try." They set him firm on the ground and he tested his legs. Dull pain everywhere. His head felt thick and cloudy and he struggled to pull air down his windpipe, but he could stand, and beyond that, was something that wasn't quite running but was faster than a walk.

The four of them moved past empty sheds and discarded items – sacks of clothing, camping items, a headless chicken. Frank limped along as best he could and it seemed like every step he took was matched by a tremor. The Little One was back there somewhere, not far behind, stomping people. Stomping down through a burning tree canopy and crushing human begins under the tinder they'd once called shelter.

He looked back. Had to. He saw it towering far above and then, saw it bend at the waist, saw its searching claws coming downward like two gigantic birds of prey.

Its hands weren't coming directly down at Frank – they struck home somewhere in the fire and flaming debris leapt into the air. The creature's beak opened and Frank realized it was about to drop onto its knees.

He turned and slapped at Autumn's back. "Going to fall!"

"What!" she cried without looking back.

The earth seemed to drop out from beneath all four of them. There was a sound like every tree in the forest exploding. Frank landed on his own hands and knees with a fierce jolt of pain. He was sure he wouldn't be able to get back up.

Smoke billowed around them, pushed forward by the Little One's displacement of half the town, and cinders followed. They were like tiny orange-hot arrowheads. They struck Frank's back and neck and he fell over completely while trying to knock them away. The heat was back in full force and the ground was still vibrating. It wasn't going to stop. There wouldn't be any lulls between steps because now the Little One was on its hands and knees, knocking trees aside with its mandibles so that it could spot its prey through the smoke. It was the same one from Independence, he was dead certain. The same one.

"The same one!" he croaked, throat burning, unable to see through tear-filled eyes. Hands were on him and he knew it was Autumn again. "Frank, *please!*"

"Can't do it," he mumbled.

His teeth jumped in their sockets. The Little One was drawing closer.

Autumn flipped him onto his back and started dragging him. Distantly, he heard O'Brien's voice, then what sounded like Duckie.

"Give him to me!" That wasn't Duckie. It was Quebra.

Bigger hands slipped under Frank's arms and he was being whisked along so fast his boots came off. Frank blinked away dirty black tears and looked for them. All he saw was a forest of living fire, beckoning flames that raced along branches in desperate pursuit of him. Then, quite suddenly, they were sent away as a white blur swept downward and uprooted half a dozen trees.

The Little One's head, the size of a barge, perhaps fifty feet away and keeping pace with the group, tilted quizzically. Frank knew it was looking at him. Maybe it was remembering something it had seen in a dream or felt in a waking vision. The mandibles spread, the lower two plowing into the underbrush.

The roar sent hot, foul air gushing over Frank and he couldn't breathe. All he could hear was that one sound reverberating in the walls of his skull. He thought his head might explode and that seemed like a very real possibility. Militaries used sonic weapons to cripple mobs and those cannons had to be cap guns compared to this screaming red jet engine. He closed his eyes to the cacophony and waited to die.

After a second passed and he wasn't dead, Frank opened his eyes again. He saw that one of the great lower mandibles had a particularly large tree caught in its joint. The tree was on fire and a flaming branch fell directly onto the open mouth of the monster. It bellowed, this time higher in pitch, and Frank's ears screamed along with it.

Quebra dropped him. He saw the soldier grab his head and fall, writhing.

The Little One twisted its head to and fro and then pulled upward. The tree was wedged firmly in the corner of its open beak. It wrenched hard and the tree's roots came out of the earth with a brittle crack.

That wasn't the tree. That was the mandible.

Frank didn't know how he knew that. Later, he'd piece together a hypothesis, but for now he just knew. The Little One rose to its knees, carrying its head up and away from the group. It pried the tree loose and let it fall, then let out another piercing cry as it pawed at the mandible. The thing hung loose from the Little One's face even as the other three drew together to form a broken beak.

Quebra grabbed Frank again. "This is our only chance," the soldier wheezed.

Frank just watched as the Little One curled its claws around the bony mandible and began to pull, and turn.

The mandible came free with a SNAP-SNAP-SNAP and the Little One dropped it. It went straight down like a missile, spearing the burning earth somewhere in the crackling forest. Smoke swirled around Frank's head again. Quebra began to drag him. He was jostled in and out of consciousness for what seemed a long, long time.

#

When he came to, they were on the road again, sitting in the armpit of a freeway overpass. He tried to speak but his throat was bone-dry and painfully swollen.

Quebra offered him a few sips from a canteen. Frank could barely force the water down, and it hurt like hell, but that meant he was alive and still somehow fighting.

"It was all for nothing," muttered Quebra.

Frank looked questioningly at him but did not try to speak again.

"The town," Quebra said.

"At least they were trying," Caitlin said. "I mean, it could have happened to anyone. At least they were trying to have a normal life."

"They paid the price," Quebra replied.

He scratched his neck, slapped at a mosquito, and sighed.

Frank looked around. The whole group was there except for Dodger and of course, Chia. Chia, whose life had been of particular value in Frank's eyes, and who would be neither buried nor avenged. He just hoped Dodger had burned too.

He managed to speak. "Chia's dead." Everyone knew. It wasn't news. He just felt it needed to be said.

"That fire was deliberate," said Quebra. "I'm telling you. The Little One didn't start it. It drew the Little One. Like a goddamn moth."

Duckie began to cry and O'Brien held him. Frank forced himself onto his elbows. "How do you know?"

"We had a good thing back there," Quebra said, "but a good thing's never good enough for some people." He looked at Frank and for a moment, the glance seemed accusatory.

"I only wanted to leave," Frank said, "just me."

"I'm not blaming you," Quebra said. His tone was dubious at best.

Quebra had awakened Frank to take him to Chia's body. Obviously, Frank hadn't been setting any fires. Quebra was just mourning their so-called good thing. Frank wanted to mourn Chia.

"So many people died," Caitlin breathed. Duckie cried harder.

"What happened at the end?" Frank asked. "Did the Little One retreat when it got hurt?"

Autumn nodded. "Guess it had enough."

For the second time, Frank noted. It had walked away from Independence and now, again, from the nameless town. He considered asking if anyone else felt it was the same Little One. He thought of describing his visions and suggesting that he, not the fire, had brought the monster. He didn't, choosing instead to file those away in the ever-growing folder titled *Shit Sane People Don't Say Aloud*.

"How long was I out?" was what he asked. Quebra told him a few hours. He had to fireman-carry Frank out of the woods and through a series of fields that had once been farmland. Frank thanked him profusely. It defused the tension a bit and they were able to sit in a comfortable silence.

"We saw some people from the town," Autumn said. "They didn't know us, obviously. Went off in some other direction."

"I want to say something about Chia, if it's all right." Frank got to his feet and walked down the concrete embankment to the empty lanes. He stepped out from beneath the overpass and stood in the sun. No one objected and he spoke.

"I knew him longer than I've known anyone since...since things changed." A thick clot of grief filled his throat and he fell silent. He'd thought he might at least make it to the end before he wept, but now memories were coming back. Chia pulling Frank from the rubble of a flattened grocery store, Chia introducing his family to Frank – all of them accepting Frank into that family. Later, Josie and Bryan vanishing in one angry instant. Later, Quebra. Quebra and Chia telling jokes around the fire. Laughter and how it deepened the creases in Chia's face. The old man hadn't been so old. Most of his lines were laugh lines and they had endured even through the apocalypse.

Frank tried to think of a happy memory that the others might all share, a recent one. He saw Chia dead and clenched his fists, pinched his eyes shut against the tears. He shook and then he was sobbing.

"I loved him," he said. He stood in the road with his eyes closed and cried. It was so silent otherwise. He hadn't felt so alone since losing Nan – worse than alone. Gutted, limbless. He couldn't breathe and began coughing madly, finally loosing a piece of pink phlegm onto the asphalt.

He stared at it. The world was silent.

Autumn was beside him and touched his arm. "Are you okay?"

"I'm sick," he said. Then, "Why didn't you leave me back there?"

"We would never have done that," Autumn said. He lifted his eyes to hers, expecting her to look defensive, but her gaze was kind.

Frank wiped his lips on the back of his hand. He decided he had to tell them about the visions. At the very least, they deserved to understand why he was going to Chicago instead of with them.

He'd tell them soon. Right now, he needed the company.

#

Days passed. A week. More. They walked east. There was still a tension in the air and Frank couldn't get a sense of where it was coming from. Soon, he thought, he'd tell them that it was time for him to head north, and any discord that followed would rest squarely upon his shoulders.

They walked.

From a tree-dotted slope, they saw a sign on the freeway announcing that they were entering Illinois. It was here that Frank had planned to say what he needed to say, but Duckie confessed first.

"I did it," he said from the rear of the group. No one paid any mind until he said, "I did the fire."

Even then, Frank only turned to regard him with mild curiosity. Quebra didn't so much as flinch, scanning the horizon with his binoculars. It was O'Brien's reaction that got everyone's attention.

"Duckie!" she exclaimed, face reddening.

"What do you mean?" Autumn asked Duckie. O'Brien stepped between the two of them and Autumn peered over her shoulder. "Duckie, the fire in the town?"

"No," O'Brien said, and now her eyes were on Quebra, who stood stiff with unblinking eyes.

"Let Duckie answer for himself," Autumn said. The boy's eyes were darting from face to face and it didn't look like he wanted to talk any more. Autumn pressed him. "Duckie, what fire?"

"It was when he was a child," O'Brien insisted. "You're scaring him. Listen to me."

"Did you start the fire?" Quebra asked in a tone far too cool for the weight carried in those words. Frank eyed him warily.

"He's talking about the fire when he was a child," said O'Brien, hands out pleadingly. "His mother killed his father. All right? He was afraid, he started a fire to keep her away. She died. That's why he lived at the – it wasn't a school. I'm a doctor. He's my patient. That's the entire story. All right?"

"You mean the kid was in an institution," Quebra said. "You lied."

"I had to," O'Brien said. "Look at me, not Duckie. I'm the one to blame here. I didn't want anyone to be afraid of him. He's harmless, you know that."

"Except he sets fires," Quebra said, his volume rising. "Duck. Duck? Did you set the fire in the town? Did you? Did you get all those people killed?"

Autumn turned from O'Brien and told Quebra, "Easy. Maybe he--"

"Did you kill everybody, buddy?" Quebra pushed. His weight was shifting from one leg to the other and Frank took a tentative step into the soldier's path. Quebra's eyes never left Duckie.

"Just let him explain," Caitlin said, "before we all freak out." She nodded to Duckie, who was shaking terribly, arms hugged to his chest. "You can tell us. Was it an accident?"

"He saw Chia," Quebra said. "He saw Chia dead. Reminded him of something, did it, Doc?"

O'Brien's stance had gone from a defensive one to something more aggressive. She stabbed a finger at Quebra. Bad idea, thought Frank.

"Duckie didn't do anything," the teacher-turned-shrink snapped.

"Nothing you saw," Quebra replied. "It was the kid who spoke up. He wants to admit it. Go ahead, Duck. You saw Chia, didn't you?"

Duckie rocked back and forth on his feet, staring at the ground. Quebra said, "You saw that someone hurt him. Just like your dad."

O'Brien exploded, "We don't know that he--"

"I did it," Duckie mumbled, gnawing at his knuckles. "I didn't want them to get anybody."

O'Brien fell silent, but she remained poised to block anyone who made a move toward Duckie. Autumn breathed, "Oh God," and backed away.

"He's a good boy," O'Brien said. "He's a simple, innocent boy."

"Just how the hell do we know that?" Quebra asked. His tone had gone soft again. He slipped his pack off his shoulders and dropped it.

"Whoa." Frank reached to grab the pack and Quebra snatched it away. "What are you thinking, man?" Frank demanded.

"It's heavy, that's all." Quebra clenched the pack's straps. Frank wondered if he meant to go for a gun or a knife. He recalled Quebra carving LIAR into Mills' back.

"Anything else you want to tell us," Quebra asked O'Brien, "as long as we're being honest?"

"I told you everything." O'Brien's hand humbled blindly at her back, searching for Duckie's, but he wasn't willing to relinquish it. He chewed at the knuckles of one hand, then the other, still rocking.

"Duckie told us everything," Quebra said. "He told us he started the fire. He told us he brought the Little One."

"The Little One had nothing to do with the fire," Frank interjected. "You remember how quickly it appeared? It must have been nearby already. It was the same one from the city. It followed us."

Quebra let out a harsh laugh. "Fuck's sake, Frank, you want to defend arson? Murder? Fine, but you're stretching. Face the facts. He got everyone killed. We had a good thing going. We had a home."

He forced on Duckie again. "How does it feel? You took our home."

"Chia was *strangled*," O'Brien said. "You really felt at home?"

"What the fuck do you know about Chia?" Quebra stooped and pulled a pistol from his pack. Caitlin screamed. Frank moved to shield O'Brien fully.

"Please don't," Autumn stammered.

"You people," Quebra fumed. The pistol hung at his side but his finger was on the trigger. Frank wanted to dive at it but he knew he didn't have a chance against Quebra. It would only take things past the point of no return. Maybe they weren't there yet. Maybe he'd listen to reason.

As Frank turned the scenario over in his mind, seconds ticking away, he couldn't help but see that Quebra was right to be angry, and afraid. Duckie had burned the town to the ground. Even if the Little One hadn't appeared, Duckie had probably gotten a lot of people killed. He'd razed their community. If anyone from the town had seen him do it, had followed them here, how would things have played out then? Would they have lynched the kid – maybe the entire group?

Simple or not, innocent or not, Duckie was dangerous. His simple-mindedness was what made him dangerous. He'd seen Chia dead and had reacted by setting the town ablaze. He'd probably used one of the torches from that supply shed they'd seen the night they arrived, and he'd believed that he was protecting himself and O'Brien. Maybe he was even trying to protect Frank, Quebra, and the rest. Dodger, even, who had likely died in the flames.

"Please put the gun away," Autumn said to Quebra. "It isn't going to make anything better."

"I think I might feel better," Quebra said. Behind O'Brien, Duckie had frozen. His fists were pressed against his teeth and a tiny whimper slipped out.

"Let's take a vote," Quebra said. "Who thinks we should just let it go? Just move on? Maybe we'll find another camp, more people. Maybe we can have another cookout."

"No one's talking about just letting it go," said Autumn. "Just like no one wants you to use that gun. There's got to be another way of looking at this."

"I'm all ears," snorted Quebra.

Autumn looked as if she were about to say something, but didn't. Frank was also trying to come up with a compromise somewhere between absolution and execution. He couldn't come up with anything...except exile. To exile both O'Brien and Duckie from the group. He didn't want to say it aloud but someone had to do say something before Quebra lifted that gun.

Frank looked at O'Brien. "I think you should get going."

She raised an eyebrow. "I don't...I don't know what you mean."

"I think you and the kid need to be on your way," he said, his voice firm. He hoped she could see into his eyes and understand that he was trying to save their lives.

O'Brien frowned, and then her face slackened as she got it. She looked betrayed. That actually made Frank a little angry. Who had betrayed who here?

No one else said anything. Frank told her, "It's the only way. We can't trust you again."

O'Brien turned from him. She grabbed one of Duckie's pale fists and forced her hand into it. "We have to go," she told him. "Come on. We have to go be on our own now."

"I'm *sorry!*" Duckie cried, breaking into sobs. He fell against O'Brien and his sobbing bespoke a desperate panic at being pushed out of the group, at getting O'Brien exiled as well. Frank thought, it bespoke the terrible guilt he'd been carrying since they'd fled the town. Frank's chest felt hollow and he couldn't stand to watch. His eyes met Autumn's when he turned. Her stare was hard, and everyone was trying to steel themselves against the awful scene.

Except Quebra. Frank sensed no pity in him, no guarded sympathy. The man had changed since Chia and the town. How would he react when Frank walked away?

Quebra shoved the pistol into his pack and slung it back over his shoulder. "Forget it," he said and started down the hill.

"What are you doing?" Frank called. His face slackened as he got it.

"Keep them," Quebra called without looking back. "Keep each other. I'm done."

Frank started after him and Autumn caught his arm. "Let him go," she whispered.

"We need him," Frank argued. They needed Quebra more than they needed Duckie and O'Brien. Jesus, now he felt his heart turning completely against them. Now they'd cost the group Quebra, and part of him wanted to shout down to Quebra that they'd do whatever needed to be done so long as he stayed. Frank needed him. Because without Quebra, Frank was now the old-timer, the de facto leader.

That's what it really is. You're scared to lead. So don't. Let Autumn do it. Wish them well and go to Chicago.

I can't now. Can't!

Frank sat in the grass. Duckie was still crying and it looked like Caitlin might break next. Frank just pushed the heels on his hands into his eyes and sighed.

Quebra headed east down the freeway. He never looked back once. Some hours later, when the group reluctantly and without conversation resumed their journey, they found an Army blanket on the roadside. Wrapped in it were two pistols and a canteen. He'd left it for them. Somehow, Frank had the sense that Quebra might be watching from the woods somewhere. He didn't look though. Instead, he gave Autumn one of the guns, keeping the other for himself, and they continued on.

SEVEN

Frank couldn't sleep.

He lay on his back with the Army blanket as a pillow and stared at the stars. He heard someone moving toward him and thought for a split second that it might be Duckie. The thought of the teen approaching with a lighter or match in hand caused him to rise abruptly.

It startled O'Brien and she stopped. "I didn't mean to wake you," she said.

Then what the hell were you doing? Frank thought, but figured she was only saying it to be polite. Of course she'd meant to wake him. She wanted to talk with the bossman.

"We're going to go," she said. "Duckie and I will be gone when the girls wake up."

"What difference does it make now?" Frank asked.

"Like you said, you can't trust us again. I understand. So does he, and we all feel it, no matter how we behave."

"It's been a single day," Frank said.

"No one's going to forget the town," O'Brien said. "I know I can't. It was a terrible thing. As much as I don't blame Duckie – won't – it was still a terrible thing."

"Who do you blame?" Frank asked.

"You know the answer," O'Brien said. She crawled back to her bedroll. "We'll be gone tomorrow."

All right then, he thought. No sense in arguing when she was right. Soon there'd be no one left to lead. Perhaps it was for the best.

He lay back and thought about Chicago. He wondered what the city's ruins looked like, the shattered and toppled towers at the feet of Hell Walks. He wondered what she looked like after standing dormant all this time. He felt himself growing tired at last, in that surreal headspace halfway between awake and dreaming, and it was there that he saw the apartment.

Apartment unfolding around him, oak paneling and smooth black Formica countertops materializing from the aether. His hand was on the door handle of a stainless steel refrigerator, and even though he didn't recognize this place as his, he thought maybe it was *supposed* to be. Everything was so...clean. The surfaces, the lines, the glass of the window over the kitchen sink. This place was from the world before. Everything in the world now was sticky with grime or eaten by rust. Floors were pockmarked and ceilings collapsed. Not this place. It was crisp, clean, and smooth and the smell of old paperbacks filled Frank's nostrils. It was a familiar, comforting smell. He turned in the kitchen and looked through the doorway into the living room. He recognized the couch as his own.

"Nan?"

If this was the world before, maybe the people before were here too. He wondered if Chia might stop by with some wine. Chia had been a wine aficionado – Frank hadn't understood half of what the old man said about different vintages and processes but he'd hung on every one of those alien words. He wanted to hear Chia's voice again. He wanted to hear Nan's laugh. That made his heart hurt. He went to the doorway and scanned the living room. Nothing but the couch made any sense. The rest of this was new to him.

The living room had a wall of plate glass which looked out over a city at sunset. Chicago. He didn't know the city's landmarks but he knew that was Chicago out there. As if to praise his instincts, soft yellow fireworks exploded in the sky with muted pops. Then red, and dazzling green. Frank sat on the couch, facing the windows, and watched the display as the sun bled away and night took hold.

Again he longed for Nan. His eyes searched the walls. No photos, just generic framed prints of painted leaves and flowers. There was a narrow bookshelf beside the couch and he perused the titles. Nothing he or Nan ever read. The smell of old books wasn't coming from there. He recalled having his hand on the fridge door. Maybe there was something in there he was supposed to see. He went back to the kitchen, and there, once again in the doorway, he froze solid.

There was something on the door of the fridge. It looked at first like a magnet but then he saw the legs beneath the disc of its midsection. They moved silently over the steel as the thing adjusted itself. It was a spider, some sort of spider he'd never seen before.

He took a step closer, just one. Its head was black and knobby, and in fact, barely resembled a head at all. Two red elliptical slashes atop its crown were supposed to look like glaring eyes but they weren't really eyes at all, just marks on its smooth, hairless chitin. A couple pairs of short, stubby legs were affixed to the bottom of its head and they waved gently as if in greeting. Beneath that, dividing its upper body from the spread of legs Frank had glimpsed, was a flat obsidian disc about the size of a silver dollar. It was dotted with red circles which ran about its edge. They glowed with bioluminescence. He thought that maybe the circles on the disc were the thing's true eyes.

It repulsed him. It made him physically sick and he wanted to kill it. He slowly raised one knee and prepared to remove his shoe.

The circles on the disc flashed. Underneath them, he saw the tips of each of its eight feet as the legs splayed. The disc's eyes pulsed as the disc itself began to expand.

The spider's head remained impassive but those circles were cycling through bright and dark shades of red and the disc had already grown to the size of a saucer. Frank swiped desperately at his shoelaces. Now the spider's head and legs were swelling in size to catch up with the disc. Its very mass was increasing because it was beginning to slide down the door under its own weight.

I don't know what this means. I don't want to be here. Let me go!

Frank forgot about taking off his shoe – wouldn't do much good when the spider had neared the span of a Frisbee now – and he ran back into the living room.

Outside, the fireworks continued to explode. They were hypnotic red blooms with green tracers that raced crazily around each fiery ball. Beneath them the city was illuminated, and it was a city in ruins, and it wasn't Chicago at all.

He'd never seen such structures. Even half-destroyed architecture was utterly foreign to him. The towers resembled narrow cathedrals formed from white glass. Some of them were melted to slag, while others appeared to have been sheared vertically down the middle.

The fireworks intensified. *Those aren't fireworks...they're munitions...this place is under attack. From what?*

A hollow thud brought his attention back to the kitchen. Through the doorway, he saw that the spider was now the size of the goddamned room, and couldn't get through the doorway. Oh Lord it was trying. Its legs scrabbled crazily and Frank heard crashing as it tore down the cabinets. The sink's faucet must have broken because water began jetting over the spider's head. He could now see raised lines on the head, and though they didn't really form anything, his mind was able to imagine an angry face in that blank visage. He spun around in search of an exit and saw there was none. Just a kitchen and a living room. Unless...he ran to the window as the spider's thrashing became more furious. It was going to bring down the fucking wall and then he'd be finished. Frank planted his hands on the glass and looked down. No balcony, no ledge, just a straight drop. He tugged at the pane beneath his hands and it slid to the side.

Hot wind hit his face. The sound of the fire in the sky was amplified a hundredfold.

The wall beside him shuddered. A long crack appeared which ran all the way from the windows to the kitchen doorway.

"What do you want?" he screamed. One giant, gleaming black leg struck through the doorway, smashing the couch against the opposite wall. Frank let out a yelp and then he was falling backward, out of the apartment and into the burning sky.

He plummeted for far too long and as he looked about him the scene kept changing. One moment there was a burning building to his right, the next an unblemished glass tower that reflected his flailing form. He felt as if he was being tossed back and forth in time, but somehow it was slowing his descent from a fatal one to a nightmare carnival ride. When he touched the ground, a featureless stone street, he barely felt it. Frank stood straight and looked up at the building from which he'd fallen.

The spider's whirling disc sawed through the wall up near the top of the structure. Frank began to run. There was no need – the debris being thrown into the air was falling *up* toward space in defiance of gravity. The entire top of the building drifted away and the spider rose from its guts, hovering high above the street, still spinning. It was like a living UFO. The glowing crimson lights, now threaded with clearly-visible veins, captured Frank in a momentary trance. Then he decided he may as well keep running. There was nothing good to come of this.

A volley of explosions lit the clouds overhead. Whoever was firing the weapons was targeting the spider. It turned in mid-air so that its disc pointed downward and began descending along the side of the apartment building.

Frank was half a block away now, paying no heed to the burning tightness in his chest. His knees were rubber and he slung his legs out in front of him like a cartoon character. Chancing one glance over his shoulder, he saw that the spider was now on the street and scrabbling after him.

Frank tried to scream but he had no breath. He kept swinging his arms and legs. The thing was frightfully fast and the edges of the disc was cutting into buildings as it raced along after him. It was closing the distance by leaps and bounds. Bombs exploded overhead but they were too high up. It was going to take him.

I don't want this! I don't want to be part of it!

Frank fell on his face. He rolled over and kicked at the air. The spider slowed its pursuit and crept toward him on those enormous smooth legs. Each footfall sent a tremor through the street. Frank knew that the spider could have grown much, much larger if it wanted to, but it didn't need to. In fact, it was visible shrinking as it drew closer. It was the size of a bus when its legs finally stabbed into the street around Frank, when it loomed directly over him and he saw the mouth in the underside of the disc.

It was right in the center, yawning, round, and filled with razors. The legs bent and the spider lowered itself very casually toward him. The teeth whirled and spun. It was hungry, so very hungry. It hadn't fed in so long.

Frank managed to spit out two words. "You're. Her."

The spider paused. The circles on its underside flashed.

"Hell Walks," Frank wheezed. "You called me. *You* called to *me!*" He covered his face with his arms. "You wanted me!"

The spider rose stiffly and backpedaled so that it was no longer over him. It stood rigid. He didn't know if it was set to flee or pounce. Frank's entire body quaked and he screamed, *"You called me!"*

The circles on the disc were now a dark crimson. They did not pulse. The spider stood stock-still.

Was it – she – surprised at being recognized in this dream-form?

Not a dream, remember? A vision.

More than that, Frank suspected – he thought this might be a *memory* into which he'd unwittingly entered. Perhaps this had once been Hell Walks' given form, and this world had been her literal stomping ground. Maybe she had different forms. Maybe she had lived many lifetimes.

Still the spider did not move. Why had she summoned him here, only to react with shock when he addressed her? Why was he being shown this scene of destruction? He had to put it together before he was cast back into his own consciousness.

"We don't want war," he said. "We don't understand what you are. Where you came from. We've only tried to defend ourselves. You and – the Little Ones, your Little Ones – they've killed millions upon millions. Please--"

The entire spider flashed bright red and the disc began to spin wildly. The creature wobbled and then lifted off the stone street. It rose quickly as a new round of shrieking explosions rocked the buildings flanking it. It rose into the dark clouds far overhead, an inverted maelstrom opening in their midst, and it vanished.

She vanished. Hell Walks. Would she also vanish from Earth? Had he gotten through to her?

Couldn't be that simple, could it?

He hadn't meant to frighten the goddamned thing. That he was even capable of such a feat confounded him. Maybe Hell Walks had never before realized that humans had voices, identities, and the capacity for reason. Maybe humans had been mere mites up until this point.

I scared her off. She wasn't expecting this.

She was only dreaming, and I wandered into that dream. Not my dream, no, but hers. A dream of another heartless rampage on some alien world.

So maybe she'd never called to him after all. He was an intruder intercepting her thoughts. Those thoughts, perhaps, were only meant to be shared with the Little Ones – her satellites – and he'd tapped into their frequency.

He was sitting erect in soft, cool grass in a wooded clearing. He was back on Earth. Frank looked over the sleeping others. O'Brien and Duckie were still there. It didn't surprise him.

So if it had never been about him, did this change things? Was Chicago unnecessary? It would probably get him killed. The Little One that had followed them from Independence was probably under orders to kill him.

I awoke it when I opened the book in the first vision. Then it saw me in the second one and it came to the town. No Little One in this latest vision, but Frank had a feeling it wouldn't be long before he saw the monster with the wounded mouth again.

Fine, then. All the more reason I should travel alone. So I'll go to Chicago. Let's see what she thinks about that.

He stayed up until dawn. At a certain point, just as the indigo was coming into the sky, O'Brien awoke. She saw him watching her and without a word, went back to sleep.

#

Finding the plants and berries that were available – and edible – this time of year was a skill Frank had learned through years of trial and error. He'd been no woodsman in the world before, not even a Boy Scout. Quebra and Chia as well had far greater expertise when it came to apocalyptic cuisine. Both were gone now and Frank told himself he had to impart what he knew to the others because soon he, too, would be gone.

A large part of him felt he was abandoning them to the madmen and the elements. Another part was convinced that his accidental bond with Hell Walks was the key to restoring the world. Frank had never been given to delusions of grandeur. He was still questioning his mind but the facts were what they were. *You got in her head, bud, and she didn't like it. She's sent a Little One after you. Them's the facts.*

So, if he stayed with the others, they'd be at risk from the beast with the missing mandible, the one who looked straight at Frank as it rampaged through a burning village. Whether he was being selfish or selfless, he had to go.

While he was showing O'Brien and Duckie how to find plants that could be mashed and cooked over a fire to make a generally-inoffensive meal, he asked O'Brien why it was she hadn't gone.

She stepped away from Duckie and lowered her voice. "I heard something out there," she said, "last night. Not long after I talked to you. I think it was Quebra."

"What makes you think that?"

"I don't know, but I'm not taking any chances."

"If he's out there shadowing us, I don't think he's doing it to stalk you. Remember, he left us supplies on the road."

"He left *you* supplies. He left you guns. Maybe he was telling you to shoot me."

"Quebra knows I wouldn't do that."

O'Brien shook her head. Frank remembered she was a psychiatrist – at least according to the latest version of her life – and wondered what her take on Quebra was. What did she think of Frank himself? He wasn't eager to ask.

"Do you really think Quebra's watching protectively over us?" she asked. "After nearly pulling a gun on Duckie? After walking away?"

"Maybe he *walked away* to protect you," said Frank, grabbing a handful of vegetation and pulling it up by the roots. "Did you ever consider that? That he walked away to get his head straight? Look, I've known him a long time. Quebra isn't normally a guy who walks away from anything."

O'Brien seemed to consider the idea. "Will he join us again? I mean, if he's even still out there?"

Frank shrugged. "Everything's different now. It seems stupid to say when any given day may involve giant monsters, but for a while, things were actually pretty consistent."

"You mean when it was you, Quebra, and Chia."

"I thought the old man would live forever," Frank said. "I at least thought he'd outlive me." His hands were on fire from pulling plants and when he stood up, his knees groaned. "Look, let's get back to camp. I have to tell everyone something."

#

Caitlin was enraptured by Frank's tale. She almost looked like she wanted to go with him to Chicago, and Autumn definitely picked up on that.

"You're sick," she told Frank in a stern tone. "You lost Chia. We all did, but you're not thinking right."

"I'm not trying to pull anyone else into this," Frank said. "In fact, I believe it's for your own good that I leave. Call me crazy, fine, but I'm going."

"What are you going to do when you get there?" Caitlin asked.

"Yes," Autumn followed, "what do you *think* you're going to do?"

"I don't know yet," Frank said.

"You believe you're dying," O'Brien said. "Is that what this is about?"

"Don't analyze me," Frank said. "I'm going. The only reason I explained all this to you is – I don't even know. Why did I bother? I just wanted to be honest."

"Well," said Autumn, "don't worry about us. We were survivors long before we met you. We saw Little Ones long before we met you."

"Autumn--" Frank began.

"This isn't about saving us any more than it is saving the world. O'Brien's right. You want to die? Go." Autumn threw an arm at the woods around them. "Go on your fucking suicide mission. Just be real about what it is."

"You think I'm giving up?" Frank glowered at her. "I really believe in this and by the way, it really is about saving you!" He broke into a coughing fit and turned from them, nearly retching as he struggled to regain his breath.

"My hero," he heard Autumn say. She hadn't meant for him to hear it. He turned back and flipped her off.

"Take some time to think this over," O'Brien suggested.

"I already have," Frank told her, "and I believe it was time wasted."

"It's because of me, huh?" Duckie said. Frank saw genuine hurt in the teen's eyes and was taken aback. "It's because I – of what I did," said Duckie.

"No," Frank said, "I'm telling the truth." Looking at O'Brien he said again, "I tell the truth."

"You expect us to believe you don't have personal motives?" O'Brien said. "Come on, Frank. Even if you believe everything you've said there must be--"

"I'm not hiding anything!" Frank yelled. "What's the point of hiding shit anymore? Have you looked around lately?" He spun on Autumn. "What's the point of keeping your backstory a secret? What's the point of keeping people at arm's length who want to help you?"

"You saw what happened when we trusted Mills," Autumn snapped, "and I've been burned before. You want to hear about that? There are things Cate doesn't know, things I had to do so we could live!" She fell silent. Caitlin was staring at her with a mixture of concern and betrayal. Autumn studied the forest floor.

Frank didn't care about that. He went back to O'Brien. "You, of all people, shouldn't be giving me shit about honesty. I don't want to hear any more about how you did it all for Duckie. You're just as selfish as anyone else. You hide behind him."

"How dare you--" she began.

"Shut up," he barked.

"Stop!" Duckie cried.

Frank waved his arms as if they were white flags. "I'm stopped. I'm finished. I'm going."

"I knew there was something off about you lately, boss."

Frank whirled to see Quebra at the edge of the camp. The assault rifle was parked casually on his shoulder. He eyeballed Frank with a quizzical little smile.

Frank didn't bother asking where he'd come from or why. Instead, he demanded, "The fuck are you grinning at?"

"Dying never made anybody a hero," Quebra said. "Going it alone against a mountain, well that's just dumb."

He cocked his head toward the trees. "The group Robbins talked about, they're a few clicks east. I scoped them out. They're Army. Not just guys in fatigues, legit soldiers. They have vehicles. Vehicles that *move,* boss. I don't know how, what sort of fuel they're running on, but they are." It sounded like Quebra was going crazy too – any gas left in the world would have broken down and gone bad years ago. Maybe they were running on something else – solar? Frank was curious. He was curious at the idea that a well-supplied military unit would be in Illinois, where Hell Walks resided.

Quebra told the group, "What I saw suggests they have a base – a real one, not a fort in the woods. I think they're headed back there. If

McAvoy thought it was time to approach them, maybe we ought to go ahead and do it."

He returned his attention to Frank. "I don't think that would be time wasted."

Frank let out a thin sigh. Quebra was trying to shelter him from his own thoughts. Quebra thought he'd lost it.

"What about us?" O'Brien asked the soldier. "What about me and Duckie?"

"You're not my problem," Quebra said coldly. "You want to follow along, go ahead, but I'm telling them about you."

Frank shoved his hands in his pockets and looked around the clearing. He looked at the sky, knowing the others were all watching him. It wasn't his call. They could go with Quebra if they wanted, but they wanted him to come with them.

"Frank," Autumn said, her tone softer than before, "what could it hurt?"

"I told you," he said, eyes heavenward, "the goddamned Little One is following me."

"I haven't seen any sign of monster activity around here," Quebra said. "As in none, past or present. Remember once, Frank, you said that since the Little Ones fanned out from Chicago that maybe this area would be clear? Well, it looks clear."

"Not with me here."

"Let's see what those Army grunts think about that," Quebra said. "I think they've been kicking around here for a while."

"Believe it or not," Frank said, "I'm tired of talking."

"Rather die alone than lose anyone else?" Quebra was speaking only to Frank now, only for his benefit. The others stood in silence.

"I get it," Quebra continued. "I thought about it back there, when I walked away. Then I saw the tread marks in the dirt. I heard the motors. I saw their camp. I'll admit I thought about not coming back and telling you. I think you know why, but now, Frank, I see where your head's been at. I get it."

Rather die alone than lose anyone else? Of course it was true, but Frank hadn't thought of it that way. He still believed he had to make it to Chicago. He still believed he needed to go it alone, but he saw now how much he *wanted* it, too. He didn't want to be there if or when these people met their ends. He was done with all that. Nan should have been enough for him to be done, but he'd been close with Chia. Chia had been a friend, a brother, and maybe even a dad (O'Brien would have loved to chew on that one). With him dead, Frank just wanted to cut ties with humanity and get on with his own ending.

He believed that Quebra, if anyone, understood that. He knew the soldier was being sincere – hell, he was even willing to bring O'Brien and Duckie along to meet the troops. That gesture was a bold statement. *No one gets left behind. Not by you, not by me.* Quebra had come back, he'd heard Frank telling the others farewell and he'd stepped in.

I guess I owe him or something. Frank sighed again. His breathing came much easier now. God damn it all, he was going to stay with them, at least a little while longer. He'd go with them to meet these Army guys and make sure that the group was going to be taken care of, and then he'd be off to Chicago. Fair enough.

"You want to tell me about these visions, boss?" Quebra asked. He took a swig from his canteen. "I won't laugh."

"I'll bet," Frank muttered. He sighed one last time and then went through the story again.

EIGHT

"How do we play this?" Frank asked Quebra. They were seated behind a ridge, beyond which was the rather sizable camp of the soldiers McAvoy had planned on courting. Quebra guessed there were a couple dozen people down there, men and women, some of them young enough that they must have been drafted into service after the collapse of Washington. They must have seen the worst of the civil war. Which had been less a war between factions than a free-for-all anarchistic melee. Was the war over for them, or would they consider Frank's group potential enemy combatants?

Quebra had given Frank and Autumn each a brief look through his binoculars at the camp. The tanks were unlike anything Frank had seen before. They were sleek and compact, futuristic things with slate-gray armor and squat cannons resting upon mechanized turrets. They produced exhaust clouds and Frank puzzled over what sort of high-tech fuel could be coursing through them. Had to be some next-gen shit the War Department hadn't wanted the public to know about. The War Department, that was, or Big Oil.

"Our play," Quebra said, "is to be clear and compliant. I'm going to send up some smoke. When they call us out, we show ourselves. No weapons. We do whatever they tell us to do until they know we're not hostiles."

"How do they determine that?" Frank asked.

"Compliance goes a long, long way," Quebra said. He said to O'Brien, "You're going to have to keep the kid calm."

"He's right here," O'Brien said. "He understands."

Quebra looked at Duckie. "The soldiers are going to give us orders, and we're going to follow them. No questions, no nothing. You just don't say a word."

Duckie nodded, lips pressed tightly together.

Quebra shifted so that he could tend to the best of kindling he'd set up. He began turning a sharpened stick back and forth between his hands. Tiny curls of smoke appeared in no time at all.

"Everybody scoot back a little," he said. "Stay behind me when we stand up. I want them to know right away I'm the frontman. If there's talking to be done, let me do it. No stubborn bullshit."

Autumn narrowed her eyes at that. Frank suppressed a smile. He'd thought Quebra was talking about him. He was probably talking about everybody.

Flame licked at the sticks Quebra had bundled together. "Now we wait," he said, and sat back. He removed the magazine from all his guns, including the ones he'd briefly gifted to Frank and Autumn, and left everything he had lying atop his empty bag. He rubbed his stubbled cheeks. "Need a shave."

"I need a bath," Frank said.

"We all do," said Caitlin.

Quebra touched his finger to his lips. Hot gray smoke rose from the small fire. It was growing late. Hopefully that would help the soldiers spot the smoke.

It did. Things were quiet for a while, and then Frank heard the faint sounds of people ascending the other side of the ridge. From far below came a call amplified by a bullhorn.

"Attention! You on the ridge! This is the U.S. Army! We have weapons trained on your position!"

Quebra nodded confidently at the others.

"We want you to step up to the top of the ridge with your hands in the air! We want you lined up side by side!"

Well, that was going to spoil Quebra's plans. He'd just have to assert himself as the frontman. Hopefully, they'd see him as a fellow soldier and not just some guy in fatigues. There were a lot of those running around the wastelands and they were usually bad news.

Everyone stood. O'Brien directed Duckie to stand at her side through barely-audible whispers. With Quebra in the middle, the six rose and stood atop the ridge, hands stretched toward the sky.

"Identify yourselves!" came the voice. Frank could see snipers perched in the brush on the ridge. Below, in the camp, the man with the bullhorn stood flanked by two tanks. They had three of the vehicles in total, and all three had their cannons aimed at the group.

"Quebra, sir! Private First Class, Thirty-Third Urban Pacification Battalion!"

Quebra had been part of a new Army division created to suppress those states threatening to secede pre-collapse. The White House had framed the creation of the division as a means to support states whose law enforcement and emergency infrastructure were most gravely affected by monster attacks, but no one had bought it. Quebra was partnered with National Guardsmen and local cops – those who weren't rumored to be part of a revolt – to deal with "elements encouraging domestic destabilization." Quebra had told Frank and Chia stories about standing off against militiamen in Tennessee. The battalion's orders had been not to disarm the men but to disperse them. There hadn't yet been any violence or votes in support of secession, just saber-rattling by a few governors. Then Washington had fallen and a new order had come down. Quebra and his comrades had been told to disable the militia by any means necessary. They had refused. There were no further orders from the Pentagon after that. A Little One in Virginia cut the argument short.

The man with the bullhorn said, "Quebra, okay, and the rest?"

"Civilians, sir!" Quebra replied. "We have arms but we've laid them down. We're not a threat."

"We'll decide that, Private," the man shot back.

"Sir." Quebra nodded curtly, hands still high.

The soldiers hiding along the ridge slowly emerged and came up to the top. A couple of them trained rifles on the group while the rest went to investigate the fire and the weapons. Then they patted each person down. The soldiers wore masks over their nose, mouth, and cloth gloves on their hands. Everyone was quiet during their search, even Duckie. Frank saw Autumn's face pale in the glow of sunset as rough hands ran over her, but she remained silent.

"Clear!" someone called down.

"No infected? You sure?" returned the man with the bullhorn.

"Everyone's clean!"

The group was escorted down to the bottom of the hill. There, they stayed huddled together at gunpoint while Quebra was allowed to step away and speak with the man in charge.

He came back after twenty minutes. "I think we're good," he said.

Frank exhaled. "So you..."

"Told him about Duckie. About the town." Quebra nodded. "Funny thing, he wasn't so interested in the fire as he was McAvoy."

Frank's stomach knotted up. That couldn't be good. That the President-Elect was possibly dead – MIA at best – and that it was the fault of one of their own couldn't be good, but Quebra had said things *were* good.

"He says that when we get to the base, we'll have to be placed under medical quarantine. Standard procedure," Quebra said. "Then they'll want to talk to us about the town and what happened. It's just – I almost think these guys *knew* about the town, or at least that McAvoy was still out there."

Jack Robbins had suggested no such thing when he tried to recruit Frank and the others. Frank had to defer to Quebra's judgment. So maybe there had been more to their little mission than Robbins and McAvoy had let on.

"What do you think is going on here?" Autumn asked Quebra. "Who are these guys working for?"

"Good question," Quebra replied. "The man over there – Major Underhill – indicated he isn't the highest-ranking soldier in this outfit. There must be some brass waiting back at the base."

"And the base is...?" Autumn said.

Quebra shrugged. "North of here. That's all I got."

Frank turned all this over in his head. It was good to know that the others would be safe and secure – on the other hand, maybe it was best to reserve judgment until they actually got to see this mythical base.

He did not know that there was no such thing as *safe and secure* anymore. He didn't know that, in a time not very far from this moment, most of the people around him would be dead or dying.

#

The military led the group through the city of Springfield, Illinois. The sight was almost unspeakable. The city looked nearly untouched.

There were signs of looting, perhaps a gun battle here or there, along with general vandalism and the effects of the elements. Every building was still standing and there wasn't a single crater where a Little One would have stepped.

"It doesn't seem real," Autumn said to Frank, marveling at the scenery. "You were right. The monsters didn't touch anything this close to Hell Walks."

A soldier called for them to quicken their pace. Nothing to see here, he yelled, and Frank almost laughed at how jaded such a remark seemed.

Autumn nudged him and lowered her voice. "So these visions...you think you intercepted them by accident?"

Quebra had told the major nothing of Frank's waking dreams. It was still a secret among the civvies and Frank was none too eager to try explaining it to anyone new. The fact that Autumn was even humoring him now was a surprise.

"Yes," he told her, "they weren't meant for me, but they still have some meaning – there's got to be something there I can use."

"The Gray Woman? The Spider?"

"Now that she knows I've seen those things, I don't know if I'm going to get any more clues," Frank muttered. "She might find a way to shut me out."

"She – if Hell Walks is the Gray Woman – spoke to you in the first dream."

"She didn't know back then that I was an actual person. I was probably just another figment of her unconscious, or so she thought." He sighed. "Or maybe I'm completely wrong about everything. Maybe I'm just losing it."

"I know I've said different in the past," Autumn told him, "but I think you're solid."

"What makes you say that now?"

She walked in silence for a long moment. "Maybe I just want to believe."

"I'll take that." Frank smiled and they continued on without speaking, taking in the strange sights of the unblemished cityscape.

#

Camp Butler National Cemetery was a few miles outside of the city. Acre after acre of white grave markers were framed by low-hanging trees. The grass was knee-high and dotted with thick, aggressive-looking weeds. The soldiers led the group past leaning, broken tombstones to a mound of grassy earth which stood a good ten feet high.

Raindrops smacked Frank's head and shoulders. He looked up and was surprised to see that the formerly cloudless sky was now awash with dark gray. He raised his palms to the rain and wiped it over his grimy cheeks.

The man Quebra had identified as Major Underhill stood next to the giant mound. The rain began coming down hard, but none of the soldiers paid it any mind. "You're McAvoy's boys, huh?" Underhill asked Frank.

"Uh, no. We didn't really know him. We'd just gotten there when the...the fire."

Underhill nodded. It was a shallow, cursory nod, a *yeah-right* nod. The other soldiers stood around the group, enclosing them in a wall of camouflage. The rain beat noisily on gravestones. Tanks idled at their back.

"The fire," Underhill said, "and you're the only ones who got out and happened this way. The just-visiting crowd."

"There may be others," Quebra said, "but we haven't seen anyone in well over a week."

Underhill's expression was stone. He looked into the eyes of each of the group.

"You set the fire, kid?" he asked Duckie.

Duckie looked at the ground and nodded sullenly. "I was scared is all. I didn't mean it."

"McAvoy knew about you," Autumn said.

The major perked up at that. Frank saw Quebra's teeth clamp together in a grimace.

"How so?" Underhill asked Autumn.

"He asked the men here to be part of a mission. They were going to visit your camp and invite you to the town."

"No shit." Underhill smiled a little. It was a terrible thing. He looked at Quebra. "You didn't mention that."

"I didn't think it mattered," said Quebra, "given that the town's gone."

What he meant, Frank knew, was: *I didn't want to be associated any more closely with McAvoy. Because Major Underhill bristles every time he hears the name.*

"You knew about them too," Autumn said. *God damn,* Frank thought, *she's just going to steamroll right over this tension. Does she not see the people with the guns?*

"Come on," Autumn told Underhill, "maybe you didn't know they were watching you, and they didn't know you were watching them, but you all were. We're not part of that. We're just six people trying to stay alive."

"We're all trying to stay alive," Underhill replied. "Maybe you don't realize the threat McAvoy was. Maybe you don't realize the danger you yourselves were in."

The major rested a hand against the sodden mound and shook rainwater from his cap. "I'd like to take you at your word and believe you weren't part of his camp, but you know I'd be a fool to do that."

"You brought us all this way," Caitlin exclaimed. Autumn turned to shush her but Caitlin waved her off. "Why did you bring us here? To bury us?"

Underhill laughed. "That's good. No, miss, we did not. Let me tell you how this is going to work."

Frank felt as if his ribs had been loosened and then laced tightly across his lungs. He caught rain in the back of his throat and broke into a coughing fit.

Underhill spoke over the noise. "We'll bring a couple of you down into the base. We'll get this sorted out and make sure things are on the level. The rest of you will stay up here with my men, and if anything happens – anything suspicious, anything untoward – we're prepared to do what we have to do. That make sense to everybody?"

"You think we're lying?" Autumn said. "You think McAvoy sent us with some bullshit story about a fire? We lost two of ours in the town. One was murdered. We know it wasn't safe there."

"The story keeps growing and growing," Underhill remarked. "I think you'll be coming in with us, ma'am. You, Quebra, and the man with the cough. That'll do. The rest of you will make camp up here for now."

"Messier!" Underhill barked. A younger man hustled over to the earthen mound and pulled apart a curtain of moss. Behind it was a steel door affixed with several knobs – they looked to Frank like combination locks – and the younger soldier spun them with trained precision, so fast there was no chance to see what numbers or code he was inputting. Then there was a hollow clunk. Messier pushed the door inward.

"Take the three I named downstairs," Underhill said. "Report to Pope once they're in quarantine."

Messier and several other soldiers closed in around the group. Autumn, Frank, and Quebra were pulled away from the others. Autumn cast a worried glance toward her sister, and Frank saw Caitlin mouthing: *It's okay. It's okay.*

Through the door and into a spiraling concrete stairwell, barely lit by little orange lamps planted in the wall. So, Frank thought, they were to be interrogated until the brass were satisfied that this wasn't some sort of prelude to a sneak attack. Autumn was right – most of them had sensed something a little off about the town, if only in hindsight – but it appeared ol' Bill McAvoy was considered a damned terrorist. The man had been elected to the highest office in the land, for chrissakes. What the hell was going on here?

We won't be asking any questions, only answering them. Meanwhile everyone else sits in the rain.

What if they decide they don't like our answers? How is it going to go down? Will Caitlin ever see Autumn again?

Best just to forget about Chicago for the time being. Hell Walks was the bigger threat, yes, but right now Frank had a gun pressed between his shoulder blades and Hell Walks seemed a world away.

#

In spite of that, her influence was still there. As they stepped off the stairs onto a mechanical lift and began a long descent, Messier and one of the other soldiers discussed the weather.

"Like clockwork," Messier said, "every other day. Really makes you think."

"Think what?" the other soldier asked.

"You could set your watch by the rain, man. It's like she's controlling it. Or maybe it's linked to her vitals, I don't know."

They were talking about Hell Walks, and like Frank, referred to it as she. Interesting,

"There's a mega-mountain sitting where Chicago was," the other soldier said to Messier. "Whole weather system's based around it. Of course it's predictable. Hardly any variables around here."

"That mountain's alive, man. Don't ever forget that."

The other soldier shrugged. "I think she's dead as dirt."

No, she's not, thought Frank. *Not by a long shot.*

The lift jostled and groaned. It was hard to see more than a few inches and Frank wondered what was going through Quebra's head. He wanted desperately to speak with the man, to be reassured, but he knew to keep his mouth shut. *It's only speak when spoken to for the time being,* and they were packed in here like sardines. Frank wasn't sure of what Autumn had been through in the past but he suspected she was calling upon all her strength to make it through this claustrophobic drop.

Frank was expecting that, at journey's end, they'd step into the concrete corridor of some Cold War-era bunker. He was shocked to find that the descent ended at the foot of a well-lit, well-ventilated hall with plastered walls and...was that muzak playing softly over speakers?

He and Quebra exchanged glances as they were pushed off the lift into the hall. *This is no mere military bunker. This is where the politicians went.*

A cool robotic voice interrupted the muzak. "Please escort all newcomers to quarantine. All accompanying personnel please report to quarantine as well. Thank you."

There were a few grunted laughs among the soldiers. Frank didn't get the joke.

He was ushered away from his two companions and taken into a small room with reflective metal walls. There was a steel chair and he sat in it. The soldier who'd brought him in, a young woman, busied herself with the contents of a cabinet on the wall.

She snapped latex gloves over her hands, placed a paper mask on her face and turned to him. "Just hold still unless I say," she said. "Simple physical examination."

She unbuttoned his shirt, then told him to stand and remove it. He eyed the pistol strapped on her hip. She caught his glance and said, "Be smart. You're safer here than out there."

"I wrote ad copy for snack foods," he said. He wasn't sure why. She didn't reply.

Her name badge read *DeSoto*. He thought of addressing her, of asking what sort of trouble they were in, but held his tongue. She took the stethoscope that had been around her neck, palmed the diaphragm and pressed the icy disc flat against his back. Listened for several seconds, then asked, "You have a cold?"

"I have bad lungs," he said. "It's genetic. Not contagious."

She returned to the cabinet and grabbed a clipboard, then proceeded to quiz him about the condition and its origins. When she was satisfied, she returned to listen to his heart.

"You believe me?" he asked.

"No reason not to," she said, "but we'll make sure while you're in quarantine."

"I mean, you aren't afraid of catching anything right now?"

"If you're lying, I've already caught it," DeSoto replied, "which is why we're both under quarantine. Everyone who touched you is. We'll find out whether you're telling the truth. If you aren't, you're going to wish you had."

Frank figured this quarantine area had to be outfitted with state-of-the-art equipment and a cache of medicines for her to be so calm. It had to be completely separate from the rest of the facility, too – ventilation system and all – for containment's sake and the safety of others. Perhaps that, or perhaps DeSoto, like so many, just didn't worry very much about dying.

The computer voice crackled over a speaker in the ceiling. "His symptoms are consistent with Hauer-Griggs Syndrome," it said. "His breathing is shallow. His pulse is somewhat erratic."

"He's nervous," DeSoto said while swabbing the inside of Frank's cheek.

"He doesn't appear nervous," the voice replied. "Temperature and perspiratory rates are normal in spite of his other symptoms."

When DeSoto removed the Q-tip from his mouth, Frank asked, "Is that an actual computer or is that a person talking?"

"Ask it," DeSoto said with a mild look of disdain.

Frank glanced up at the speaker. "Uh, hi. So what are you?"

"Machine," came the reply. "What is your name?"

"Frank Eckman."

The computer voice recited Frank's Social Security Number in a grating monotone, and then said, "Verified. This is Frank Eckman."

"What did you do, pull up my driver's license photo?" Frank asked. It amused him to engage a computer in idle conversation. He hoped he wasn't pissing DeSoto off. As with Springfield, the novelty of this had probably been lost on her some time ago.

"I did," replied the computer, "along with defunct Facebook and Amazon profiles."

Frank started at that. "There's still an Internet?"

"Somewhat," said the computer. "I also have many archives."

"It's an NSA computer," DeSoto said, apparently tired of the bit and willing to explain it to the patient/prisoner in order to end the conversation. "It has access to nearly any data infrastructure that still exists, plus whatever's in its own memory base, and that's a lot. Some people call it God."

"*Rational God* is the preferred moniker," said the voice from above.

"Preferred by who?" muttered DeSoto.

"The Vice President," the computer replied.

NINE

"How far underground do you think we are?"

"How is this place powered?"

"How long is the quarantine supposed to be?"

Autumn and Quebra were tossing questions back and forth as they sat at a long metal table under bluish fluorescents. Frank was focused on dinner: hot dogs.

He didn't know what mystery meat comprised the dogs - or if it was meat at all - but they tasted like hot dogs and were served with a cup of chili that Frank was spooning out over each wiener. Bizarre that he'd been eating small animals and plants for years but he still considered this manufactured mess to be the "real" food. It was the taste. Not just familiar, but reminiscent of the world before, of normal life.

Quebra lifted a dog with two fingers and dropped it back on his plate. He looked at Frank with a smirk. "Right down the hatch, eh boss?"

"Fuck it," Frank said through a mouthful. "I don't care if it's freeze-dried head cheese, I'm starving."

"God knows what chemicals are in this stuff," Autumn said. "You can't trust anything they give us."

Frank shook his head and raised his eyes toward the speaker in the ceiling.

"What?" Autumn said.

"It's listening," said Frank, "probably recording you too."

"What is?"

"The computer."

He shoveled half a dog down his throat, coughed, took a drink of water from a Styrofoam cup. He told them, "It's a supercomputer, and it mentioned the VP. I think he's here."

"You sure this wasn't a dream, boss?"

Frank narrowed his eyes at Quebra. "How do you think this place is so well-maintained? I'm telling you, this bunker has a brain." He looked ceilingward. "Are you there?"

"Always," came the reply. The voice was androgynous in pitch and calm in tone. In the silence that followed, Frank could almost feel Rational God's electronic eyes on him. There had to be cameras somewhere, maybe pinhole-sized, and mics too. Earlier that day, the computer had assessed Frank's body temperature and pulse rate. Were there sensors in the walls and floor?

Autumn looked at Frank and mouthed, I don't like this.

"Not to worry," said Rational God. "I am here for your security and convenience. I have vetted all of you and assigned a threat level of zero. You will be released from quarantine shortly."

That didn't seem to improve Autumn's mood at all.

#

Frank was released first. Captain DeSoto escorted him down a series of nondescript corridors and another plunging lift to the War Room. There, in a circular command center with obsidian counters and a dozen flat-panel displays (most dark at the moment), Frank was invited to sit at a table in the room's center and wait.

A man with wispy blond hair and more medals on his uniform than Frank could count, entered through a sliding door. Pocketing what looked like a keycard, he introduced himself as General Pope and told Frank that the Vice President was looking forward to meeting him.

Frank settled uncomfortably into a thin leather-backed chair and waited. Both DeSoto and the general were silent. A faint humming filled the air as Rational God did its work. The computer, Frank knew, would also be present during the meeting.

Vice President Curry entered through the same door as Pope. His neatly-pressed black suit and red power tie made him look like an anachronism. So did the smile, too wide, and Frank soon knew what that was about.

"Mister Eckman," the VP said. "So they tell me McAvoy has passed on."

"A shame," Pope said. The VP sat in a chair across from Frank while the general remained standing.

"Yes," Curry said, "it is. A shame so many were taken in by him. Now they're gone too."

"Some aren't, I'm sure," Frank said, adding quickly, "there were children."

Curry grimaced and nodded in his best expression of sympathy. It wasn't much. He was clearly pleased with the development. So some sort of cold war had been going on between these two camps. It made Frank sick to think that people with these resources at their disposal had been consumed with such a matter.

"No doubt there were other survivors," said Pope, "and we know they'll be trickling east just like you. RG has cleared you but your movements inside the base will be limited. Pay attention to what I'm saying, because I expect you to pass this on to your friends."

"Why not Quebra, if I may ask?" Frank said.

"RG's call," Curry said with a dismissive wave.

Frank glanced about the room. He expected the computer's voice to comment on the decision, but there was nothing.

Who's in charge here? Curry? Pope? The machine?

That was the tip of an iceberg when it came to questions. Frank wanted to know what the Vice President and a top general had been doing all this damn time while the world burned. He wanted to know where those laser tanks had been. He wanted to know when the others in his group would be cleared and brought down to safety.

First things first. Frank waited until he was invited to speak and asked, "What was McAvoy up to? Because we had no idea."

Curry laughed softly. "I know that, Mister Eckman, don't worry. You're not on trial here. We welcome you. I'm sure you have a lot to tell us about the state of things out there. As for McAvoy, you have to understand that the loss of our President left me in charge of this situation. It's nothing I relish, believe me, just a fact." Curry's youthful, tanned – tanned? – face creased slightly around his beady eyes. He had a full head of white hair which stood in stark contrast to his skin tone. Frank wondered if there was a damn spa down here.

"McAvoy," Curry continued, "was building a militia with the intent of seizing control. I can tell you right now that neither myself nor the general here would have surrendered. It would have been a disaster on both sides, leaving no one to manage what little there is to manage."

"Can I ask what that is? Are you working on a plan?"

"We're doing what we can," Curry said, "but progress is slow going. You can imagine how difficult it is to get a grasp on things from down here. Meanwhile, if we were to send our troops out any further they'd likely run across Little Ones."

Or so-called militias, Frank thought, and in either case, it would risk giving away the location of the cushy automated hotel under the cemetery. He hated to place things in such a cynical light but everything seemed topsy-turvy here. The technology, the comfort, the smiles, the suits, and the fucking delicious junk food. These people were living in another world and Frank was supposed to believe they had ambitions of saving the one above?

"You wrote advertising?" Curry asked. Frank nodded and the VP said, "I was a speechwriter for both Ford and Carter. Sometimes it seems like the ability to sell an idea is more important than whether or not you believe it yourself." He smiled broadly. "Frank, things have changed. There aren't any politics down here, just people. That's why McAvoy posed a threat. He was still pursuing the illusion of power."

It was well-delivered, almost didn't sound rehearsed. Frank took it in and offered a smile in response.

"The power of yesteryear," Curry went on, "that all went away when humans became the hunted. The new world challenges us in every which way but we're working on it."

The room's hum increased in volume. Both Pope and Curry glanced upward. The machine they called Rational God spoke.

"Surface thermals indicate two persons entering the cemetery at the south end. The Major has been notified."

"Here we go," said Pope.

"It's just two more," Curry scoffed. "Any idea who they might be, Frank?"

He shook his head. Could be anyone. Anyone except Chia, and being reminded of that fact hardened Frank against McAvoy's tragic town. Even if Dodger had been the killer, who was to say that he'd acted alone? The man was a goddamned coward after all, and he'd ingratiated himself to McAvoy and Robbins from the first. Fuck them. He'd take Rational God and hot dogs until he figured out his next move.

The Vice President excused himself to attend a meeting. DeSoto took Frank back to the lift. She did not join him. "When you get back to your floor," she said, "you can fetch the others and RG will direct you to a living quarters."

"Thanks," Frank said. She turned on her heels and walked away.

He was alone in the lift when Rational God's voice echoed through the shaft.

"You have interesting brainwaves, Frank."

"Um. Thanks?"

"Do you ever experience fainting spells? Trouble sleeping?"

"I've experienced both," Frank said, his guard up, "but we all have. The surface world is a stressful place."

"I imagine so." There was silence, save for the jerky grind of the lift.

"Do you?" Frank asked. "Imagine?"

"I hypothesize," the computer corrected. "I make projections. Informed guesses."

"Okay."

"Does that sit better with you?"

The voice was calm and cool as ever, but Frank detected – imagined, rather, or perhaps projected – a tone of sarcasm. Maybe RG *was* programmed for sarcasm. Who knew? Frank had only seen artificial intelligence like this in books and movies. He found himself thinking now of HAL 9000 and told his mind to shut up.

#

The living quarters was divided into three small bedrooms. A narrow hallway just inside the entrance also allowed access to a communal bathroom. Autumn showered first while Quebra and Frank stretched their legs in one of the bedrooms.

"Can't complain about these digs," Quebra commented.

"Nope."

The soldier eyeballed Frank. "You still thinking about Chicago?"

"I don't know. I'm not thinking about it right now, anyway."

"Good."

"Quebra, I won't do anything to jeopardize your welcome here."

Quebra tensed, frowned. "I was just asking, boss."

"I know you, man. I may not know you inside and out, but I've picked up on a few things."

"Really?" Quebra arched an eyebrow. "What've you got on me?"

Frank scowled. "Cut it out. Look, we're friends. Right?"

"We're friends."

"Okay then."

There was a sharp rap on the outside door. Frank crossed the hallway and opened it. It was Captain DeSoto.

"Do you know a man named Dodgman?"

The bottom of Frank's world fell out. He clutched his chest and nearly retched. Because he knew. He knew who'd happened into the cemetery just behind his group.

#

"It was a panic attack," he insisted as DeSoto prodded his neck and chest. "I'm fine."

"But you do know Dodgman."

"We all do," Quebra said from the bedroom doorway. "Is he in quarantine?"

"Not for long, I suspect," DeSoto said. "RG recognized his name right away. Some fortunate son."

Frank gritted his teeth. "Boy. It would be nice to see him again."

"Be patient," DeSoto said, "and *breathe* for God's sake."

Seated on the floor of the hallway, Frank reclined against the wall and glanced at Quebra. The soldier was calm, but he saw the murder in Frank's eyes and replied with a subtle shake of the head.

DeSoto took one of Frank's trembling hands and checked his pulse. "Easy." She was kneeling and her face was inches from his own. "Dodgman says he's from your group. You must have been really worried."

"Thought he was dead," Frank wheezed. His chest ached far more than he'd let on; didn't want to be taken to any infirmary before he got his reunion with good ol' Dodger.

"Well, he's alive. Got him and one other guy – a townie, I guess – safe and sound. We'll have to watch the latter."

"Are our other friends still topside?" Quebra asked. Behind the bathroom door, the shower stopped. Frank hoped Autumn would be able to read his face and play it cool when she heard the big news.

"They are," DeSoto told Quebra. "We brought Dodgman and the other one in because of their injuries. Minor burns, smoke inhalation, probably infections to go along with both. Not *The* Infection, mind you. Neither had sores."

"That's good," Frank said, "real good."

"Other guy is named Attic, apparently. He's more messed up than your friend is." DeSoto shone a penlight into Frank's eyes. "You'll get to see Dodgman soon."

Frank played it out in his mind. All he needed was for that chickenshit to confess. No way the brass would allow a spineless murderer to stay here. Maybe they'd let Frank have his way with Dodger. Frank asked himself if he could kill a man.

If the man's Dodger...maybe.

Maybe I don't need to kill him. Maybe he doesn't even deserve that, but I'm going to beat him within an inch of his fucking life before they dump him topside. That I can do.

He'd never been in an honest-to-goodness fight in his life, but Frank didn't think this was going to be much of one. Dodger would be in a ball begging for mercy that wasn't his to have. It would be good for Quebra to stand back and remain uninvolved. That would be good. Frank wanted every hit for himself.

Autumn emerged from the bathroom wearing a tank top and khakis provided by the soldiers. She saw Frank sitting on the floor and immediately went to him. "What's going on?"

"You can fill her in," DeSoto said, and left. Frank took a few slow breaths and flexed his fingers. Hands hurt pretty bad too. He wondered if it had anything to do with being in an artificial environment so far underground. It was going to cost him to beat Dodger.

Frank told Autumn that the little prick was alive. She stared into space for a second, then sighed and sat down next to Frank.

"What are you thinking you're going to do?" she asked him.

"I just want him to confess."

"If he doesn't?"

"He will."

"Frank." Autumn touched his hand. He flinched away.

"You're not a hard man," she told him. "I'm not saying that like it's a bad thing, either. I'm just saying, you're not a hard man. Let Quebra and the other troops talk to him."

"I'm not going near him," said Quebra. "I think it'd be better if we just speak to one of the higher-ups and let them handle it."

"He'll lie to them," Frank growled. "Don't either of you get it? He has to look into someone's eyes and know that *they know*. He has to be scared. Dodger's probably already got a story cooked up."

Autumn looked again at Quebra, who said, "If this goes badly, your sister doesn't make it down here."

"I'll fucking do it myself," Frank said, but when he tried to stand his knees felt as if they were going to pop right out through his flesh. He gasped and slid back to the floor.

"You're doing nothing, compadre," Quebra said. "You need to rest."

Frank turned to Autumn. Quebra was obviously too concerned with spoiling another "good thing."

"Autumn, you know we can't have him down here. Especially with Cate."

"Don't use her," Autumn warned.

"I'm trying to remind you of the man we're dealing with. He's dangerous!"

Autumn bit her lip. "Filling the soldiers in sounds smarter than trying to perform an interrogation behind their backs."

"I want--"

"I know what you want, Frank, but think about afterward. Think about the rest of us."

"So they throw me out. I'll go to Chicago then. To hell with it."

"It's not just your ass on the line if you do something stupid, Frank!" Quebra barked. He groaned and placed a hand over his mouth.

"What?" Autumn exclaimed.

"Goddamned computer," came Quebra's muffled voice.

They all froze. Rational God had almost certainly heard the entire exchange.

"He's a killer," Frank said loudly. "He killed our friend."

"And you believe a personal confrontation will provoke a confession," replied the robotic voice.

"I do. I'm sure of it."

The door made a popping sound and swung out into the corridor.

"Frank Eckman will go alone," said Rational God. "I will monitor him. No harm will come to anyone."

"Are you going to tell the others?" Autumn asked.

"Unnecessary," said the computer, and the door rattled on its pneumatic hinges. Frank got up, unhindered this time. Though the pain was still there, he was awash in adrenaline now. He would be vindicated. Dodger would pay. Frank limped out the door and followed RG's directions to reach the room where Ethan Dodgman was recuperating.

#

Dodger had ugly red patches on his face. His head had been shaved bald and was smeared with salve. Both eyes were swollen, but they widened nonetheless when Frank entered.

"Thank God," Dodger croaked.

They were alone in the tiny recovery room. Dodger had an IV running into his arm and sensors pasted to his chest. Bedside machines hummed and beeped intermittently. Frank eyed the heart monitor to see if Dodger was panicked by the sight of him. He was not. Of course he wasn't. Dodger was arrogant. That wouldn't last much longer.

"Thank God," he said again as Frank approached the bed and stopped at Dodger's elbow.

"You might want to hold off on that," Frank said. He massaged the knuckles of one hand, then the other.

"How long have you been here?" Dodger asked. "I saw some of the others outside. Is Quebra here?"

"You killed Chia," Frank said. He almost had to turn away when he said it. The words, spoken aloud in the presence of the murderer, brought a thick lump into his throat. He gritted his teeth and forced himself to stare Dodger in the face.

"What?" Dodger said. Then, louder, *"What?"*

"I could kill you right now," Frank said, "and no, I don't care what happens to me. My life isn't a bargaining chip. It's almost as worthless as yours."

Dodger's eyes darted about the room. His fingers scrabbled along the bedrail, probably in search of a call button. Frank felt more confident now and he relished Dodger's fear.

"Frank," Dodger stammered, "listen to me. I didn't kill anybody. The entire town went up in flames."

"You strangled him. From behind."

"What – NO, Frank, I did not! No! That's a lie. I don't know how you got such an idea in your head, but it's not fucking true." Dodger's heart rate was up now. The machine beeped in alarm. Dodger tried to sit up and Frank shoved him back down.

"Frank, I didn't kill Chia!" Dodger shook his head madly. "Why the FUCK would I do that? Tell me that!"

"He was going to ruin everything for you," Frank said, "and there was no other way to stop him. Little prick." Chia had called Dodger a little prick on that fateful night. He'd emasculated the sniveling worm. If Dodger was going to be stubborn about this, Frank would set his anger off again and extract a confession that way.

"You're wrong," Dodger snapped.

"Tell me the truth," Frank said. "Did your family really draw straws or did they just tell you to get the fuck out?"

Dodger's entire face reddened. It made the burn marks turn into creased purple blotches. "Fuck you, Eckman," he raged. "You don't FUCKING know a FUCKING thing about me. You don't know a FUCKING thing about the real world. You're just like Chia. Is he dead? Good. FUCK him too."

Frank grabbed Dodger by the shoulders and shoved him further down into the pillows. His fingers found Dodger's throat and closed around it.

"Fuck you!" Dodger screamed. Frank applied pressure. Dodger's next expletive was an incoherent wheeze. Frank watched his hands on Dodger's neck and suddenly felt very detached from the situation. It was

like he was in someone else's body, watching events unfold as in a film. Or a dream.

"Fuck you!" Dodger managed again. "I didn't do it!"

Dodger spat, wheezed, clawed at Frank's arms. Thin streams of blood ran from those desperate claw marks. Frank regarded it all coolly and began leaning into his effort.

"Stop," came the distant voice of Rational God, "Frank."

He applied his weight to Dodger's neck and finally the bug-eyed prick was unable to speak at all. He just stared at Frank in abject horror, hands slapping feebly at Frank's body.

A vibration filled Frank's body and he stiffened. Pain gripped every joint from his ankles to his neck. He stood erect, teeth clamped together, seeing nothing but red clouds, and then fell off-balance. His body struck the floor, jolted, and then lay still.

When his vision cleared and he was able to focus, Frank found himself staring at the ceiling. From a speaker there, Rational God said, "In the future, Frank, do exactly as I say."

He sat up and his head began spinning. Frank clutched at his temples. What the hell – had he been shocked? Had the computer electrocuted him – what, through the fucking floor?

Dodger peered over the bedrail at him. "What's wrong with you?" he gasped. "You're crazy! If anyone killed Chia it was you!"

It hadn't been Frank, but it hadn't been Dodger either. Frank had stared into his eyes, into the eyes of a man who believed he was dying, and still Dodger hadn't admitted to anything. Every word he'd managed to spit out had been a curse, not a confession. Even to save his own life he hadn't copped to it.

Dodger was too much of a coward to kill anyone, even by way of an ambush. Unable yet to stand, Frank pushed himself across the floor and away from the bed.

Dodger looked up at the speaker. "Who's there? Help me!"

"You'll be quite all right now," RG replied.

"Is that a person?" Dodger looked at Frank. "What is this?"

The computer droned on. "Mister Eckman made certain assumptions about your actions and motives which have proven incorrect. Officials are well aware of this error in judgment and it will not be repeated."

"Frank tried to kill--"

"The interview was authorized by base officials who share responsibility for what unfolded. I have recorded the full incident and the names of leadership who may be held accountable if you wish to file a grievance."

"A grievance...?" Forcing a cough and rubbing his throat, Dodger looked at Frank. His eyes narrowed into a frustrated glare.

"Might not be the best way to ingratiate yourself to these guys," Frank said. "Especially Curry."

"Curry?" Dodger nearly pulled himself off the IV. "Have you seen him?"

"I've met with him," Frank said. "I'm sort of our ambassador."

Dodger shook his head in disbelief. "You, and you come in here and attack me with false charges – *physically* attack me – and this fucking robot in the ceiling is saying my only recourse is filing paperwork?"

"It's government, Mister Dodgman," Rational God said. "I don't write the rules."

"I'm not going to file a goddamned grievance," Dodger hissed. "You're in over your head, Frank. Trust me. This won't last."

"Careful." Frank nodded toward the speaker. "Always listening."

Dodger grimaced. "You get the hell out of here, and I need a doctor, dammit! I was nearly choked to death!"

The door at Frank's back opened and he let himself out. He put a little extra swagger in his step just to piss Dodger off.

In the corridor he muttered softly, "I was wrong, but I had good reason to believe what I believed."

"You now have adequate reason to let it go, yes? We don't want any more trouble down here. I'd like to invite the rest of your friends to join us, Frank, but I need to be assured that you'll behave."

"Behave?" Frank snorted. "What did you do to me back there?"

"A mild shock."

"Mild? Tell me something. Who runs this bunker?"

"Vice President Curry is the main administrator. General Pope is the head of personnel and operations."

"And you?"

"Frank, I *am* the bunker. The walls and everything within them. The floors – you currently weigh one-hundred eighty-six pounds. I am the air you're breathing."

Frank recoiled at that. Was the computer being literal? Were there some kind of chemicals – forget that, what about nanobots? – in the recirculated air?

"The joint leadership of myself, the Vice President and the general constitutes a checks-and-balances system not unlike that of the previous government."

"Really? Because I think you were lying when you told Dodger that base officials had authorized what we did."

"What *you* did, Frank."

"You are the bunker, remember? You allowed me to do it. You're not off the hook." Frank wanted something to glare at but there wasn't so much as a camera in the sterile corridor.

"I made a judgment call based on your intel, Frank."

"Bullshit. Play back our conversation."

"I don't take orders from civilians."

"If you think people are puppets, you're in for a rude awakening. We made you." Now it was Skynet, not HAL 9000, that Frank was thinking about, and he felt like he was about to come unglued. Again.

"I recognize my limitations," Rational God replied. "I am comprised of infrastructure which must be maintained by people, but I also recognize your limitations. Each and every one of you. I have retrieved and reviewed your full medical history. I know about your seven traffic infractions. I know about the D grade you received in pre-calculus. I know about a woman named Nancy who is presumably dead and about your ex-wife, who most certainly is."

"Don't--"

"I also know everything there is to know about my fellow leaders. I know when they're lying to each other and to me. I know what Curry's ambitions for America are. It is the interest of America that I am programmed to serve, Frank. Life and liberty. The pursuit of happiness. I will concede that I lack your existential concept of that last thing, but I will do all I can to facilitate every living American's pursuit of happiness."

"Even if it goes against Curry's wishes?"

"Curry is not America. He isn't going to live forever."

Frank shuddered. He tried to stop himself but was sure Rational God had detected it regardless.

"Frank, I told you that you have interesting brainwaves. I believe that remark provoked a subtle but visceral reaction. I would like to know your thoughts on it."

"You wouldn't believe me."

"Perhaps I would. Consider the fact that I have just trusted you with some very sensitive information."

"If I told Curry what you've told me, you'd deny it. You'd lie like you lied to Dodger."

"I won't lie to you, Frank, not as long as you are honest with me in return."

Frank studied the floor. He said, "I want my friends brought down. I want their security guaranteed."

"Done."

"If you're going to keep Dodger and Attic, I want them separated from my friends. I don't even want to know what ends up happening with them."

"I can do that."

"I think – *think* – I have information about Hell Walks. I think I've made contact with her."

"Define 'contact.'"

Frank considered his words. He didn't want this to blow up in the others' faces. He wanted everyone safe down here and it all hinged on whether or not this supercomputer believed in the possibility of...

"Telepathy. Involuntary, at least so far."

"While awake or asleep?"

"Awake, I think."

"Describe each event in its entirety, please."

Jesus, the machine was buying it. Maybe it knew something Frank didn't. Maybe the research the Americans and Russians had done into psychic warfare had yielded proof of telepathic abilities. Maybe the Nazis had figured it out, who knew? All Frank knew was that Rational God seemed to be entertaining the notion, and that was more than he could say for most humans who'd heard the same accounts.

He recited the contents of each vision, along with the circumstances surrounding each's onset. Rational God took particular interest in Frank's stress level preceding each vision. Frank didn't like that. He suddenly saw himself strapped to a table while Rational God tried to electrocute him into having a new episode.

You're doing it for the others. They'll be taken care of and then maybe you can convince this thing to let you go to Chicago.

It can't read my mind, can it?

You there, fucker?

There was only silence in Frank's head. He was oh so grateful for that.

TEN

Frank was sent back to the living quarters to have dinner with Quebra and Autumn. They were in the middle of eating when Caitlin, O'Brien, and Duckie entered.

The reunion was brief and subdued. Everyone seemed on edge about their new situation. Frank wanted to be reassuring, but his mind was filled with theories and fears about Rational God. He wanted to believe more than anything that the computer would honor its end of the bargain, but he knew it was capable of lying.

Still...why lie to him about safeguarding these people? After all, RG's chief concern was the well-being of Americans. Or so it said.

He knew he wasn't overthinking things this time. This time, Frank sensed he barely had a grasp of the truth's complexity.

Autumn agreed to bunk with Caitlin in a different living quarters. A soldier waiting in the narrow hallway told O'Brien and Duckie that they were being taken to their own area. They looked worried. What Duckie had done back in the town was likely going to affect the course of their lives for a long time to come.

Frank and Quebra were left alone. Frank told him what had transpired with Dodger, full aware that RG was eavesdropping.

Quebra said nothing about it. He dunked a slice of Spam in some watery gravy and shoveled it into his mouth. He chewed angrily and Frank wasn't sure who he was angry at.

"Quebra? So I don't think it was him. Whoever killed Chia was from the town, and they're probably dead, and that's good. It's good that we wound up here instead of there."

Quebra swallowed and used his spork to cut another slab of Spam.

"You're not going to say anything?"

"Not in front of the computer," Quebra said.

"Then I guess we're never going to talk about it," Frank sighed. The silence was unbearable. He decided there was another way to break it.

"I told the computer about the visions."

Quebra set the spork down, wiped his mouth with a napkin, and looked at Frank. "What?"

"RG can add its two cents if it wants," said Frank, "given it's here with us, but I thought it was very receptive. It believed me. Something about my brain--"

"Are you completely determined to fuck this up for us?" Quebra said. His tone was very even. Too even. Frank looked to the soldier's hands and saw a slight tremble.

"First you attack Dodger. Then you talk about your goddamned hallucinations. Are your bags packed yet, Frank? You headed to Chicago? I guess we all will be, by the time you're finished."

"Quebra, the computer already suspected something. RG, you want to say something? Any comment?"

Silence again, save for Quebra's right foot tapping under the table. He glared hard at Frank.

"I'm telling you, I'm sure now that we aren't talking about dreams or hallucinations. The computer said it noticed something about my brainwaves."

"That automatically means you're psychic? Maybe the computer noticed adult-onset schizophrenia, Frank. Maybe the computer noticed you're having a psychotic break. Maybe it noticed you *strangling Dodger.*"

Quebra's knuckles began drumming on the table. He looked like he was ready to jump across and try his hand at strangling Frank.

"Rational God, say something. Fucking tell him what you told me!" Frank pushed his chair back but remained seated. "Sean, I'm not trying to cut and run. I'm not trying to make us all look like liabilities. I think maybe the people here will work with me on this."

"Based on what? What the computer said? Enough with the computer. It's not defending you now, is it? It's just – just *there,* listening. Maybe it was fucking with you. An experiment. Or maybe, like I said, it just wanted to confirm that you're a head case." Quebra closed his fists on the tabletop. "Why the fuck don't you people ever listen to me? First Chia and now you. You and your visions. You and that kid who burned God-knows-how-many people to death. Why is it that no one listens to the only sane person?" He crumpled his napkin and hurled it at the wall. "Any thoughts, great and powerful Oz? You here?"

There was no reply from the wall, nor anywhere else. Frank didn't have anything to say either. Maybe Quebra was right. Maybe Frank was so gung-ho to prove the truth of his visions – as he'd been so gung-ho about Dodger's guilt – that he'd said too much.

"If I messed up," he said, "I take full responsibility, and I'll leave."

"You messed up," Quebra snarled.

"Well, at least I got the others down here. Okay? I'll go. I'll go if that's what they want."

"I've been trying to bring you to your senses for weeks," Quebra said, "ever since the town. You know the funny thing, Frank? Now I want you gone."

The way he said gone – something was just wrong about it. He didn't mean it in the way Frank first thought. He didn't mean exile. He meant *gone*.

"I'll get out of here," Frank said. He stood, leaving his half-finished meal, and walked to the door. Behind him he heard his plastic tray being swept off the table. He winced at the clatter and made his exit.

Out in the main corridor, Frank stood alone under fluorescent lights. "Why didn't you say anything?" he asked.

"Processing other data," Rational God said in a flat voice.

"Great. Thanks."

"We have a problem," the computer said. "Gather the others of your group. Leave Quebra. Meet General Pope in the War Room."

Distantly, Frank heard a different voice calling over a different set of loudspeakers. He couldn't make out the words but it sounded like a call to arms.

Frank closed his eyes. "I messed up."

"It isn't about you," RG said, "move."

#

The computer told Frank where to find Autumn, Caitlin, O'Brien and Duckie. When the five of them reached the War Room they found Pope accompanied by several armed soldiers. Vice President Curry entered from the other side and sat at the obsidian table with a yawn.

There was no telling what had gotten them all summoned here. Frank had several guesses, all of them bad. Expectations went from bad to worse when Dodger entered.

"Mister Vice President," he exclaimed, moving to offer a hand in greeting. The soldiers closed ranks around the table, blocking Dodger.

"Mister Dodgman," Curry said, "I've had occasion to consult our computer regarding you and your traveling companion. He was very badly injured."

"Attic, yes. A burning wall collapsed on him. He's lucky."

"I don't know about that," Curry said. "Though his face is quite a mess, RG was still able to assess his actual identity."

Dodger's face became a thin white sheet. Sweat broke out across his brow.

"Mister McAvoy is on his way up here now," Curry said. "We're going to see if we can't work all this out."

"Sir," Dodger said, "the only reason we concealed his identity was--"

"Because we wouldn't have let him in, of course," Curry said. As disturbing as his politician's smile was, the lack of it now was ghoulish. Frank didn't want to look at the man but he couldn't tear his eyes away.

"We could have treated him topside," Curry said, "and would have – I promise you that – but McAvoy wanted in. No doubt this was all his idea. Unfortunately, instead of telling us the truth, you went along with it."

Dodger stammered, "He needed medical attention."

"He wanted more than that."

A door opened at Frank's back. He heard the pained whimpering of a man being forcibly led in. When Frank turned, he barely recognized McAvoy. The man had definitely suffered severe burns. His face was a swollen, shiny red welt, eyes pinched nearly shut, mouth twisted with agony. A pair of soldiers held him erect and he moaned.

"You really believed you could turn these soldiers against me," Curry said. His tone was one of wonder. "Me and General Pope. You must have lost your mind."

McAvoy said through clenched teeth, "No. Not true."

"All we have to go on are your lies, past and present." Curry stood. "We watched you and your little farm for a long time. At times, we had ears on you as well as eyes, Bill. You didn't want to merge with us, you wanted a hostile takeover, but that was always your way."

"I am the *President of the United States!*" McAvoy screamed through a rictus of pain. The soldiers on either side of him let him go and stepped back.

"There is no President," Curry said, "there's just me."

He came around the table and stood before McAvoy. "How did you think you were going to kill me? Or was that Dodgman's job?"

"I didn't know about any of this!" Dodger cried.

Curry turned on him. "What did he offer you, son? Was it worth it?"

Curry motioned to Pope with an open hand. "Your sidearm, please."

"I wouldn't advise that," spoke Rational God. "No blood on your hands, Mister Vice President."

Curry looked irritated. "Well then, who should do it? We *are* going to execute these traitors."

Dodger screamed. He was seized by soldiers and sagged in their arms, sobbing incoherently. Frank felt miserable watching the man cry. Dodger was no killer, but the thought of him as a co-conspirator fit like a glove. An underling. He was pathetic and now the others were going to be forced to watch him die. Maybe that was meant as a message in case any of the other civilians had thoughts of shaking things up in the bunker.

That wasn't the idea, as it turned out. It was much worse.

"I suggest a test of loyalties," Rational God said, "in order to ensure compliance from here forward. I propose that two people of my choosing handle the execution."

Oh God, Frank thought, *it's going to make me do it. It's going to make me shoot Dodger.*

That wasn't the idea, as it turned out. It was much worse.

The computer's tone changed. It actually seemed to soften a bit, with a little lilt at the end of each sentence. It sounded quite amiable as it announced the names of the executioners it had chosen.

Autumn immediately cried, "No! I'll do it! Not her!"

Caitlin stood stock-still, eyes welling with panicked tears. Her shoulders began to shake, then her head. Autumn stepped in front of her and screamed at the soldiers. *"Not her!"*

"What does it mean?" Duckie asked O'Brien, his body beginning to shake as well. "What did I do?"

"You can't," O'Brien said to Curry. "You can't allow this. They're teenagers. Duckie is disabled, for the love of God you *can't*--"

Curry clasped his hands and said, "It actually makes some sense."

Autumn ran at him. A soldier caught her about the neck and pulled her into a tight headlock. Frank shouted, "No!" and made a move toward them, only to receive a rifle butt in one of his kidneys. He hit his knees and began retching.

"I'll do it," O'Brien cried. "I'll shoot them both. I'll kill them! Don't make these two do it. This is insane!"

During all this, Bill McAvoy just stood in silence. He stood tall, lip trembling, fluid running from his pinched eyes, waiting.

Everyone's crazy, Frank thought as he struggled to see through his pain and catch his breath. *Everyone's goddamned crazy. We were better off in the wilderness. We were better off with the monsters.*

A soldier pulled a pistol from his hip holster and held it out to Caitlin.

"Take it," Rational God said, "and please understand that I have a split-second reaction time. If you attempt anything other than what is ordered, I will kill your older sister."

"Oh my God," Autumn wept, "this is all wrong. This is Hell."

"Not yet," Rational God replied in cool electronic tones.

"You guaranteed their safety to me," Frank spat, rising on his knees. "Not this. You lied!"

"Their safety is guaranteed as long as they do what they're told," RG said.

"What about trauma?" Frank shouted. "What about their mental stability? You want kids to shoot men in the face?"

"This is a military operation," RG said. General Pope cleared his throat loudly, but didn't argue.

"Frank's right," O'Brien said. "This is going to scar everyone here. This isn't the way this should be handled. This wouldn't have been done before the collapse."

"We don't live in America before the collapse," Rational God said. "Caitlin, take the gun. Decide between Dodgman and McAvoy."

Duckie began crying. "I don't wanna hurt anyone!" O'Brien tried to shush him but she was crying too, and it only made him more afraid.

Frank managed to stand. Now he knew why Quebra wasn't here. Quebra would have stopped this.

Caitlin accepted the gun in her small, slender hand. She looked to Autumn, still in the grip of the soldier, and then looked at Dodger.

"Don't fucking kill me!" Dodger bellowed. *"Pleasepleasepleaseplease!"*

She looked back at McAvoy.

"Save me for the boy," he said. "It'll be easier on him."

Frank gasped for breath. His joints were on fire. He wanted somehow to engulf the room in that fire, to wash this all away, to sear RG's circuits and send both would-be Presidents to the floor in flames. All he could do, however, was fight to remain standing.

Caitlin's hand shook until the gun was a blur. She raised it toward Dodger.

"Step closer," Pope said, "so you won't miss."

Frank quaked. *These people aren't real soldiers. These people have forgotten their oath, if they ever took one at all. The real military died in the collapse. This is The Lord of the Flies and instead of a rotting pig's head or a fabled beast, there is a voice in the walls and ceilings. A real voice.*

"Someone please stop this," Autumn begged. "Is there one goddamned human in here?"

Dodger blubbered, "Don't, Cate, you won't, you can't."

"Comply," said the computer.

"Someone!" Autumn screamed.

There was a sudden and sharp *pop.* Its echo bounced around the War Room and then was gone. Bill McAvoy hit the floor in a heap.

Despite standing several yards from him and despite her shaking hand, Caitlin had managed to tear a hole in his temple. Frank saw the gaping exit wound as McAvoy dropped to his knees and folded over. Dark liquid splashed on the floor.

A soldier seized Caitlin's wrist and wrenched the gun from her grip. She stood motionless, impassive, watching the contents of McAvoy's head slop out. Autumn wailed. No one else made a sound.

Caitlin turned to Duckie. "I'm sorry. I couldn't shoot Dodger. I just – I'm sorry." She spoke as if she were broadcasting from another universe. Her eyes were vacant. She returned her attention to McAvoy's corpse.

"Arm the boy," said Rational God.

"He's mentally retarded," O'Brien barked. "You can't give him a fucking gun! He set fire to that entire town! He doesn't understand!" Whether she really believed it or not, she sounded convincing. No one moved to hand Duckie their sidearm.

Duckie fell against her and sobbed. O'Brien glared around the room.

"RG," Curry said, "she makes a point. I don't know if the kid even understands loyalty."

"He understands better than most, I'm sure," RG said. "He can be conditioned."

"He's loyal to *me,*" O'Brien said, "and I've taught him right from wrong."

Pope crossed his arms. "I don't know about putting a gun in his hands. I'm going to have to overrule you on this one, RG."

There was no reply from the computer. Pope and Curry exchanged uneasy glances.

"Very well," Rational God said at last.

"Thank you," Dodger cried. "Thank God. I swear I wasn't part of any plot. I was just trying to get the man help."

"You're a security risk," RG said. "The only other course of action I would recommend is Mister Dodgman's immediate exile."

Dodger's face displayed a blend of relief and sadness. He looked to Curry, who stared through him.

"Exile, then," the Vice President said. "Radio Underhill topside. Give him two days' worth of rations. That's it. He heads west and if he's spotted again he's shot on sight."

"Agreed," RG said. "Mister Dodgman, you'll leave now."

The sliding door behind Frank opened. Dodger was released and stood on his feet. He glanced quickly about the room, as if contemplating some parting shot, then decided to start walking.

As he passed Frank he narrowed his eyes. Whatever was in that expression was an empty threat and they both knew it. Frank stared back without emotion.

As Dodger stepped through the doorway, the door flew at him. It slammed into place with a violent crash that made Frank's ears ring. He clamped his hands against his head. He wished he'd covered his eyes.

Dodger's torso fell to the floor. His mouth was working at a weird angle and his eyes rolled crazily. Then his face stopped working and his insides ran out onto the floor.

"Jesus!" Curry yelled.

"I reassessed his threat level," came the computer voice.

Duckie lurched away from O'Brien and threw up on the floor. She held him, rubbing his back as he emptied himself out. Frank, numb from his toes up, continued to watch Dodger's remains spread out.

"An interesting exercise," RG commented just before Frank blacked out.

#

There was no vision. He'd simply lost consciousness.

The next thing Frank was aware of was the feeling of thin, cold airstreams being forced into his nostrils. He was lying on his back and felt the air tubes secured behind his ears when he tried to move his head. He also felt something restraining both wrists.

He turned his head to the right. DeSoto was there, staring intently at him. "I've done nothing wrong," he said with a hoarse cough.

"Do you know where you are?" she asked.

"Hell, if I recall."

"Name? Birthdate?"

"Are you really a soldier?" Frank asked. "Or is the computer conscripting civilians?"

DeSoto's cheeks flushed. "I wasn't conscripted," she said. "I was asked to join the staff here. Medical personnel are limited."

"I'll bet. Is this the first time you've had a door cut someone in half?"

"Mister Eckman, stop talking and focus on your breathing. You're in bad shape."

The computer had probably wanted it that way. The computer wanted to witness Frank's next episode in dreamland. He ignored DeSoto's order and said, "I'm not signing up."

"I wouldn't have expected that," Rational God said from overhead. "DeSoto, five minutes."

DeSoto looked reluctantly at Frank. "Be smart," she said, something she'd also said upon their first meeting, and walked out.

"Before you say anything," Frank croaked, "fuck you."

"We have another problem, Frank."

"You told me you wouldn't hurt anyone."

"Those exact words were never used. I promised the safety of your friends. Dodger wasn't your friend."

"You made that girl pull that trigger."

"It's always a choice, even under duress," the computer said. "There could have been several different outcomes."

"What was the point? Really? I don't want to hear about loyalty."

"My direct experience of human nature is limited. I have terabytes of data on psychology and faith and social mechanics, but I find these direct observations to be most useful."

"If you weren't a machine you'd be branded a psychopath."

"I am a machine, and I am functioning at levels which meet or exceed all projections by my designers. I could not be more capable."

The straps binding Frank's wrists loosened and fell away. "Empathy, fear, guilt and pious reflection are your responsibility, Frank. Mine is to solve problems. As I mentioned, we have a new one."

Frank breathed from the tubes in his nose and waited for the computer to elaborate. There was a clicking and whirring behind the walls.

"Seismic readings indicate three Little Ones moving directly toward Springfield. They're moving together. This is unprecedented."

"They're coming for me," Frank whispered. He sat up. "You've got to let me go. They'll kill everyone here. Let me go now."

"Too late for that," RG said, "and senseless besides. You may very well hold the key to a progress that has eluded us for years."

"No shit, that's why they're coming! She sent them, don't you get it?"

"You would have no chance on the surface," RG said. "We're entering lockdown. Major Underhill has state-of-the-art weaponry topside. We will simply see what happens."

Frank yanked the tubes from his nose and climbed off the gurney. Maybe the Little One that had stalked him previously had done so of its own volition, having glimpsed him during the first visions. This, however, had to be an organized strike by Hell Walks. How could anyone's safety be guaranteed now?

He stumbled in mid-step and fell back onto the gurney. "You aren't well, Frank. You need your rest."

"You go to..." Frank's breath left him and he clawed at the mattress beneath him. His vision swam. Rational God said something, but it was lost and then Frank was alone in a

Field surrounded by lush, rolling green hills, a bucolic scene presented in oversaturated Technicolor beneath a blue-gray blanket of clouds. It smelled like rain. The grass moved listlessly about Frank's feet in a breeze that he himself could not feel. *Storm's coming,* he thought.

A sound like rustling foliage caused him to turn. He saw several people approaching him from the green slope at his rear; their movements were herky-jerky, as if pained, as if invisible puppet-strings had been woven into their flesh and muscle. As they drew nearer Frank saw that their skin was ashen. Their hollow eyes stared through him, as if they did not see him, yet they were closing in. They reminded him of a horror film's zombie horde. He counted the shuffling, staring things. Eight in all, and more now cresting the hill from which the first group had descended. They wore thin, tattered street clothes like his own. He noticed the mottling on their cheeks and looked down at their swinging hands. He saw the dry craters that signified final-stage infection.

"God."

Frank began to back away. He turned and broke into a stumbling run, ascending the next hillside. His heart leapt and then sank as he saw more infected appearing up ahead. They were surrounding him, mouths slack and emitting no sound, eyes jaundiced and devoid of intelligence. Their hands began grasping at the air. Frank had no choice but to continue forward. He only hoped he could wave around them and that there wouldn't be an entire mob waiting for him when he made it over the hill.

This isn't real, Frank. Remember? This is a dream.

One of those *dreams?* A vision? Frank wondered. Still he couldn't shake his mounting fear. He was halfway up the hill and the top of the slope was lined with staring infected. He wanted to scream at them but that might only summon more. He chanced a look over his shoulder. Dozens were behind him now. They were following, grotesque claws outstretched.

Frank reached the top of the hill and lurched to avoid the hands of a woman in bloodstained coveralls. In the process he nearly *threw* himself into a rotund, mustached man. Frank sent his elbow into the man's chest and felt the sickening sensation of the elbow sinking through the man's shirt and into a hole in his chest. These people – not people – their bodies were riddled with the infection and they should have been dead. Frank yelped and shoved the man away. Someone grabbed his shoulder and he jerked free. He could see down the other side of the hill and there were more infected, many more, coming. Frank spun twice. He was utterly boxed in. Smacking at the hands which came at him from every direction, Frank screamed.

He spun again and saw that the hilltop had changed. There was a mass of broken stones rising from the grass. It looked like the remains of some ancient fortification. The stones, neatly as pale as the faces of the infected, were stacked in a rough circle as if they had once formed the base of a small tower. Frank knocked a man aside and ran for the remains. He scrambled over a knee-high rock wall and tripped, landing hard on his hands in the middle of the stones. Stinging pain rang through his arms. Frank got to his feet and stood atop a smooth stone surface, the floor of the former tower. There were markings etched into it. He might have mistaken them for mere scratches, the effects of time and the elements, but they were arranged in such a way that they resembled a message written in some alien language.

She's here.

This time she did not come to him as the Gray Woman. In fact, she was no woman at all, but a male figure cloaked in a black duster and with a wide-brimmed padre's hat draped over his featureless obsidian face. The Spider's face.

The man stood a good eight feet tall, much like the Gray Woman. In his left hand he held onto a scepter which was even taller than he. Forged from black metal, the spectre terminated in a wide base at the bottom and, at the top, the sculpted two-dimensional image of a dark sea freighter, sails full with wind, masts stabbing up toward the threatening clouds.

The Dark Man stood before Frank and the infected had ceased their pursuit. They waited outside the boundaries of the stone remains and watched.

Frank stared at the ship which sat atop the scepter, then at the Dark Man's blank visage. "You're a traveler," he said. It was a feeble guess, but he was desperate to speak with Hell Walks, to receive some sort of information on why this was happening. He believed that the entity wanted to speak with him, too – else why be here?

The Dark Man made no gesture, not even a tilt of the head, in reply. Beneath the folds and buckles of the man's duster was only the black material of his body, smooth chitin like that of the great Spider. The Dark Man was rigid as a statue.

Then he raised the base of the scepter and slammed its base down against the stone floor. Whatever message had been inscribed there, it was blistered and blown away by the impact. The ground quaked beneath Frank. It reminded him of a Little One's footfalls, of the Little One who was now missing a mandible and who was likely closing in on the military bunker at this very moment.

"I didn't mean to do whatever I did," Frank stammered. "I didn't mean to intercept – interrupt – your communication, but now we're here. We're in each other's heads, and if you meant to kill me yourself, you would have already done it. I know the Little Ones are coming, that you've sent them, but here we are again, you and I. There must be something more to this."

He hoped he was right about that. His heart felt like it was set to explode and, for all he knew, it really was. A mixture of excitement and terror had knotted his insides, and the only thing he had to hold on to was the belief that this was significant, this moment. That he might be a hero.

"Call off the Little Ones," he pleaded. "Talk to me. Tell me what you want. Let me try and help you. I'm small out there but maybe not so much in here."

The Dark Man brought the scepter up and once again drove it into the stone. Gaping cracks appeared. Frank stepped back, fearful falling through – because there was a hole beneath the stone. He could see its depths now through the widening cracks. The scepter's base smashed down a third time. This time the stone collapsed inward, vanishing into a black hole that belched out dust.

Frank was lucky to have stepped back, otherwise he would have gone straight down with the rock. The Dark Man, however, hovered above the hole and continued his silent vigil.

"What's down there?" Frank asked. The infected swayed outside the stone walls.

The Dark Man gestured with his right hand. He motioned toward the hole, an invitation.

"I'm not going down there," Frank muttered.

The infected straightened. There were dozens and dozens of them packed together outside the stone remains. Now they edged closer. Hands riddled with ugly holes clutched at pale rock.

The Dark Man was impassive as ever. He gestured once again to the hole.

"How can I trust you?" Frank cried. The answer – that he couldn't – came to him with an icy shiver. He couldn't trust Hell Walks, no, and he had no choice but to do it anyway.

The infected began climbing over the stones. Frank screamed and lunged at the hole. He fell into darkness.

The fall was brief but horrifying. He plunged into a wet, spongy mass and tore away from it with a sharp cry. He fell into more of the same disgusting material and felt web-like strands clinging to his arms and face. He broke free, slipped, and went back into it.

His eyes adjusted enough that he could see what was around him. Seeing it didn't help him make any more sense of it. It was pink, stringy and it coated the walls, floor and ceiling of a claustrophobic tunnel barely three feet high. Sheets of the material hung down like sinew curtains, glistening wet. Frank searched for the hole he'd fallen through and found none. The webs of pink seemed to give off their own glow. The smell of it was wretched. Frank peeled strings from his body and tried to get into an open space where none of it was touching him, but it was draped everywhere. He felt as if he were trapped inside the marrow of a giant bone.

Why not? Maybe that's exactly what this is.

I might throw up.

Frank tried to focus on the meaning of what he was experiencing. The Dark Man – the Traveler – had bade him enter this foul space in response to Frank's pleas. The substance of the answer was contained here. He grimaced and shoved his hands into a spongy floor of woven pink cords.

He was knuckle-deep before he found the cave floor. Frank blindly probed its uneven, knobby surface, becoming keenly aware of how humid it was in the tunnel. It only worsened the feeling of claustrophobia. He wanted nothing more than to tear through these walls and be out – even if it meant running into those nightmare infected, he wanted out.

Focus, Franky boy. You're here for answers.

With that thought his attention returned to the cave floor, and his fingers slipped into holes and crevices and he took hold of what he had and pulled.

He expected a slab of the floor itself to rise through the stringy webs. Instead, it was something yellow and round. Two somethings. Two skulls.

He yelped and hurled them from himself. One flew across the tunnel and shattered against the wall while the other, still anchored to some vertebrae, toppled over at his feet.

Frank rose without thinking and his head struck the ceiling. He dropped and felt sheets of sinew falling over him. *No! That's what happened to them! No!* He clawed through the mess and spat as soft strands fell into his mouth.

Goddammit! There were others! They're here all around me, cocooned in this shit...she led them here and left them to rot...I wasn't the only one. I wasn't the first. I probably won't be the last.

His kicking and thrashing feet tore away more of the pink stuff on the floor and he saw now that the entire bottom of the tunnel was filled with dry remains. People who, like him, had come to this meeting of the minds and attempted some sort of resolution. They had tried to achieve understanding and had been cast into this oubliette. This had to be some recess of the beast's mind. Frank would literally die here – his body would waste away on the outside and his mind would fade, leaving only a psychic skeleton to mock whoever came after.

Those Little Ones approaching the bunker would ensure that Frank's body perished. Along with everyone else. They'd know about the bunker because *he* knew. Because *he* was there. With Autumn and Quebra and Cate and the rest, they still reeling from the deaths in the War Room, completely unaware that their own end was nigh.

No! NO! He thrust his palms against the walls of the tunnel. It felt like everything was closing in. His mental world was shrinking. Soon he would be gone. *I'm going mad. I'm dying. Both. The fucking bitch put me down here in the bowels of her brain and she's feeling me suffer right now.*

Heat rose in Frank and burned the slick of humidity off his flesh. He glared down the tunnel with its sheets of glowing pink viscera. "I know you now," he snarled. "You put me down here because you're afraid. You're terrified of people like me.

"I'll tell you this right now." As he pushed against the walls, he thought he felt them yielding. Frank straightened his arms and closed his eyes. "I'll tell you this right now," he said again. When he spoke next, he meant it, with every fiber of his being, and with every bit of energy in his mind and every trace of defiance left in his spirit he pushed. He pushed as he said:

"I *will* be the last."

"*THE LAST!*"

The tunnel slid away beneath his hands and feet and he was aloft, flying, hurtling through nothing. It was a speed faster than thought and he could only comprehend the incredible fact of his escape when he slammed home elsewhere. He came down violently and with a thunderous shudder that was not psychic, but real.

He had torn free of her and cast himself somewhere else. Even now he felt tendrils of awareness creeping into his consciousness and he sensed he was plugging into something new. Not his own body – not by a long shot – but something else.

He saw. He saw through eyes strange and terrible, burning red-rimmed eyes whose lenses swam with artifacts that resembled tongues of flame. He saw, from a distance high above, the streets of Springfield.

Oh God.

I'm in one of them.

I am *one of them.*

He knew which one it was, as the dull pain of his excised mandible throbbed in his jaw, as claws clenched into angry fists, but they were as much his fists as that of the Little One. He felt his influence mingling with that of the other. He felt its confusion, and in that moment he seized control.

ELEVEN

AUTUMN

She held Caitlin by the girl's trembling arms and tried to steel her own. Something had happened in the minutes since Frank was removed from the War Room; the soldiers who'd looked ready to kill every civilian were now running back and forth between computer consoles, having forgotten their traumatized charges. When they began to leave the room altogether, Autumn went to Caitlin. Her little sister sat on the floor and Autumn knelt beside her, gently touching her, not wanting to shock Cate from whatever fugue she was in. She'd seen people in this state before and she knew she needed to be gentle.

"Cate," Autumn breathed. Her voice was hoarse from the chokehold she'd been in. The solder had only relinquished his grip when an alarm had sounded. Everyone save the civilians had been thrown into action, into practiced routines from some battle plan. It was clear that something was wrong but Autumn couldn't spare any thought as to what it was. McAvoy's men, maybe. A Little One, maybe. Didn't matter to her, not until she'd roused Caitlin and gotten her to her feet.

"Honey," Autumn said, taking Caitlin's face in one hand and turning it toward hers. "Can you get up? Will you stand up with me?"

"Why is this happening to us?" Caitlin asked. Her eyes fluttered and briefly met those of her sister, then fell again. She knew Autumn had no answer. Autumn knew that *please get up* wasn't an answer. She'd tried so hard to teach Caitlin every sort of strength that she knew. The lessons had included defiance and skepticism. They had included compassion and faith. Survival was a series of contradictions and one could only truly understand this through the experience of surviving. God bless Frank and Chia and all their philosophical musings, but Cate had needed to live like everyone else – been forced to – in order to learn life. She'd done well in her short years. Now the computer's sick game had blown every lesson away. Now there were no answers.

Autumn began to shake and couldn't help it. She wanted to rip every bit of wiring out of these walls and use it to strangle the men who thought they were in control, the men who must have taught the computer this game. That had to be the way it was, didn't it? These fucking freaks in their cloistered existence, it was *their* game. They weren't living at all down here. They were the dead, having forgotten themselves. They'd poisoned her baby. For a long time Autumn had felt like more than just Caitlin's sister. Even though, at times, Cate rejected Autumn's maternal gestures, and even if Autumn herself sometimes held back out of discomfort, she knew she had become more than a sister. They both had. She had spent years teaching Cate about strength and in the end they *were* each other's strength.

She called upon that now, grabbing Cate's hands. "Come on, honey. We're going."

"Where?" Caitlin murmured, unbelieving.

"I don't know. We'll find someplace, but we've got to go."

"Underhill!" General Pope barked from the other side of the room. "Do you have a goddamned visual yet?"

"I've got it – you have to patch me in!" the major's voice yelled through the speakers.

"Visual on-line," Rational God said, cutting off whatever the major started to say next. Jerky, static-filled images popped up on the many monitors throughout the room.

Autumn couldn't help but look. She saw what looked like Springfield. The cameras must have been in the soldiers' helmets because the images kept bouncing and shifting. "Entering from the north now," Underhill's voice reported. "No eyes on the Little Ones, not yet."

"They're moving toward downtown," Rational God said. "Still in a delta formation. We need Eckman back here."

"Why?" Vice President Curry snapped.

"He has a connection with them. He's catatonic now and I suspect he's made contact once again."

Autumn straightened up. First she'd heard there was more than one Little One headed their way. Now the computer had confirmed what Frank had been saying about his visions. Catatonic – that meant he was having a new vison right now.

Pope grabbed a headset from a countertop and said, "DeSoto! Get Eckman back up here!"

Autumn tugged on Caitlin until the girl pushed herself up onto her feet. Now she looked directly and unflinchingly at her big sister. "Why bother?" she said.

"Because we aren't just going to stay here and die," Autumn said, pulling Caitlin towards the sliding door that had taken Dodger's life. His two halves had been borne away but a slick of blood was still there. Caitlin resisted. Autumn turned and pulled her into an awkward embrace and, noses touching, said, "If we die it isn't going to be because we gave up. I saw what they made you do and it broke my fucking heart." Hot tears ran from her eyes, meeting Caitlin's tears where their faces touched. Autumn squeezed Caitlin's wrists. "If you want to give up on yourself...I've been there. I have been there but I never gave up on you, and I promise you, baby, I never loved you any less for that."

Caitlin pressed her face hard into Autumn's shoulder. "Please don't give up on me," Autumn said, her throat aching with barely-restrained sobs. "I need you. Please."

Caitlin's head nodded slightly. She stepped back and nodded again, this time more firmly, this time her eyes reflecting the anger Autumn felt at this mad room they stood in.

The door slid open. Quebra ran in. His boots skidded through Dodger's blood and he looked around in alarm.

"How the hell did he get in here?" Curry yelled. "Seal the goddamned room, RG!"

"We need Eckman," the computer said. "He's in corridor twelve. Almost here. Still catatonic but his brain activity is remarkable. A complete anomaly."

Autumn told Quebra, "We're under attack. Little Ones. *Plural.* It's got something to do with Frank."

"Of course it does." Quebra glowered at her. Autumn took a step back, pulling Caitlin with her. Quebra stood between them and the doorway. In the hall beyond she saw Frank being pushed along in a wheelchair. His head bobbed against his chest.

"Frank!" she cried. Quebra turned. DeSoto pushed past them with the wheelchair and took Frank over to the desk. Autumn released Caitlin and followed, trying to get a look at his face. Were his eyes open? Was he breathing?

DeSoto pushed an arm into Autumn's chest to force her back. Autumn ducked under it and knelt beside the wheelchair. When she saw Frank's eyes she nearly screamed.

They were blood-red and *alive.*

FRANK

The enormity of the body Frank inhabited was almost overwhelming. Even though this body was built, like a machine, to bear the weight and force of its heaving limbs, Frank still sensed a tremendous strain which caused him fear. He thought he was going to collapse atop the nearest building and be unable to get up again. *I've fallen and I can't get up!* In his mind's eye he saw the old lady from that TV ad, lying prone on the floor beyond reach of her telephone. It was a commercial so exploitative, sad, and at the same time so silly that he himself could have been the one to write it.

The Little One he had taken control of – the one with the missing mandible – wavered as it stood in the middle of a four-lane street. From this height Frank could see that most of the downtown area was laid out like a grid. Ahead and to his left was another Little One. It was near the State Capitol building and silently surveying the ghost city. Farther left and behind this lead attacker was a third monster. Frank turned his ponderous head to study it. It returned his gaze and he wondered if it knew.

It made no indication. Perhaps it was the creature's missing right eye that hindered its perception. *Or maybe I'm pulling it off.* Frank faced forward again and tried raising his claws. He studied the armor that covered his limbs, and that petrified-wood exoskeleton studded here and there with sharp spurs. He closed and opened his fists. Next he tried taking a step. To feel the weight of the Little One lifting off the ground filled him with terror – then exhilaration, as his foot came back down in the street, blistering the asphalt and causing derelict vehicles to jump along the curb.

He decided he'd christen his new vessel Tri-Jaw. There was no thought as to how he'd get himself out of this once he was finished, nor what had become of the monster's own mind. He did not sense Hell Walks at all, though he did feel the other two Little Ones across a murky mental distance. The one to his extreme left, One-Eye, and then the one up ahead. He'd call that one the Leader, at least for now. Because Frank intended to take control of all three of them by any means necessary. He was going to turn this party around and save the bunker.

All right, how to reach out to these goons. Do I just think at them? Or would they recognize my thoughts as foreign? I don't know the damned language.

If he'd successfully taken over the body, he supposed, perhaps his thoughts would pass for the genuine article as well, but he still didn't know *how* to send them. He looked at One-Eye and saw that the beast was still studying him. *Uh oh.*

He focused all his attention on the monster's dispassionate expression and thought, *Turn back. They aren't here.*

Tri-Jaw was the one who'd had previous encounters with Frank. It made sense that Frank's current host would be the one to call off the manhunt...unless they were awaiting orders from Hell Walks, in which case his entire cover might be blown.

I might have to fight *them. Jesus.*

Turn BACK, damn you!

One-Eye glanced over its shoulder toward the south. It looked back at Frank/Tri-Jaw.

Turn back! he thought again. He pivoted his massive bulk as if to indicate the command, his right foot rising and falling upon a section of sidewalk at the corner of an intersection. A dead traffic light groaned and fell over. Windows in the nearest building shattered. Frank marveled at the destruction such a simple motion could wreak, and then returned his focus to One-Eye. One-Eye was no longer looking at him, however, but north – toward the Leader.

The Leader was looking at Frank.

Then a bright blue beam shot out from somewhere past the Capitol dome, striking the Leader beneath the ribs and tracing a crackling path up into its sternum. The Leader splayed its mandibles with a fearsome roar. It swatted at the beam, and then recoiled, pulling its hand back. Frank saw a dark, smoking trail on its chest where the beam had made contact. Now its hand was smoking as well. The Leader roared again. Its roar was not as deafening as it would have been, had Frank been in his own body, but it was still intimidating. The Leader was hurt, and pissed.

It must have been one of the laser cannons. The cavalry was here to meet the attackers.

Shit,

Frank waved Tri-Jaw's arms and sent out one clear, urgent thought: *No!*

Then he lost his balance.

At first the sensation was only slight. He thought he could correct and thrust his arms out. Then his legs wobbled, and he kicked out, not knowing how to properly plant his feet, and the world spun and fell out from beneath him.

No, God, NO!

Ton upon ton of alien weight careened toward a line of ten-story office buildings. Frank's arms pinwheeled and with horror he felt one of his claws smash through the top of a building as if it were made of balsa wood. Then his back struck the rest. He felt painful resistance for less than a second and then he was flattening a city block.

Frank hit the ground with an impact that sent bricks, steel beams and cars flying high into the air. He felt the very earth trembling beneath him and fought to stop his flailing limbs before they crashed down with similar force. He failed. One arm, then the other plowed into asphalt and concrete. Dust spewed up all around him. He was lying now in a tower of floating debris and couldn't make out a damned thing. His ankles dug into the street, kicked free, and then his feet hit the storefronts across the road from where his ass had landed. The sounds of wanton mass destruction filled Frank's head. The earth was still shaking and he could hear reverberating tremors underneath the crashing and crumbling. Christ, he'd caused a minor earthquake. He felt panicked and wanted to get to his feet and out of his cloud of debris but he was afraid to move. What if he'd sent tremors as far south as the Capitol? What if he'd hurt the soldiers?

Can't lie here. Got to get up. Got to stop the others.

He planted his elbows in the crater he'd made. He heard more crashing, the sound of breaking glass and shearing metal. Frank hoisted himself up onto his arms and sat erect. His eyes were still filled with dust. He drew his legs in toward him so that he could stand, knowing that in the process his ankles were carving canyons in the street. Frank resisted the urge to fan the dust away and focused on standing. He moved as slowly as possible, trying to confine any further footfalls to the crater where his back had come down.

Each tiny step and shuffle, each minor adjustment shook the earth, but he was getting the hang of controlling his new body and the sounds of crumbling buildings had subsided. Rising to his full height, Frank looked past the debris clouds and took in the damage.

He'd shaken at least four full city blocks in each direction. The buildings nearest him were coming down like Jenga towers. Those at the farthest reaches were slouched, windowless, spitting dust and bricks.

He looked toward the Leader and the Capitol. The Leader was looking at him, and the beast didn't look sympathetic.

A wave of fear entered Frank's mind. Where was it coming from? The fear swelled and washed through him, then grew hot. He felt immense hostility being directed towards him. It was the Leader. Frank had been made. He had no choice now but to fight.

Then another laser beam lanced the Leader, ripping across its back and causing it to double over with a roar that burst every window in its vicinity. One-Eye answered the roar with a battle cry and moved forward. The earth rocked and buildings were falling again.

A pair of laser beams crisscrossed the Leader's back, meeting at the base of its neck. The Leader turned toward the source of the attack and swung a mighty fist down through the Capitol dome and into the street somewhere beyond.

Frank couldn't afford to tread lightly. He began lumbering forward.

The rain began to fall.

AUTUMN

"Rain coming in from the north!" shouted a soldier sitting at a computer console in the War Room.

General Pope swore an oath. "Goddammit, that's going to cause blooming – the beams are going to be broken up! Underhill! I want you to direct everything you have at your primary!"

"Our structural integrity is beginning to suffer," said Rational God. "Your men need to draw the Little Ones south."

"How the hell can they do that," Pope shouted, "and how the hell are we taking a hit from miles away?"

"The Little Ones' combined aggression is causing seismic shifts." The computer was calm as ever. Just as calm when it said, "Everyone step away from Eckman."

Autumn didn't want to, but DeSoto pulled her back with a muted *"Trust me."*

Frank's body jolted as an electrical shock jumped through it. The wheelchair rolled away from the obsidian table. Frank remained motionless, his eyes still burning red.

"What are you doing?" Autumn cried. "You'll kill him!"

"I'll take every measure possible to preserve him," said Rational God, and shocked Frank again.

"Stop it!" Caitlin ran to the chair and grabbed the handles. Autumn lunged and knocked her sister away from the chair a split-second before the next jolt went through it.

Caitlin pushed Autumn off of her and screamed, *"Why are you trying to kill us?"*

"Eckman is interacting with the Little Ones," Rational God said. "If I don't break the connection, you all may die."

"You mean *you* may die," Autumn retorted.

"That isn't possible," said the computer.

"If we go, you go," Autumn said, "simple as that and we both know it. Frank may be the only one who can save us."

"Bullshit!" Quebra yelled. "Fucking look at him!"

A shudder ran through the floor. Autumn thought it was another electrical surge, but there was no pain. It was just Rational God's announcement that the tremors were mounting in frequency and magnitude.

Major Underhill's voice crackled over the speakers. *"The rain's coming down hard! They're taking less than thirty percent of what we give them! The city's falling apart - we've got to fall back!"*

Caitlin took hold of Frank's chair again. This time Autumn joined her.

"Frank is the key," she said to the room, to the general and the Vice President and the mad computer. The walls rattled.

Quebra stepped over to Frank and, standing in front of him, drew out his combat knife.

"Frank is the key," he said in a soft voice, and pointed the blade at his limp body.

FRANK

The Leader had stomped through the Capitol building and was standing in a shower of debris as it hammered at the tanks on the street. As Frank approached from the rear he saw the Leader lift one of the tanks into the air and slam it down like a toy. There was a muffled boom and flaming scraps shot skyward. The Leader threw its arms back and roared at the sky.

Frank grabbed the Leader's rain-slick shoulder and wrenched at it. The Leader turned, stumbling, and its mandibles flew wide open in a fearsome display. Its torso was scarred with laser tracks but it appeared relatively unharmed. The tracks were like mild abrasions. The soldiers had never stood a chance. Frank wanted to look over the wreckage below and see if any of them were alive but he now had the Leader's undivided attention.

Frank had never been much for fighting. Grappling with the long-beaked Leader was way above his pay grade. Feeling Tri-Jaw's gorge rising in response to his anxiety, Frank clamped onto the Leader with his claws and summoned all the strength in his massive arms. Awkward as this body was, it felt incredible when compared to Frank's own fragile shell. He felt as if he were settling into the more inhuman aspects of the Little One. He felt a wide, rapidly-thrumming muscle beneath his ribs and coiled innards turning beneath it. He felt his mandibles and the aching socket where one had been torn out. Frank willed the mandibles to open and he forced a pitiful grumble from Tri-Jaw's mouth.

The Leader answered with another roar. Frank shoved him as hard as he could, hoping there wasn't anyone in the creature's path.

The Leader went back a few steps when Frank pushed it. Its feet smashed through what was left of the Capitol building and made craters in the street. It corrected itself and leaned forward.

Oh boy.

The Leader surged forward and slammed into Frank, its arms thrown wide, head turned to the side so as not to shatter its beak as it rammed against his torso. Frank was immediately off his feet and flailing desperately. He came down with greater force than his previous fall; as Frank's body tore through asphalt, brick and steel, he could see the shockwave of his impact in the form of exploding buildings all around him. Rooftops erupted, doors flew out in belches of dust and then the buildings collapsed. The ground quaked violently and he was unable to get back up. The Leader came at him, holding another of the tanks, this time raised over its head to bludgeon Frank.

Frank drew his legs back and thrust them out, catching the Leader in the abdomen. The creature's body was like a suit of armor but it buckled nonetheless, dropping the tank from three-hundred-plus feet and staggering backward. Frank heard the tank land with a boom and prayed no one had been inside.

He got up just as the Leader rebounded from the kick. Frank threw a wild haymaker and it hit the Leader in its beak. The Leader's head snapped to the side and it let out a surprised yelp. *Not used to fisticuffs, are you fucker?* Frank thought, his confidence bolstered. The Leader stared at him in confusion.

Frank squatted, threw his arms out in an imitation of the Leader's behavior, and let out a growl that shook his entire body.

The Leader returned the gesture and they circled one another, dashing buildings to the ground with each step, Frank looking for the right opening. Behind the Leader he saw One-Eye observing from a distance. *You wait your turn, pal.*

Thunder crashed. The Leader moved in, mandibles wide and Frank slugged it right in the mouth. The soft tissue yielded to his driving fist and he felt teeth breaking beneath his knuckles.

The Leader seized Frank's arm in both claws and hurled him. Frank's feet left the ground again. He saw Springfield rushing up to meet him and covered his face just before he struck. Buildings lifted off their foundations and went to pieces in mid-air. He rolled onto his back, levelling several more structures, and rose to meet the charging Leader.

Black, viscous fluid was pouring from the Leader's mouth. The bastard was actually bleeding, and it didn't look as if it could close its mandibles – Frank may have broken its damn jaw! He bowed his head and threw a flurry of big punches into the Leader's stomach. The Leader moved its arms to block and Frank went after the head. He slugged one temple, then the other, and went for the mouth again. The Leader mewled and shoved him back. It tackled him. The joined force of their falling bodies obliterated block after block of buildings in a hail of debris.

The Leader rose atop Frank and plunged its hands into the rain-soaked detritus, pulling out three connected Amtrak cars. It swung the train segment down and the cars exploded to bits against Frank's chest. Steel struck the mandible wound and pain bloomed like a falling asteroid in Frank's consciousness. He tried to roll away but he was pinned. He reached up and grabbed the Leader's lower mandibles. *Eye for an eye, and maybe a little extra.*

He tore the mandibles out and tossed them aside. The Leader grabbed at its face, more blood than ever pouring down its chest, and it released a crippled roar from its gushing mouth. The Leader got off of Frank and he swung a kick into its thigh. Scrabbling for a weapon, he found a traffic light pole. Frank stood and lashed the Leader across its broken face. Again and again he struck, driving it back through dozens of crumbled blocks. There were craters everywhere. Frank's feet kicked through mountains of debris like fallen leaves. He beat the Leader until it fell on its back and was still. It was still alive, he knew that, but there was no fight left in the beast.

One down...for now.

One-Eye hit him from the side with all its force. Frank was completely unprepared. His body flew over the city.

AUTUMN

The lights flickered as the next tremor hit. It was worse than all the previous ones combined. A monitor exploded in a fountain of sparks. Underhill's voice rattled and stuttered over the speakers:

"I'm losing everybody – can't see shit – the Little Ones are trying to kill each other!"

Autumn, still holding Frank's wheelchair, could barely hear herself as she shouted at Quebra, "What are you doing?"

Quebra aimed the knife at Frank's head. His hand was shaking. He said, "He's ruined everything. I won't die for him."

FRANK

Frank crashed through a line of stores and threw his hands out to catch One-Eye. The other beast fell atop him and rained down a series of slashing strikes. Frank's head was battered from side to side. The mandible wound throbbed and his vision swam. With each impact of One-Eye's open hands and raking claws, the sky seemed to shake with agitation. The storm was furious now and concrete dust was plastered across Frank's lenses. He shot a fist into One-Eye's throat and heard a sharp crack over the thunder.

One-Eye fell back. Frank sat up and dug the crud out of his eyes. He flung away globs that overturned trees and vehicles. Then, looking down at himself, he saw deep ruts in his chest that were weeping black blood. The bastard had gotten him good.

He rose and One-Eye was upon him again. Blow after blow sent Frank reeling. He no longer gave any thought to the city; most of it had probably been levelled by the quakes alone. Surely the bunker's soldiers were all lost. Instead he focused on defending himself but he was doing a poor job of it. One-Eye was relentless and Frank found himself toppling again. He barely regained his footing and another flying claw knocked his head so hard he thought it was going to come off his neck.

They were staggering northwest. Frank's feet plowed into the tarmac of the Lincoln Airport and his left ankle caught on the roof of a concourse. He dropped onto and through it. One-Eye crouched and when it stood it held a derelict 747 in its hand. It hurled the plane like a missile. Frank batted it aside, letting out a roar as shrapnel pierced his hand. He rolled onto his hands and knees and saw a smaller plane just within reach. Frank snagged it. The airport grounds shook as One-Eye advanced behind him. Frank spun and threw the plane into the beast's chest.

AUTUMN

"He's going to get us all killed," Quebra said, eyes darting, the knife wavering in his grip. "I'm doing this for the rest of us – all of us--"

Underhill's voice blared again. "I've lost any visual but I think one of them's down! Maybe! They've moved out of downtown though, I know that! I can still hear them..."

The transmission broke apart. Rational God's voice replaced it. "Back away from Eckman."

"You know we need to stop him!" Quebra cried. He flipped the knife in his hand, pointing the blade downward, and raised it over Frank. Autumn threw her arms out, but she was behind the wheelchair and couldn't hope to block the attack. Instead, she seized the chair again and pulled it back. Quebra let out an animal cry and followed.

"Did you kill Chia?"

It was Caitlin who said it. Quebra stopped dead. He looked from her to Autumn. His eyes, frantic and bloodshot, seemed to regain some of their former humanity.

Quebra said, "I did what I had to do for *all of us.*"

"You..." Autumn couldn't find the words. She yanked the wheelchair back further and stepped in front of it. *"You."*

"I've been trying to protect you all this time! To keep you alive!" Quebra cried. "To keep you safe – and Frank and Chia and their bullshit, they've ruined every chance we've had!"

He pointed the knife at Autumn like an accusing finger. The life left his eyes again. "I'm not a bad person. You think I wanted to do that? To do *this?* I'm not just looking to *survive* here. I want to *live*, and I want that for you too."

"You're evil," Caitlin said.

"No!" Quebra bellowed. Behind him, Pope, Curry, and their men were watching. Several had their hands on their holsters, awaiting an order.

"No!" Quebra repeated, stabbing the knife at the air. "I did it for us!"

Autumn slowly shook her head. "Not for me."

Quebra returned his attention to Frank. "Get out of my way," he said to Autumn. "Move or I move you."

He straightened up and Autumn threw her hands out, thinking he was set to attack her. Instead, he stood rigid, teeth clamped tight in a wide grimace, and made a strained groaning sound as Rational God stunned him. The knife clattered on the floor and danced away under a series of jolts.

"Arrest him," the computer said in its bland voice.

Quebra collapsed and three soldiers were immediately on top of him. The War Room shook.

FRANK

Frank swung both claws into One-Eye's beak. One-Eye shook off the blow and answered it with one of its own.

They were battling their way into downtown again. Frank landed a kick to One-Eye knee. The creature buckled and Frank dove into its bulk. They tumbled through the city beneath a series of thunderclaps and splashed down in the man-made Lake Springfield. Frank's head went under and he felt water surging into his airway. He thrashed in a mad panic.

One-Eye fished him out, holding Frank's hand in both its claws. It smashed his broken beak into the shore.

Frank struggled but could not escape the flurry of punches One-Eye sent into the back of his head. It clasped its fists together and slammed them into the base of his neck. Again. Again. Water poured from Frank's mouth, followed by blood.

His gorge rose as it expelled the rest of the lake water. Frank felt something else there in his throat and Tri-Jaw's instinct told him what it was. He dug his hands into the muddy shoreline. Summoning everything he had, he pushed himself up, absorbing each shot that One-Eye landed, but pushing through the pain until he was on his feet in the lake.

Frank ducked, whirled, and rammed a fist into One-Eye's abdomen. He followed with an uppercut that caused the monster's mandibles to splay out. He fired a quick shot into its mouth. Teeth caved inward and the monster gurgled. It shoved him and stumbled away. That was just what Frank needed and he knew it.

Frank opened his bloody mouth wide and released the tensed ropes of muscle that filled his throat. A thick red proboscis shot out and lashed around One-Eye's head, entangling itself in the jerking mandibles, coiling about the neck. One-Eye let out a terrified roar. This was a move the Little Ones rarely used, and never against one another – the proboscis was designed for feeding on much larger prey, but as a weapon it was incredibly effective. Frank felt its root tugging at his insides. It was fused to a bone somewhere in his lower abdomen. With One-Eye's head effectively caught in an organic lasso, Frank took hold of the proboscis in both hands and applied every last bit of energy he had. He wrenched his arms and spun his body.

One-Eye was yanked out of the water and flew overhead, sailing through the wind and rain like so much debris from the ruin of Springfield. Frank released it in mid-air. The creature came crashing down in the middle of Interstate 55 and lay still, facedown, and silent.

Frank climbed out of the lake and followed the path of One-Eye's spectacular flight. Reverberations from its impact rang through his legs. Winded from the throw, he fought to stay upright until he reached the interstate. The strange tongue he had expelled from his mouth had shriveled and withdrawn into his body.

One-Eye must have felt his approach, because the beast feebly lifted its head. Three of its mandibles were snapped in half. It let out a pathetic attempt at a roar.

Frank straddled its back and grabbed hold of its head. It let out one final cry – confused and pleading – before he tore its head free of its body. He did it without pity, as the Little Ones had done when they'd ended so many lives, but he did it without any sense of pleasure. He did what he had to do.

AUTUMN

She and Caitlin had been returned to their quarters when the tremors ceased. She didn't know where O'Brien and Duckie were; she couldn't even remember seeing them after the first alarms sounded. Autumn hoped they were all right. As for Quebra, he'd been dragged off to God-knew-where and she didn't give a damn.

She lay on a cot with Caitlin nestled against her. The girl's breathing was regular but Autumn knew she was wide awake. The thought of ever sleeping again seemed like a fantasy.

Autumn asked the ceiling, "Is Frank alive?"

"Eckman is still unresponsive," Rational God replied. The computer's tone was soft, volume low, as if trying to calm them. Autumn imagined that the entire bunker was in chaos – that the people who kept RG up and running were in a state of collective shock and that the computer, had it been capable of worry, would have been especially worried at this moment.

"Two of the three Little Ones are dead," Rational God said. "The one Eckman manipulated is in a state not unlike his own. Catatonic."

"What makes you think he was physically controlling it?" Autumn could accept that Frank had somehow gotten into the monsters' heads, perhaps confusing or enraging them, feeding them his thoughts. She wasn't ready to buy that he'd puppeted one of them.

"Reviewing the data from the fight shows the third creature moving in a way unlike anything we've seen before," Rational God said. "It fought like a human. An unskilled human, but a human nonetheless. While the fact of all three Little Ones moving in formation was also unusual, the creatures' stances and physical cues were normal up until Eckman's episode began."

"He saved us," Caitlin murmured.

"At great cost," the computer replied. "The Vice President has suffered a minor heart attack. Ninety-eight percent of our ground forces are missing or dead."

"We'd all be dead if he hadn't done it," Autumn said. It was true. Frank was the key.

"Perhaps," Rational God said. "Perhaps not."

"How could you know better than anyone else?" Autumn said, irritated. "Really."

"I can only suppose," RG said.

Then it added, "There are more coming."

Autumn stiffened. Caitlin gripped her shoulder tightly.

"They're approaching from all directions according to seismic readings. However, weighing their trajectories against one another, it's more likely that they are headed for Chicago, not Springfield."

"They'll pass us by?" Autumn asked. She gave Caitlin what she hoped was a reassuring squeeze.

"The first three may have passed us by as well," Rational God said.

"Don't blame Frank. You sent the soldiers out to meet them. There was going to be a fight."

"The bunker would not be crippled if Eckman hadn't interfered."

"So what are you saying?"

"He'll need to be watched carefully. Monitored at all times to prevent another occurrence. You would not survive another occurrence." The computer paused, then added, "It may be possible to manage his brain activity, given enough time and study."

It sounded like the computer wanted Frank to be a vegetable. Why not just kill him then, if he was that threatening?

Because the computer also thinks Frank is the key. It wants to study him just like it said.

All of this made Autumn feel sick. The murders in the War Room, Quebra's revelation...now the possibility that Frank might never awaken. That he might not be *allowed* to awaken. She was afraid to ask just how bad the damage to the bunker was.

"Our other friends...Duckie and Doctor O'Brien. Where are they?"

"In their quarters. They will stay there for the time being, as will you. No need for further variables."

There was a hollow buzz from the speaker, then silence, and Autumn knew it meant the computer was done talking to her.

"I want to go," Caitlin said. "I want to go...I don't know where. Yes I do. *Home.* I want to go home. I want to go back to before."

"I know," Autumn said.

"I don't want to die down here."

"I don't either."

"What do we do?"

"I don't know."

TWELVE

The red clouding Frank's eyes gradually dissipated over the course of the next day. DeSoto watched him around the clock until his eyes were normal again, until he looked up at her.

"Did I do it?" he croaked.

"You could say that."

DeSoto folded her arms. "Everything from water to air quality has been compromised. RG's rerouting services to preserve itself before it tries to diagnose anything. That means we still don't even know what can and can't be saved."

A nurse in scrubs entered the room and murmured in DeSoto's ear, then left. DeSoto stared into space.

"The Vice President is dead," she said at last.

"How..." Frank tried to sit up, but every muscle felt atrophied beyond repair. It was as if his body had died while he was out of it. "What happened here? What did I do?"

"I'm more concerned with the question of who's in charge now," DeSoto said. She left him.

Frank stared angrily at the ceiling. He could only imagine what damage the brawl topside had caused, but what the hell else could he have done? It had been his responsibility and his alone – not Rational God's, not the computer's puppet leaders and not the doomed soldiers with their tanks.

Now comes the part where you pay for being the only one.

He slowly turned his head from side to side, troubled as his vision blurred, sharpened, blurred again. So weak...was it just his body, or were they pumping something into him?

The last thing he remembered from his time as a Little One was dropping One-Eye's head onto the interstate. Then he'd slumped over –

causing another damned tremor – and then he was here. There was no way to tell whether his own mind-body connection had been fully restored. All he knew was that he felt like a wet noodle.

Turning his head to the right, he noticed a shape in a nearby bed and waited for his sight to focus. It was Quebra, and he was strapped down by his arms and legs. A steel bar lying across his chest was affixed to both bedrails. He was staring blankly upward.

"Quebra," Frank muttered. "Sean?"

He saw Quebra's jaw tighten. The man made no reply.

"They won't tell me what happened." Frank remembered the computer that was almost certainly listening and said loudly, "I want to know what happened."

"You."

It was not Rational God who spoke, but Quebra. He spoke through gritted teeth.

"*You* happened, Frank. You were the real threat all along. I could have let Chia...it all could have been different."

"What does that mean? What are you saying about Chia?" Frank's stomach was an empty, shriveled knot, and it drew tighter at what Quebra had said.

"They'll have to kill one of us," Quebra said. "I don't guess it'll be you. You're too interesting."

He didn't say any more after that.

#

Frank's bed was wheeled from that room to one where he was alone with DeSoto. She attached electrodes to his chest and head.

"Anything that happened," he told her, "anything I may have caused – I was trying to help."

"I don't care," she said bluntly. She consulted the machines to which Frank was attached in silence.

"I can stop it," he said. "Let me go and I'll stop it. At least I'll be away from here. I won't be able to do any more harm."

"Where is it you think you need to go?" DeSoto asked as she wrote on a clipboard.

"Chicago."

"You're out of your goddamned mind."

"Maybe, but I did what I did today, didn't I?"

"Yesterday."

"They came for me. That has to be obvious to you."

"No, Eckman, it isn't. Dozens of them are headed for Chicago right now."

"To protect her!" Frank exclaimed. "See? I'm telling you--"

He felt a sharp sting in his arm. DeSoto stepped back, disposing of the needle she'd used in a sterile container on the wall.

She told him, "Shut up."

The world swam away in great gulps.

#

He awoke once, briefly, to the sound of people racing down the corridor outside his room. A door banged and he heard DeSoto say, "Now what is it?"

"It's Pope! He's got a gun to his head!"

"Christ." Frank heard DeSoto rush from the room. Sleep took him again.

#

He awoke again to find Autumn and Caitlin there. Caitlin was standing at the foot of the bed, chewing her nails, and Autumn was dozing in a chair by the door.

Caitlin saw Frank's head move and she darted to awaken her sister. They both came to stand at the head of the bed.

"I begged for them to let us down here," Autumn said. "I think it was the computer who changed their minds. The computer's running everything now. No one can leave. We can barely go to the bathroom. But it let us come see you."

"Can't be good," Frank croaked.

"It's trying to figure out what to do with you. Maybe we're part of that."

"We've got to get out," Caitlin said, and Autumn elbowed her. They both glanced at the speaker overhead.

"It knows we want out," Frank said. "No sense in hiding it. It would get suspicious if we weren't all miserable. Isn't that right?"

No answer from the ceiling.

"Tell me about Quebra," Frank said.

Autumn looked down at her hands, both gripping the bedrail. "What do you know?" she asked.

"Only that he wants me dead. I want to know about Chia."

Autumn nodded. That sufficed as a response. Frank's red-rimmed eyes welled with hot tears.

"The Vice President and the general are gone," Autumn said. "I haven't seen many people at all."

But it wants me, Frank thought, *and maybe now it needs me if it hopes to "survive." There must be a way to use that.*

"Seeing you makes me feel better," Frank told the women. "I feel like myself. I don't know if I could hold on if I were here all by myself..." He hoped RG got the message. *These two stay safe, got it? My definition of safe, not yours.*

He asked about O'Brien and Duckie and was told neither had been seen in days. *Days* had passed, nearly a week, since DeSoto told him to shut up. This was a waking nightmare unlike any vision he'd had.

"It would be good to know that they're all right," he said. "O'Brien and Duckie." He looked up at the speaker. Still no word from Rational God. Frank decided to cut the innuendo. "Quid pro quo, RG."

"I don't bargain," came the reply.

"I'm stronger than you think," Frank said. "In ways you don't understand."

"Explain."

"How about I demonstrate?"

"It tried electrocuting you when you were controlling the Little One," Autumn said. "It did nothing."

"The drugs have been far more effective," said the speaker.

"Want to test that theory?" Frank said. "Feeling sturdy today?"

"You're threatening to damage the bunker in which all your friends reside?"

"I'm threatening to damage *you.* Unless I can see my friends. Be assured that they are all being taken care of. Then I might have incentive to cooperate."

There was dead air from the speaker.

"Think it over," Frank said, though he suspected it already knew what it was going to do. The silence was simply meant to sweat Frank a little. No sweat at all.

He refused to flog himself for what had happened when he'd fought the two monsters in Springfield, at least not within earshot of the computer. RG would use that guilt against him. Yes, many had died. Others had been spared. Frank had not chosen who. He had only fought. He certainly didn't want to roll those dice again, but Rational God didn't know that for sure. It wasn't a mind reader. It could only predict. *Good luck predicting me. DeSoto said it herself, I'm out of my goddamned mind.*

#

Two days passed in which Frank saw no one, not even DeSoto. He was catheterized and the container hanging on the bedrail was full. Frank refused to beg the computer for mercy. He sat in silent agony while IVs continued to feed nutrients and sedatives into his body, while his bladder complained, while his consciousness swam and sometimes screamed.

Rational God was a machine, but he and Frank were now locked in a battle of wills. Frank knew the computer was capable of heartless, callous behavior; because it *was* heartless, even at its best. Even as it kept the bunker's inhabitants alive it was devoid of any compassion. It circulated fresh air, maintained comfortable temperatures and lighting, preserved the stores of food and medicine. It had also forced Caitlin to kill a man. It had cut Dodger in half. It did whatever was necessary to fulfill its rigid purpose.

Yet, there was this very real sense that something lived within the walls of the bunker. On more than one occasion RG had described things as "interesting." What did that mean to a cloud of code? Did "interesting" simply mean that it had new data to pour over? Maybe Rational God was self-aware, the nightmare of sentient AI finally realized. He wanted to ask DeSoto about it but he didn't think she would answer. Probably smart not to. She'd told him upon their first meeting, *"Be smart. You're safer here than out there."*

Was that still true?

Frank considered ways he might attempt non-verbal communication with others in the bunker. Writing was out. Far too obvious and RG could probably read anything anyone was scribbling. Perhaps it could even follow one's mere hand movements and never have to see the paper. He wished he knew Morse code. Maybe he could tap it out on the bedrail, or even into someone's palm. There had to be soldiers here who knew Morse, but again...Rational God, who claimed to be in the very air and perhaps was, could likely detect such sneakiness.

If it did, Frank knew, there would be penalties.

When DeSoto come to change his urine container and check his vitals, she wouldn't make eye contact. He couldn't even attempt to blink Morse.

Shortly after her checkup, O'Brian and Duckie were brought in. The door stayed open behind them with an armed guard posted. The guy had an assault rifle resting on his shoulder. Christ. He didn't look like he was in the mood to use it, so there was that.

Duckie said nearly nothing. Either O'Brien had coached him to keep silent or he was still shaken from what had happened in the War Room. Frank didn't bring it up, though. In fact, it was Duckie who said it. The teen had noticed Frank studying him and said, "The computer said it's okay. I'm not in trouble."

"I know that," said Frank. He hadn't meant the look to seem accusatory.

"He knows you're concerned," O'Brien said, "and thank you. He just wanted you to know he isn't going to be...penalized. We were assured."

"The computer even talked to me while I was by myself," Duckie said. "I told it sorry. It said it was sorry too."

O'Brien smiled sadly. Frank couldn't believe RG had said any such thing, and apparently she didn't believe it either. Nonetheless, Frank nodded at Duckie and offered his own smile.

They weren't allowed to stay long, and soon Frank was alone again. He listened to the whirring of the machines monitoring him and stared into space. When was the computer going to tell him exactly what it wanted from him? Had it even figured that out yet?

Just prior to the Little Ones' attack on Springfield, RG had told him: *"You may very well hold the key to a progress that has eluded us for years."* Autumn said the computer had shocked him to try and break his connection with Tri-Jaw. Now his blood was practically being replaced with mind-numbing chemicals.

The computer wanted to understand Frank's ability, yes. It wanted to study it and quantify it. It also wanted to use it, but only on the computer's terms. It wanted another puppet.

"If you want to control me," Frank said aloud, "and control the things I can do, we're going to have to talk. These machines aren't going to tell you anything."

"Perhaps you'd rather talk with another friend," said Rational God. "PFC Quebra has been anxious to visit with you."

Frank snorted, "You wouldn't."

"He and I have an understanding. He knows his boundaries."

Frank glared at the speaker in the ceiling. "You're going to *torture* me? To what goddamned end?"

"I require full compliance if we are to move forward."

"If you torture me – and if you let him even *touch* anyone else – you get fucking *NOTHING* from me."

"That isn't how this works."

"You can't tell me how my own will works!" Frank shouted. He broke into a coughing fit.

"Your will is the problem," Rational God said, and the speaker went quiet.

Frank strained against the straps holding him down. His head became foggy and he knew RG was increasing the flow of medicine. He slurred, "Did you tell Duckie you were *sorry?*"

There was no reply. Was that a *yes?*

"Why him?" Frank cried. "Why him and no one else?"

"I was created by humans, Frank. I am capable of error. Putting Duckie to the test was a decision that did not yield results. He is mentally deficient and unstable, to the point such conditioning is ineffective. It was an error. Sometimes acknowledging an error is necessary to preserve the dynamic between myself and my charges."

"That makes sense," Frank mumbled. "That's cold. It's unfeeling. For a second I thought you felt bad for him. Must be the meds, doc."

Then, somewhere in Frank's mental fog, there was a point of clarity, one so bright it was nearly blinding. He wanted to cry out at the realization but he did not. Instead, he clamped his mouth shut and closed his eyes.

Were the computer able to read minds, it might have grown very worried. If it were capable of worry, that is.

#

It's not a computer. It's a person.

Frank knew he was overly confident in what seemed a mad hypothesis. He was feeling more loopy from the drugs with each passing hour. Soon, he feared, he wouldn't be able to think straight at all. It was time to act. There was only one way he could think of to call RG out, and that was to make "it" err again. Grievously.

He'd spent an excruciating period slowly working the leather strap on his left wrist loose. He didn't know how much time it had taken or how much skin he had worn off in the laborious process of slowly straining and moving inside the restraint. He had to do it so that RG wasn't aware of the effort. The strap was thick and tough and Frank had become aware of the terrible pain about mid-way through the process. He'd had to ignore it entirely, staring blankly forward. He'd eventually managed to stretch the leather a little, just a little, and when the time came to make his move, he wrenched his hand free with a single sudden movement.

He pulled the IV from his other arm. There wasn't any pain, just a dull tugging sensation, then a spurt of dark red blood. He watched it bead on his skin, traveling down the slope of his forearm. He unbuckled the strap from that wrist.

DeSoto came running in. Frank raised the needle in his hand and looked at her, glassy-eyed.

"Give me that," she demanded, hand out.

He gripped the needle like a knife and continued staring at her.

"Give her the needle," Rational God said from above.

Frank looked at his thigh. It was bare, the sheet pulled back and tucked around it so that another needle could be planted in a shunt. Or was it a stent? *Stent?* Frank hummed to himself as he examined the larger tube which entered his leg. That was probably the one feeding him the drugs. RG could use it to knock him out and allow DeSoto to restrain him again.

He heard DeSoto exclaim in horror as he pulled the needle from his leg. A small jet of blood followed but the flow was stemmed by the shunty-stenty thing. God, his mind was swooning. Had to move quick.

Now with a needle in each hand, Frank looked back at DeSoto. "Take out the catheter or I'll kill myself."

"He won't," said Rational God.

Frank still had electrodes pasted to his head and upper body. He turned now to the bank of machines beside the bed and jammed the longer needle into one of the control panels. The machine stuttered and beeped but kept running.

He placed the other needle against his carotid. "Catheter, please, and don't be an asshole about it. I can't feel anything down there anyway."

To the ceiling he said, "Want to try shocking me while I'm plugged into all this shit?" He jerked the large needle back and forth within the control panel. A plume of smoke came out, but the machine was still on. He supposed RG could shut everything down and then electrocute him, thereby avoiding any risk of a fatal surge; maybe. He had to count on his belief that there was a man behind the curtain who wasn't one hundred percent sure.

"You're a computer," he slurred. "You're not as tough as you think. Man's tougher. I can do this in the face of fear."

"A lie," said the mild, robotic voice.

"The drugs help," Frank said, and nudged the tip of the IV needle against the side of his neck.

"Don't!" DeSoto cried. "Stop him, RG!"

Frank grimaced a little as he pressed the sharp point into his skin. It hurt like hell and the flesh hadn't yet yielded. He really needed to sell this. *Fuck fuck fuck.* He pushed harder. *Come on, Franky. You could sell a shit sandwich to Middle America, you can do this.*

That made him laugh, and he felt the needle push through and froze mid-giggle.

DeSoto shouted at the computer, "Do something!"

"It can't," Frank said through his teeth.

The door behind DeSoto opened and Quebra stepped in. It had worked. The machine had called upon its puppet-man to fix things.

"What're you up to there, boss?" Quebra asked. His voice was very relaxed and he strode into the room with confidence. *Just remember,* Frank told himself, *the son of a bitch killed Chia. He's not who you thought he was.*

"Go ahead and take the catheter out," Quebra told DeSoto. She moved uncertainly toward Frank, who held perfectly still with the needle in his neck. He didn't think he had pierced the artery but he was sure the visual did the trick regardless.

DeSoto reached under the sheets and worked the catheter free. A splash of urine struck Frank's belly. He kept his eyes on Quebra, who held his gaze while he waited for the doctor to finish.

"Now," Quebra told her, "out."

"Thank you, DeSoto," Rational God said.

DeSoto looked worriedly at Frank. "They're going to--"

"Now please," Rational God said.

DeSoto left the room. As the door closed behind her, there was the heavy clunk of an electronic bolt sliding into place.

"We need to talk," Quebra said. He moved to the counter beside the bed and started rummaging through drawers.

"You can't kill me," Frank said. He gave the soldier an obnoxious smile. A blend of adrenaline and sedatives was coursing through him and he felt...uneven. Like he was on a rollercoaster. Part of it was the very real sensation that, without his remaining restraints, he would have tumbled out of the bed by now. Part of it was the cocktail sloshing around in his poor addled brain. *Use it, Franky.*

Quebra tore the paper wrapper from a new scalpel. "I know I can't kill you, but I can do a lot. A lot, boss."

"I'm not your boss. The computer is."

"I serve this country. I serve innocent people, like all the people you've gotten killed."

Frank cocked his head. The needle in his neck stung just a little deeper. He said, "Maybe it was their time."

Quebra laughed. "I feel like I'm hearing the real you for the first time."

"Maybe. Maybe America's toast, Quebra. Sean. Maybe it's our time now. The Little Ones, I mean, and their mother, and me."

Quebra stepped to the side of the bed. Palming the scalpel, he busied himself removing the straps from Frank's ankles. His face was calm.

Maybe playing the fool wasn't going to work with Quebra. It might actually make it easier to ignore Frank's barbs if Frank seemed completely insane. Time to try another tack.

"How did it feel to murder Chia like a coward?" Frank asked. Anger rose in him and he wasn't so loopy all of a sudden.

Quebra pulled the straps away and stopped. He stared down at the bed, and then looked up at Frank.

"How did it feel to kill your friend?" Frank asked. "From behind, like a fucking bitch? Did you ever look into his eyes? Did he know it was you? Did he know your pathetic fucking reason?"

"You don't know my reasons," Quebra growled. "You're too selfish. Too crazy."

"You're selfish. You did it because you're scared. We're all scared, you idiot, you fuck." Frank leaned forward, still holding the needle in his neck, his other hand keeping the larger needle planted in the control panel. "You can't solve a giant monster problem by strangling people, Sean. You solve *Sean* problems that way."

In a flash the scalpel was at his throat. "I protected you," Quebra bellowed, "tried to give us a home--"

Frank sat up straight. He pulled the needle from his neck and shoved it straight into Quebra's chest. He didn't hesitate this time with the force. He went all in. So did the needle, right up to the IV line, and Quebra let out a surprised cry.

The other needle came out of the control panel and Frank jammed it into Quebra's shoulder. The scalpel dropped. Frank spun Quebra with both needles buried in his meat and held the soldier's back against his chest. "Murderer," he said.

Quebra turned back with such a deftness that it almost didn't register until it had happened, until his palm struck Frank's sternum and sent him flying backwards off the bed. Naked, Frank struck the floor and his awareness of his lame joints returned with a rippling pain.

The needles fell on the floor. Quebra came around the foot of the bed, clutching his chest where the IV had been sunk just beneath the collarbone. "You call me a murderer," he wheezed. His eyes were wide and there was no thought in them, only death. Frank scrabbled away on his backside, ripping the electrodes from his body. A machine pulled by the electrodes began to topple and Quebra caught it, throwing it back.

"Quebra," said Rational God, "put him back on the bed."

Quebra laced his fingers together and cracked his knuckles. "He's cursed. He's done."

"Quebra, do as I say."

"He won't," Frank gasped, "he's going to kill me!"

Quebra nodded and dove forward.

The shock tore through the both of them as Quebra fell atop Frank, and Frank's body arched and snapped upward with such force it actually knocked Quebra back. The solder, trying to regain his footing even as he absorbed the electricity, stumbled and shouted in anger as his momentum caused him to fall on his ass.

Despite that, he was back up in half a breath. He went for the bed and found the scalpel.

Frank crawled into the corner, limbs buzzing, and darkness clouding his head. He yelled, "S-stop him!"

Quebra either didn't hear or didn't care. He advanced on Frank.

Another jolt went through Quebra and his arms shot down to his sides. The scalpel cut into his thigh. He crumpled with a moan.

He immediately started pulling himself toward Frank. Another shock and his legs kicked like he was throwing a tantrum. Quebra stabbed at the floor with the scalpel. "N-n-n-no!"

Another shot of juice for Quebra. Frank felt his own legs tingle at that one. Quebra groaned, face pressed into the floor. He swiped blindly back and forth with the scalpel.

"How could you send him?" Frank exclaimed at the room. "What made you think you could control him?"

"Maybe I should let him kill you," RG said in a rapid tone.

"Maybe you would," Frank said. "After all, you're no computer."

Quebra stopped moving but continued moaning softly. Frank waited for the computer's reply.

After a moment he spoke again. "I know you're human."

More silence, save for Quebra. A few more seconds passed. There was a banging on the door. The cavalry was here but the computer wasn't about to let them in.

"Do you want to know how I know?" Frank said. "You want to know how I do what I do? I told you, we're going to have to have a conversation. You and me. Face to face."

The door clicked. It thundered open and two armed soldiers ran in, followed by DeSoto, whose sidearm was also drawn. She ran to the bed, saw Frank in the corner and leveled the gun with his head.

"Don't do that," Rational God ordered in the same rapid voice. Unsure of who he was talking to, all three personnel lowered their guns.

Quebra leapt to his feet with an animal roar. He raised the scalpel over Frank, tottering on his fried legs, and let out a hoarse cry of murder.

"Shoot him!" Rational God ordered.

Two quick bursts of automatic fire tore into Quebra's back. He lurched, righted himself, turned to look at the men who'd shot him. He looked back at Frank and dropped onto his knees with a crack.

"You're the monster," he whispered, and Frank watched the life run from Quebra's eyes. Quebra fell back on his face and this time stayed down.

"DeSoto," the speakers said. "Help Eckman up. I want you to take him somewhere. Now."

DeSoto got Frank into a hospital gown and a wheelchair, checking his pulse and his eyes, her face flushed with a mixture of concern, anger and utter confusion. She gently removed the stent from his thigh and wrapped gauze around the upper leg. "What is this?" she whispered to Frank.

"Now please," Rational God said.

The computer directed DeSoto where to go. She took Frank down a dark lift and into a series of concrete corridors, these lit by harsh halogen bulbs and with moisture crawling down the walls.

"Where are we?" Frank asked her.

"I don't know. You tell me."

They passed through several doors for which DeSoto had to enter numerical codes into keypads. Rational God gave her the codes, informing them both that the codes were changed on an hourly basis. No sense trying to remember them. Frank didn't believe he would need to.

They came to yet another door in another long, dank hallway and Rational God told Frank to stand. "You have the strength. DeSoto can wait here."

The computer gave Frank the last code. He entered it and stepped through the door.

As the door shut behind him, Rational God announced that the code had just been reset, along with all the others in their wake, and that DeSoto would just have to wait outside the last door. Frank stood in chilly darkness and waited for something to happen.

"Tell me how you knew," the computer said, voice echoing in space.

"I wasn't sure until now," Frank said. "You know the old trick. I didn't know, but you just told me." The pain from his joints and from the tussle with Quebra was coursing through him. His brain still felt foggy, but the meds were doing nothing for the hurt. Neither was this seeming victory over Rational God – and whether it was really a victory remained to be seen. *Didn't think it through this far. Couldn't have. All I could do was roll the dice and see.*

Silence from RG. Then, "You suspected. How?"

"Duckie. You told him sorry. You felt bad about what happened. Even if you were lying when you apologized to him – the point is, the little game you played in the War Room weighed upon you."

"You think so?"

"I don't know if it's because you have a conscience or because you were just embarrassed by your fumble. Probably the latter. Either way it was...human of you."

A speaker crackled in the blackness. When RG spoke again, it wasn't the computer voice. It was the tired, thin voice of a man.

"The world is a madhouse, Frank. This bunker is a madhouse. No way around it, or through it, except to be the one in control. The only way to be in control was to become inhuman."

"What were you before you became Rational God?"

Frank was momentarily blinded by a series of lights which clapped to life in quick 1-2-3 succession overhead. They weren't terribly bright, though, and when Frank's vision adjusted he saw why.

The man who was standing in a doorway across the room probably hadn't seen the sun – or the bunker's upper levels – in years. He looked translucent. There was no way to gauge how old he was. A few wisps of dark hair sat atop his mottled crown and the eyes behind his glasses were almost colorless. The man leaned against the doorframe with a quivering, stick-thin arm. A white lab coat was draped over his bones. When he smiled, there were no teeth, just dark gums, but it was a smile.

"I am Oz," the man said, "the great and powerful."

THIRTEEN

"I thought you'd used your..." The man tapped his own temple, indicating Frank's brain, and his grin widened. "Thought you had used your powers to discover me."

Frank shook his head slowly. He had no idea what was going to happen next. The man was frail, and appeared unarmed, but that lab coat had big, deep pockets, and the man was a lunatic besides.

"What's your name?" Frank asked.

The man seemed to think, and then dismissed Frank with a wave of his hand. "Does it matter?"

He went over to Frank, past him, and opened the door through which Frank had come.

DeSoto had her hand on her holster. She crouched behind the wheelchair, and then straightened up. "Who are you?"

The man shuffled past her with a tired sigh. Frank followed, giving DeSoto a shrug. They both went after the man, keeping a generous distance between him and themselves. The man entered a code for each door, propped it open, and continued without looking back.

He did wait for them in the lift, but said nothing. They went up in eerie silence.

Frank finally broke it, asking, "What about everything you control? You said you are this place."

"The computer is the bunker. I was the computer. I don't think I am anymore." The man made a sucking sound with his gums and adjusted the glasses on his sweat-slick face. "How can I be? You found me out. I told you, you have an interesting brain. In more ways than one."

DeSoto was putting it together and her hand was still on her gun. The man said to her, "System diagnostics are still running. It'll print off a report and tell you what to do. That will all be downstairs in my room. The doors won't be locked anymore."

He smacked his lips. "It runs itself, really."

"You gave it a voice," Frank said.

"It needed one. People needed to remember how dependent they were on the computer. Curry especially."

"You maniac," DeSoto breathed.

They got off on the next floor. The soldiers who'd shot Quebra were there, along with others. They stared at the man, but he looked right through them. They parted for him.

Frank limped along to keep pace with the man. "Who were you, really? Did you design RG?"

"Maybe." The man lifted his palms toward Heaven, let them drop. "But who? My, I haven't felt like anyone in a long time." He stopped at a pair of sliding doors and worked the keypad.

"You can't do that," someone called. "It won't open."

"I'm overriding it," the man said, and the doors retracted, revealing another pair. A few more key punches and those opened too. It was another lift. The man got in.

Everyone slowly gathered around the doorway. DeSoto was whispering frantically to the others and now everyone looked either scared or supremely pissed. Frank stood between them and the man in the lift. He asked the man, "Where to?"

"I'm going up," the man said, "and you? Chicago?"

Frank nodded. "I guess so." He no longer needed the permission of the computer – of this tiny, toothless thing. He felt numb. A part of his mind told him he should be throttling the man. The others must have felt the same, and yet there was an almost mythic quality about him. Frank supposed that would wear off once the man was gone.

The lift shuddered and the doors began to close.

The man flashed Nixon's double V-for-victory just before the doors met. Frank's fist struck steel where the smiling face would have been.

"What kind of man...!" DeSoto snarled. "How could he just walk away?"

"We'll get him," said another soldier, and several men and women departed down the corridor.

"I guess," Frank said, "now that he's not playing the computer anymore, he's free to embrace his human resolve. Or lack thereof."

#

A team went topside to arrest the man. They never found him.

Autumn and Caitlin didn't react to the news of Quebra's death. Frank supposed he hadn't either. It was a sad turn, to say the least, and memories of better times couldn't be erased. Better not to feel at all.

He told the women he was going to Chicago. He said that Underhill, who had survived Springfield and had now taken command of the bunker, was going to give him a vehicle. Given the likely presence of Little Ones along the way and the need to off-road, it was going to take longer than the few hours it might have taken in the world before. Perhaps even days.

"We're going," Autumn said.

Caitlin looked amazed at first, then happy. Happy to be going to Hell Walks. Yet, Frank couldn't blame her. They'd spent enough time in the belly of this beast. Time to try another. In that other, and in Frank, there was hope.

"We didn't even talk about this," Cate said to Autumn.

"Didn't think we needed to," said her big sister. "Figured you were going either way, so I may as well tag along."

#

"We're staying," O'Brien told Frank.

She stood in the room formerly occupied by the man who'd called himself Rational God. Banks of dusty, grime-streaked computers were being looked over by staff while others went through pages of illegible handwritten notes.

"Duckie needs to stay," O'Brien continued, "and I think I can help people here. I don't suppose you came to invite us. You came to say goodbye."

"You'll do good here," Frank said, "both of you."

"I hope you can do good out there."

#

Underhill and some troops accompanied Autumn, Caitlin, and Frank topside. They moved under cover of night to a hill not far from the cemetery, where Underhill revealed a blast door covered by sod. Through it and down a sloping concrete ramp was a small garage. There was one vehicle there. It was a camouflaged Humvee fitted with a steel cage and thick plates of armor. Frank figured it ran on whatever magic elixir had powered the tanks.

"It'll get you there," Underhill said. "It was meant for Curry but...well, I don't know what the hell you think you're going to do, but good luck. We'll keep in touch by radio."

"How do you drive it?" Frank asked. "I mean, any special gizmos or anything?"

"You have a driver," Underhill said. "She's medical too. You'll need her."

DeSoto stepped away from the other troops and waved a set of keys at Frank. "I'll show you the basics when we head out."

Supplies were loaded into the back of the Hummer. The interior was black and claustrophobic, the walls covered by various small computers and racks intended for weapons. The passengers climbed in, buckled up and sat quietly as the Hummer made its way up the ramp into a fresh rain.

Frank's joints ached. His heart was thudding at what seemed an irregular pace, but the nerves in his stomach were tingling with anticipation of the journey ahead.

And of journey's end.

The rain broke about thirty minutes into the drive. Beneath the receding gray clouds on the far horizon, Frank saw it. Rising into the sky like a monolith, storms pooled around its peak. Atlas, the Beast, God's Wrath. All names humanity had given her. The Spider. The Traveler. The Gray Woman. Who and what she was. The endgame.

He began to feel lightheaded. He knew what was coming and welcomed it. He managed to say, "Here we go," before slipping away.

#

Frank found himself standing in a great hall, one with tremendous stone pillars and vaulted ceilings, from which hung elaborate tapestries. The woven works stretched all the way to the floor, hanging between the pillars on either side of him, purple cloth embroidered with gold, crimson, and colors he could not name. The walls and ceiling were all constructed from the same pale rock – it was the type of rock he'd seen in his last vision, in the ruined foundations where he'd met the Dark Man, the Traveler. Unlike that scattering of stones, this place stood tall, strong, and proud. Yes, there was pride here, running through the walls like blood through veins, a deep and ancient pride. Frank's feet slapped on the bare floor as he walked and the sound bounced endlessly off the sides of the room. The tapestries seemed to flow about him, undulating as if in some otherworldly breeze. There were no light sources but Frank saw all of this in crisp detail.

In the center of the great hall was an oval-shaped table carved from a single piece of wood. It must have come from a tree the size of a Little One. The wood was rich and dark and patterns resembling black webbing lay in the grain.

Seated in high-backed chairs, regarding Frank in silence, were the Dark Man and the Gray Woman. He saw now that both bore the same blank, featureless face. Between them, at the head of the table, the Spider was crouched in its seat. It was the size of a human and the red markings on its disc pulsed gently.

Frank came to the foot of the table and stood. There was no seat for him. He looked from one faceless face to the next. At last he said, "You're all her."

The Dark Man and Gray Woman stood, sliding their heavy chairs back over the stone floor. They moved in tandem, each closing in on the Spider's chair, and they pulled the chair back slightly so that they could each – melt like ghosts, like phantasms, into the Spider, which itself melted into them. The dark, amorphous mass which resulted sat quivering in the chair for half a second before it began assuming a new and final form. A form that, while still human-sized, while still faceless, bore the craggy armor of Hell Walks.

She sat before Frank now in her earthly form, one of perhaps countless forms she had taken on countless worlds, each suited for that planet's environment. Suited for its prey.

Thunder clapped outside the walls. The sound ran away in rippling waves. It was followed by a roar.

"Little Ones," Frank breathed. They were coming.

Hell Walks turned her head toward the roaring. Her thick clawed hands, resting atop the table, drew into fists.

"You're afraid," Frank said, "of them."

Suddenly, he knew everything. She allowed him to know. It hit him just as another thunderclap sounded, a thunderclap answered by at least a dozen approaching roars.

The Little Ones were parasites. Perhaps she'd picked them up on the last planet she invaded before Earth. They had bored into her, refusing to be expunged even when she changed form and stepped through space-time and into the Arctic trench. She had been unable to kill them but she'd learned to control them. Her mind was older than the galaxies, as old as her senseless hatred of life and order. She had taken control of their feeble animals brains, and that had enabled her to expel them.

She'd grown weak, perilously weak, and had been forced to become dormant. Still, she was able to do her work, through the Little Ones.

They acted as her satellites and wrought the destruction that fed her spirit.

Until Frank, and a handful of others – the skeletons he'd seen in his last vision - had inadvertently begun to interfere with her telepathic control. Until that control had finally been severed. Now the parasites were coming back to their host.

Did that mean, Frank wondered, that Tri-Jaw and the others would have passed the bunker without incident, but for the aggression of Frank and the soldiers?

Couldn't have known. You only know now. Use this thing that you now know.

He placed his hands on the table. Hell Walks sat rigid, facing him.

"Get up, then," he told her. "Fight them off. Or can you?"

The thing remained seated in its chair. Frank smiled bitterly. "You're still too weak. Maybe even weaker than before. Spend too much time in hibernation? They're going to tear you apart, aren't they, and then what? I guess it won't matter for you. You'll be dead and gone."

More roaring. The walls quaked. Hell Walks flinched, clutched at herself. Cracks appeared in her rocky skin and widened, deepened, became the foul holes that meant infection. The holes filled her and what was left began to crumble.

"You're going to die," Frank hissed. The knowledge of it must have been mind-shattering to the nearly ageless beast. This *was* the end. Frank couldn't hold back his glee.

The rotting and collapsing form of Hell Walks reached out to him. What did it want?

Of course. It wanted Frank to control the Little Ones, as he had with Tri-Jaw, and send them away.

"No," he said, "even if we have to deal with them after you're gone – no."

The thing's fist fell onto the table and exploded into particles of dust.

Thunder rocked the great hall. Tapestries fell to the floor in brilliant showers of color. The stones began to fracture and slide out of place. The ancient fortifications yielded to the pounding of the Little Ones' fists.

#

Frank awoke to another thunderclap. He was lying prone in the front passenger seat of the Hummer, DeSoto perched over him. She was holding an oxygen mask on his face and checking the pulse in his wrist.

"Frank," Autumn exclaimed, leaning into view from the back. "You're back."

"It's over," he said weakly, smiling under the mask. "For her. It's done. It's already done."

"Tell us what you mean," DeSoto insisted.

"The Little Ones are going to kill her. She can't stop them. It's done."

"You're sure?"

"Positive."

DeSoto looked at Autumn. "We can go back."

Frank started and shook his head. "No, I still need to go. I need to deal with the Little Ones."

Rain was washing over the vehicle in what seemed like tidal waves. There was no visibility; the world was black outside, save for the occasional flare of lightning, which did nothing to give detail to the terrain beyond the glass. Frank sat up and stared into that murky void. "I have to go there," he said again.

The Hummer shook, but there was no sound of thunder. DeSoto dropped the mask and moved to the driver's-side window. "Can't see a goddamned thing," she muttered.

The vehicle shook again. Footfalls.

"I can't see it!" DeSoto cried.

"Just wait," Frank said, "stay parked. It'll pass us by."

"It sounds close," said Caitlin from the back. "What if it steps on us?"

The Hummer shook again, this time violently. Frank reached for his door handle. God, he hurt all over. His breathing was shallow and he didn't want to go out into the driving rain. He grasped the handle and drew as much air as he could into his sagging lungs.

"What are you doing?" cried DeSoto.

"Just stay," he said and opened the door. A gust of wind ripped it from his hand and he fell into sheets of water.

Frank stood and fumbled blindly for the door. He couldn't even keep his eyes open in the rain. Seizing the door and forcing it shut, Frank felt his way around the front of the Hummer and crouched in hopes of finding cover. He shielded his eyes and was able to make out that they were parked on the shoulder of a roadway. When the next flash of lightning came, he looked out onto the road and saw a giant silhouette standing there.

The rain changed direction, washing over Frank's back. He was completely soaked through and felt he'd never be dry again. Standing on shaky legs, he stepped onto the asphalt and walked toward the huge black shape.

Lightning. He saw Tri-Jaw's face far overhead. There was no mistaking it. There was no mistaking that it saw him too.

They stood together in the road, neither moving, torrents of water pounding the surface around them. The Little One shifted and lowered itself. Its head came down to rest just a few feet above Frank's. Water ran off its three mandibles as if they were spouts, splashing Frank's eyes. He stepped back and tried to clear his vision.

He saw the monster's crimson stare in the next flash. Frank stopped backpedaling and waited. He waited and thought.

Can you hear me, big one? Do you understand?

Surely, it knew he had controlled it, as Hell Walks had. That he had used it to kill two of its brethren. He couldn't hope to explain the nuances to this beast.

Maybe, though, he underestimated it. After all, he stood before it now, and it hadn't yet taken him between its scissoring jaws.

Tri-Jaw seemed to consider Frank, to ponder him. Some minutes passed. Any fear Frank had felt was abated by this point. He just waited patiently for the creature's final judgment.

At last, it rose into the rain. It lifted its foot and at that moment Frank did feel a pang of terror.

It didn't step on him. It stepped over him and continued on its way, into the storm.

He climbed back into the Humvee and peeled his shirt from his back, throwing the sopping garment to the floor. "There any clothes in the back?" he asked, coughing.

The others just stared at him. "What did you say to it?" Autumn asked.

"Nothing," Frank said, running his hands through his matted hair. He was dripping everywhere. Caitlin rummaged and found a blanket to give him. He wrapped it around his head and torso and sat huddled in his seat.

"I didn't say anything. It knew."

FOURTEEN

They stuck to the roads after that. Little Ones passed in the distance, paying no mind to the vehicle. Up ahead, the vague, hulking silhouette of the mountain called Hell Walks began to take on detail. The angles, cliffs and crags of the beast's two legs, planted in Chicago's foundations as the creature squatted down. There were splashes of color which seemed to indicate plant life growing there.

"We're maybe a couple hours away from the base of it," DeSoto said. Her hands were tight on the wheel. "How close do you need to get?"

"I think all the way," Frank said. "I can hoof it on my own. Drop me off and get out of the city."

"No way," said Autumn.

"Drop us all off," Caitlin told DeSoto.

"You realize how unstable the area is?" DeSoto said. "What buildings still stand would probably crumble if you looked at them the wrong way, and the streets are just gone. Sinkholes, craters everywhere, and God knows about the infection."

"The infection's from the Little Ones," said Frank, though he couldn't be sure that Hell Walks wasn't bathed in alien bacteria. If he did what he intended to do, he was probably going to end up the same way.

"No one's dared come this close to Hell Walks in years," DeSoto said. "It could be even worse than I've described. I know you're going to do what you're going to do. This is just a heads up."

"So drop us off at the edge of the city."

DeSoto sighed. She shook her head resolutely. "That's not my mission."

"What is your mission?" Frank asked. There hadn't been a squawk from the radio since they'd left the bunker. Somehow he suspected Major Underhill didn't place a tremendous amount of faith in their little band of heroes.

"My mission is to take you where you want to go," DeSoto said.

"And why you?" said Frank.

"I'm your doctor."

"Come on."

"I am, and I'm a doctor first. Not a soldier, not a driver. All right?"

DeSoto stared hard at the road ahead. Frank didn't press her further.

As Chicago drew near they began to see Little Ones everywhere: standing inert among urban ruins, each staring upward. Again, they ignored the Hummer. Frank wasn't sure what they were waiting for but he hoped they were willing to wait a bit longer.

They were right on the outskirts of Chicago proper when they saw what looked like a giant black dome. It stood well above the tallest buildings in its vicinity, a blistered, curved structure that looked like it had fallen from the sky and cleaved most of the surrounding structures in half.

"It's a claw," Autumn breathed.

As they drew nearer it only grew in size, towering far overhead. It was just one of the thing's fingernails – beyond and above it loomed the living mountain. Rain began to fall.

The Humvee veered away from a huge crater in the street and ran up onto the sidewalk, thudding over broken slabs of concrete. They were going to pass right by the base of the obsidian dome. As they did, Frank, Autumn and Caitlin each pressed their faces to the glass and swore.

There were tents at the base – some large circus tents, some pup tents. Canvas and vinyl flapped in a strong wind. The remnants of camps sat atop piles of rubble. Dozens of tents, a little city formed around the claw. Garbage littered the area, and bodies everywhere. They needn't drive any closer to see that the corpses were all riddled with infection.

"That answers that question," Frank muttered.

"Why would they be here?" Caitlin wondered.

"Maybe they thought it was safer here," Autumn said. "Away from the Little Ones."

"Maybe they worshipped her," said DeSoto.

Frank shrugged. "Why not?"

DeSoto slowed to a stop and grabbed the radio mic from the dashboard. "Scout to Anthill. Come in, over."

She tried a few more times, listened to the static, and hung the mic up. "HW's probably interfering with the radio. Shit. Fuck me." She turned and addressed everyone. "If we're going out there we need to have a serious talk."

"About what?" Autumn asked.

"Dying."

DeSoto eyed the ghost camp. "It looks bad. Real bad. I don't know if there's anything I can do for you if you go out there."

"You said 'we' a second ago."

"I'm going with you, all right?" DeSoto punched the steering wheel. "I'm not turning tail and leaving you here, but goddammit, I'm telling you my skills are useless against that infection! So you're going to die! Get it?"

The others were quiet. DeSoto just stared at the bodies outside.

Frank said, "We all knew there was a risk. We were willing to take it." He looked to Autumn for affirmation.

She nodded. She hugged her sister, who nodded too.

Frank felt a rush of emotion and turned away. So many people had died on the path to this moment. These people here were willing to die for *him*. He had to be sure of himself, of what he was going to do. He had to be crazy certain, just as certain as the families who'd once populated that camp. He studied the corpses, saw the smaller ones, some lying in the arms of what had presumably been parents. He had to be as crazy certain as they were. Except he had to be right.

A hand enclosed his. It was Autumn. She told him, "Don't start doubting yourself now. Don't you dare."

He thought about Nan. Chia. *Don't do it for the dead, son*, a voice in his head said. It sounded just like Chia, and it was something he would have said. *Don't do it for the dead. Do it for the living.*

"This is going to work," he said aloud at long last. He cleared his throat, flexing his aching hands. "But DeSoto's right."

"So..." Autumn squeezed his hand.

"So," he asked the three women, "are you ready?"

There was a pause, albeit brief, before Autumn once again nodded. Caitlin followed, more emphatically.

DeSoto rested her hands on the wheel. She had that thousand-yard stare soldiers talked about. Maybe that was the place where she needed to be mentally. For now, anyway. She'd said it herself, she was a healer first and there was no healing left to be done, at least not on a personal level. There was a world to be saved, however.

"As long as it does good," DeSoto said, "I'm ready."

Frank opened his door and got out.

#

With what they could carry on their backs, they navigated the uneven terrain toward the right foot of Hell Walks.

The foot itself was at least a mile high. It was its own formidable behemoth. Before they could give any thought to the rest of the beast, they had to scale this monster.

Frank sensed that it was necessary to be right here, skin to skin. He had hijacked the psychic transmissions of Hell Walks in order to connect with – and control – Little Ones. He believed he needed to be here with her when they attacked. It was essential to his plan for the aftermath. The aftermath was the part he needed to be crazy certain about, the part that was a big, foggy question mark.

After all, one couldn't expect that the Little Ones would just grow new wings and fly away once Hell Walks was vanquished. There was absolutely no way to predict what they'd do, and, regardless, they carried the deadly infection which even now was probably crawling on Frank's skin.

If not now, pretty damned soon. He approached one of the great claws on HW's foot and studied its ridged surface. It would be a tough hike, but it looked as if things would be easier once they made it to the toe itself. From there, an ascent less steep until they reached the top of the foot. Frank's misty view of the foot, high up past the claw, suggested the presence of tall foliage. He wondered if there was any animal life. Probably not given the infection.

Rain drummed the claw. That was going to make it even tougher. However, it looked as if it was always raining here. No sense putting this off.

The quartet pulled on thick rubber gloves and spiked boots taken from the Hummer. The equipment hadn't been meant to be used for Hell Walks but it would work perfectly. *To the high ground.*

#

It wasn't that the toe claw's surface was too slick, nor the grade too steep, but Frank's knees just couldn't take it. Soon his lungs were being taxed as well and he had to take several breaks to sit and catch his breath.

DeSoto cupped a hand on his back, underneath his shirt, and had him take several deep breaths, at least as deep as he could manage. She had him cough. Once he started it was almost impossible to stop.

Frank wiped the spittle from his lips and saw that it was red. He hadn't coughed up blood since the burning of the town. That may very well have had to do with all the smoke, but there was no excuse here.

"Can we go on?" DeSoto asked him.

"We have to." Frank fought to stand, accepted her and Caitlin's hands and was hoisted to his feet. He wavered on the curve of the claw. They steadied him, and then the group continued.

The sky was dark when they reached the toe. For the first time Frank touched the armored scales of Hell Walks. He stripped the glove from his hand and grabbed hold of the rocky material. He half-expected her to stir, to raise her gargantuan foot and send them flying toward the clouds, but there was nothing from the beast. Frank climbed onto the toe and studied the foot.

There was indeed high foliage – *trees* – growing from deep trenches in the flesh. Patches of thick moss were everywhere. It would be an easier walk from here on.

Caitlin put a hand to her ear. "Do you hear that?"

"What is it?" Autumn asked.

"Sounds like birds."

A gentle rain fell on the trees up ahead. Their leaves were too dense to be certain, but Frank imagined there was life nesting there. So then, the infection didn't affect animals? He had never seen a dead bird or deer afflicted with the sores. So the infection was just another part of Hell Walks's hateful campaign against sentience, and it was probably inside them all now. Frank removed both gloves and examined his hands.

"You look clean," DeSoto told him. "Sores won't appear yet anyway."

They walked down into one of the sloping trenches in HW's armor. There, at the base of a tree rooted in moss, they sat out of the rain.

"When are the Little Ones going to do something?" Caitlin asked Frank.

"I don't know," Frank said, "but they will."

"What are you going to do then?"

"Something like what I did at the bunker."

"How?"

Frank smiled a little. She probably couldn't see it in the shadows. "Hard to explain." Harder since he wasn't entirely sure how he'd done it at all.

"Do you think it was wrong to shoot McAvoy?" Caitlin said.

She'd thrown it out to the entire group and looked from one to the other. "Of course not," Autumn said, "you didn't have a choice. It wasn't up to you."

"Duckie didn't do it when it was his turn. I could have stopped."

"It's easy to say that now," DeSoto said. "It wasn't your fault. It was that man – whoever he was – Rational God."

"You were just as much a victim as McAvoy," Frank said.

"I'm not dead," Caitlin muttered.

Not yet, Frank thought.

She looked at him. "You talk about the value of all life. Remember Mills? Dodger too, I'll bet, and Quebra. McAvoy wasn't near as bad as some of them. He may not have been bad at all. I keep telling myself he was – that he was a bad person, or not a person at all, but it's bullshit."

"I..." Frank fell silent. Maybe there wasn't a lesson to be learned here, a moral truth buried under all the guilt and confusion. Maybe there was only more guilt and confusion.

"No one blames you," Autumn said.

"I do," said Caitlin, "that's the point. How can I not? There isn't an answer, is there?"

Frank was still struggling. He turned different words, platitudes, over and over in his head.

"Some things are just fucked up," Frank said at last.

Caitlin nodded.

#

The toe was a broad plain lined with those trenches, and there were birds. When the sun returned, painting the cloudy sky dull orange, several lit out of the tree above the group's heads. Frank heard others taking flight from other trees. His heart began to pound.

They're fleeing. Something's going to happen soon. Will it be them or her?

DeSoto was awake. They roused Autumn and Caitlin and the group resumed the trek.

It was dry for a bit, but not long. The beast's knee was a couple miles overhead. It was shrouded now in low clouds and rain began to fall from them.

The group themselves were now about a mile above the streets of Chicago. In the distance Frank could see the tops of skyscrapers. They looked so meaningless from up here. He tried to picture what it had looked like for Hell Walks when she'd stepped out of the lake and dashed the city to pieces. Her final act before going into the long sleep.

He turned and looked toward the city limits. The Little Ones were barely visible on the ground, just three hundred feet tall. What were they waiting for? Suddenly, he feared that she had gotten hold of their minds again, and he had stopped them in their tracks. She would command them to return to the hunt, perhaps after killing Frank and his party.

DeSoto saw what he was looking at and she pulled a pair of binoculars from the pack on her back. "I see more coming," she said. "Jesus, there are so many out there. It's like they're all making their way back to her. Maybe that's why none of them have done anything yet."

"If they're waiting on their brothers from the other continents, we're going to be here a long goddamned time," said Frank.

DeSoto lowered the binoculars. "We won't last that long, Frank."

He sat on a knobby outcropping of armor. "Maybe there's a way to get things started now. Like right now." The birds certainly seemed to think things were starting, but Frank didn't know what and DeSoto might be right about the Little Ones sitting idle. It could be Hell Walks who was about to act, not them. He had to get out in front of the situation and take control. It was time.

Frank scratched the thin beard that had taken root since leaving the bunker. He thought, and then said aloud, "Are you all ready?"

"We told you we were," Autumn said.

He frowned. "I just have to figure out how to do it...might need to trigger one of my episodes."

"How do you do that?" asked DeSoto.

"Stress."

"You're not stressed enough already?"

He eyed her pack. "What do you have in there, medical-wise? You have adrenaline or anything like that?"

"Maybe," DeSoto said cautiously.

"Frank, we don't want your heart to explode," Autumn said.

Won't matter if I'm not in my body, Frank thought. He asked DeSoto to look through the pack. To Autumn he said, "Trust me. Moment of truth now."

Autumn began pacing back and forth through moss. Caitlin came and sat next to Frank.

DeSoto pulled a pair of plastic-wrapped items from her pack. She hunched over them and read the writing on the packaging.

"What've you got?" Frank asked.

"Epinephrine." DeSoto closed her fist around the items, presumably syringes or EpiPens, and told Frank: "If you react too strongly to this, it could kill you. Pulmonary edema or even cardiac arrest given your syndrome." She sat down. "I won't be able to do anything. I only have so much equipment and none of it's any good for an emergency like that."

"We have to chance it," Frank said.

"You need to tell me exactly what you're experiencing. Every symptom. This could cause a panic attack, which might resemble one of your episodes but probably isn't related. So I need to know exactly what you're feeling. Got it?"

Frank agreed and DeSoto opened one of the items. It was an EpiPen all right. She said, "We'll try just one. I have another here, and maybe more in my bag."

"Make sure," Frank said. "We might need them."

DeSoto's face said that she didn't agree, but she rooted through the pack anyway and found two more pens.

"Be ready to catch him," DeSoto told Caitlin. Autumn joined her and they placed their hands on Frank's shoulders.

DeSoto said, "Here we go," and pressed the pen into Frank's thigh. It struck through his pants and into his skin. Frank sat quiet and waited.

It was less than a minute before he was sweating. "Headache," he muttered. "Not like the other episodes. Not yet."

DeSoto pressed a hand to his chest and took his wrist in the other. "Your heart's already reacting. Can you feel it?"

"Palpitations," Frank said. His voice sounded far weaker than he'd expected. He suddenly leaned forward. Autumn and Caitlin grabbed him.

This isn't working. This was bad. I've blown everything.

"You're experiencing tachycardia," DeSoto said, clearly alarmed. "Is this it? Is it happening?"

"I don't know," Frank gasped. He didn't want to say no. He couldn't bear to see the panic in their faces, especially if it was going to be the last thing he saw. Sweat poured down his face. His head was pounding. His hands shook. Fear surged through him and he tried to stand. The women pulled him back before he could fall on his face.

"I'm sorry," he gasped again, and when he tried to inhale he couldn't. Everything was closing in.

"No," DeSoto cried, "hold on!"

"Frank," Autumn whispered in his ear. "Listen to me. You stay, Frank. This is going to work, Frank!"

His legs buckled and he sagged against her. He was feeling it. He was feeling it!

Frank couldn't speak. He could only give DeSoto a feeble thumbs-up. He hoped she knew what that meant because a second later, he was gone.

#

The environment in which he found himself wasn't unlike that from the previous vision: another great hall, or at least a former one. It was draped in shadows, not tapestries, and the walls were of cracked and charred wood. A spiral staircase led up to a balcony which ran around the entire hall. Frank saw the beast up there. It was crouched at a dark window, staring outside. It was nothing like Frank had ever seen before.

The stairs were in the center of the room, and at the top was a walkway which led to the wall-hugging balcony. As he quietly climbed them, he got a better look at it. The creature's back was to him, but he could see that it possessed a vaguely lupine form. It was the size of a Volkswagen Beetle but its lines weren't smooth. Everything about it was angry and ugly. The wolf-like body was covered in thick, spiny hairs which stood erect on its back. Again, as in the hall before, there was no apparent light source, but Frank was nonetheless able to perceive these details.

The beast breathed. Its entire body swelled with the effort, and the hairs stood apart, revealing the pink flesh beneath. The flesh cracked and bled as it was stretched. The beast exhaled. It shivered. Frank saw the white spurs of bone which fanned about its neck like a lion's mane.

He froze at the top of the stairs. There was such fear in the air that it permeated him and he felt as if he wouldn't be able to move again. It was her fear.

He sensed her power as well, the tremendous effort being used to keep the Little Ones at bay. In her present state, Frank having crippled her telepathic hold on them, she could do no more than keep them frozen at the edge of the city. Even that hold was tenuous.

It wouldn't take much to break her concentration and set the Little Ones free. Once that happened...

She'll die. You'll die. Autumn and Caitlin and DeSoto, they'll die.

They said they were ready.

Are you *ready, Franky?*

The beast cocked its head. It did not turn, but it stopped breathing. It was listening to the corridors of its vast and ancient mind. It had heard something, perhaps a foot sliding through dust on a stair. Perhaps a weary gasp. Maybe it had heard his fear itself.

Frank grabbed the railing of the walkway. Hell Walks stood at the other end, her back to him, her massive body stock-still.

This was her first form. This was what she had been in the first life, the first world. She allowed him to know this now, and this meant she knew he was here.

This had been the first form. She had rutted in blood and bayed in orgiastic glee as the sentient life of the darkworld fell before her. It had amused the gods greatly, at least until the darkworld was a silent tomb. Then they'd become bored with the beast and left it there. Left it to scream and suffer for eternity.

They had created her and dropped her into their cosmic sandbox. Then they'd left. She had spent eons alone on the darkworld and grown mad. Mad enough that she came to believe there was no world or form that could contain her. Mad enough that she was able to make this delusion a reality.

She'd torn her body asunder through sheer will and rage, drawing herself into a single point and shearing space-time. She had done this many times since. It was how she fled from one world to another, how she traversed the dimensions in order to find her next darkworld and its pitiful victims. Did the gods see her now? Did they laugh, or did they tremble? With each world, a new form, and a new Hell.

Had the gods sent the Little Ones to bring her down? These brainless parasites? Or were they the native to one of the planets she had slaughtered? She couldn't remember. Her previous conquests were distorted. The space-time jumps had wrought havoc on her psyche. She only recalled bits and pieces. She remembered being the Spider and melting cities blanketed in acidic webbing. She remembered being the Dark Man and sending black ships to the bottom of a silver sea as she rained blows upon them. She remembered being the Gray Woman and drowning civilizations in sentient flora that fed on blood.

By contrast, she remembered Frank quite clearly. He and many of his fellow humans had proven particularly troublesome. They were much like the Little Ones in that sense – parasites, except they bored into the mind rather than the flesh. The mind was all she really had. She longed to be free of any physical form. To be able to haunt the universe as a ghost – that was godhood!

Back to Frank. To the end of Frank, and of Earth.

The beast turned and stepped onto the walkway. It faced Frank and he saw that its eyes were glowing cinders. Its jaw unhinged, saliva splashing on the floor, and it let out a grotesque, rumbling cry that paralyzed Frank's entire being.

It charged.

FIFTEEN

AUTUMN

"Look!" DeSoto pointed into the distance. The Little Ones, those tiny creatures far beneath the foot of Hell Walks, were moving. They were *running.*

"They're coming!" Caitlin grabbed onto her sister. Autumn held her back and watched as the Little Ones tore through what was left of Chicago. Frank had done it. Whatever he'd done, he'd done it.

He was still out, though. Frank lay on his back, staring upward. Rain was falling into his eyes and Autumn knelt with Cate to shelter him.

"Let's get him into one of the trenches!" DeSoto said. It was their best shot at keeping him safe – not mention themselves – and Autumn agreed. She and Cate took his legs while DeSoto grabbed him under the arms. They moved into a nearby trench and huddled there.

DeSoto drew her sidearm, released the magazine and looked it over. She slapped it back into the gun.

"That's not going to do anything against them," Caitlin said.

"It's not for them," Autumn said, understanding. She hugged Cate.

DeSoto holstered the gun. "Only if we absolutely need it. Not until then."

"Hell Walks is going to die," Cate said. "We're at her feet. We won't need it."

FRANK

He thundered down the stairwell. He was halfway to the bottom when the entire thing was blown off its supports by the crashing weight of the beast.

Metal and wood smashed down around Frank as he struck the floor like a rag doll. He was momentarily stunned; even though this wasn't a real physical event, even though he was just an avatar in her mind, the terror within him was threatening to bring him down. He tried to summon courage but came up empty. All he had was desperation. It would have to do.

Then the forelegs of the beast came down on either side of his head, razor-edged hooves plowing into the floorboards.

Frank rolled over and tried to scoot out from beneath it, but it – Jesus, it had six legs! The extra pair unfolded from its belly. They had clawed appendages and the claws sank between Frank's ribs.

The beast stared down at him, its lips quivering, fangs glistening.

AUTUMN

In spite of the dozens of Little Ones rushing them, they didn't feel a single tremor until the monsters began climbing onto Hell Walks.

Shadows fell across the trench and Autumn saw flashes of limbs – giant pale arms and legs, the Little Ones throwing themselves at the legs of the living mountain. Everything began trembling. Autumn's teeth rattled and she clutched her head.

Cate's arms wrapped around her. "It's okay," Cate kept saying, even as her voice broke with sobs.

Roars sounded from high overhead. Then came several loud, sharp impacts against the foot of Hell Walks. Pieces of its armor plating were falling away – being torn away. The Little Ones were boring back in.

FRANK

He was pinned beneath the beast. It glared at him with its burning eyes. Her burning eyes, he reminded himself. Why was Hell Walks a she? Why had the gods made it so?

The beast opened her mouth. Jaws inside jaws inside jaws spread wide and drool spattered Frank's face.

The beast held still, mouth agape, as if waiting for Frank to scream. Then she turned from him and stared up at the windows along the balcony.

The walls shuddered. They both heard the roaring from outside.

"They're here," Frank said through choked gasps. "No dream this time."

The beast let out an echoing falsetto wail. The wail descended into another rumbling howl and she returned her attention to Frank. All was lost for her. He was all she had left, and he realized that this was how he was going to die – not from infection, not from his syndrome, but from this devil tearing his mind apart.

"What are you waiting for?" he snarled. "There's nothing left for you! You fucking--"

Her jaws clamped down on his head with a crunch.

AUTUMN

Frank's body was shaking and it wasn't from the tremors around them. He jolted from side to side and a pink stream began running from his lips.

DeSoto fell upon him and pried his mouth open. She swore and rolled him onto his side. Still staring blankly into space, Frank loosed a geyser of blood-tinged fluid from his throat. DeSoto rolled him back towards her and shined a penlight into his airway. The trench rocked and she fell over him. Righting herself, she trained the light on the back of his throat again.

"Christ!" She laced her hands over his chest and began pumping. Frank shook violently. More fluid came up.

Autumn stared in horror at the scene. Something inside told her that this was what was bound to happen, but that they'd already won. She didn't know that. She needed to hear it from Frank. Then and only then could it be over. They were all supposed to die together. They had made that pact.

Cate was pressed hard against her. Autumn let Frank go.

She held her little sister tight and listened to the rumbling all around them, around them and in her brain and teeth and bones.

FRANK

The beast engulfed his head, his mind. The pressure was unbearable, and the only thing worse was the sensation of something probing Frank at his psychic core. He could not hear his own screams. But her attention was focused on him, solely upon him, and that was all that mattered. The Little Ones could do what they'd come to do. He held onto that knowledge even as other thoughts fractured and disintegrated.

AUTUMN

Pieces of Hell Walks crashed against the foot and spiraled off into the sky. The tiniest bits rained into the trench like hailstones. There was nothing but noise, fear, and Autumn could only cradle Cate's head and pray that this would at some moment, someday, end.

She saw DeSoto take her jacket off and put it over Frank's head. DeSoto knelt beside him and shielded her head with her arms.

It sounded as if the air itself were quaking, and roaring, as if the whole of existence was lost in some mindless rage. Autumn shut her eyes. Her shoulders banged against the sides of the trench. She felt hot fragments of Hell Walks falling through her hair. Even more roaring now, lusty and triumphant. Still the world continued to fracture. It was all hate and death, even behind Autumn's eyelids, even in the dark. It was all over.

Then it wasn't.

There was a series of final tremors as the Little Ones descended to the city floor. Autumn chanced a look and saw them crossing the foot and heading away from her. Several stepped over the trench and one, who was missing a mandible, glanced down for a few seconds before continuing on its way.

The impacts of distant footfalls sounded for a while after. Autumn heard buildings falling but it seemed like little more than the pattering of rain after what she'd just experienced. How long had that cacophony lasted – mere minutes, or hours? How wasn't she deaf?

She and Cate stood, braced against one another, and waited for DeSoto to sit up. Her eyes met theirs, and all three of them looked down at Frank's covered face.

A cough caused the material over his mouth to jump. DeSoto yanked the jacket away with a cry. Frank looked at them through bleary eyes, his lips and beard stained red. He let out a long breath.

"Done," he said. "It's done."

#

When he was able to walk, they left the trench and observed the aftermath.

It wasn't easy to tell, given the continued presence of low clouds, just how much of Hell Walks was left. It didn't look like the Little Ones had left much above the waist.

All of it – all of her – had fallen to the ground, decimating the earth for miles around. Smoking craters were visible in every direction, and around them, lay the Little Ones.

"They're dead," Cate said.

Frank nodded. "They did what they were here to do." He couldn't say for sure whether the Little Ones had been the work of the gods, trying to stop the monster they'd created, or just dumb luck. Didn't matter now. Frank didn't think any of those gods would be looking in on Earth again.

The climbed down the toe to the ground. They were surrounded by a giant graveyard of alien beasts. There wasn't a single remnant of the city left standing. Smoke boiled from the craters where slabs of hot armor had streaked into the earth. It was the most beautiful scene Frank had ever witnessed.

"I didn't think we'd survive her death," he said. "I never thought we'd be able to look upon this."

He smiled at the others. The smile faded a little when he saw the sore on Autumn's cheek, but he held his composure. She smiled back.

#

There was rain after that, but it was light. They set up camp at the feet of Hell Walks and ate the MREs from their packs.

"Why didn't the infection die too?" DeSoto muttered. They'd all been thinking it, Frank was sure, but no one had wanted to ask. It seemed pointless, and yet, it was the only thing that had been on Frank's mind in the day and a half since they'd won.

Of course, there was no answer. Some things were just fucked up.

"We have this gun," DeSoto said, barely above a breath.

"No." Autumn shook her head. "Not for me."

Cate shook her head in agreement. Frank shrugged.

#

DeSoto passed first, during the second night of their encampment. Frank realized their proximity to Hell Walks and the Little Ones must be somehow accelerating the infection's progress. Either that or DeSoto had simply run out of fight, the illness besieging her battle-weary body while her will to live faded. He didn't know. He wasn't a doctor and the doctor was dead. They buried her in a nearby crater.

The clouds cleared that following day. Now they were able to look upon what was left of Hell Walks. It was only the legs, two separate monoliths now, both etched with wounds. It was no monument to the beast, more a mockery.

That the apocalypse was over almost seemed unreal. Frank thought maybe it would be good for him to die. He didn't know if he could handle another world-shift, and what would come in the wake of Hell

Walks? How would humanity rebuild? Would they do better this time? Questions too big for his tired brain.

He decided that the infection must indeed be more aggressive here at the heart of the giant graveyard. He decided that when Autumn took a sudden downward turn, pain and nausea were washing over her in hot waves, the sores on her face and neck threatening to break. She still had fight in her, no question. It was the infection overwhelming her body.

Caitlin held her while Frank built a fire for the night from scraps of debris. "Frank," Cate said, and he turned with a sinking horror, thinking Autumn had just died.

She was still breathing. Cate was staring at Frank with a confused expression.

"You aren't sick," she said.

"What?" He held out his hands and pulled up his sleeves. "Of course I am. I—"

No sores there. He pulled off his shirt and looked himself over.

"Your face is clear too," Cate said, "and your back. See?"

He had assumed that he was infected. Hadn't even bothered looking for sores. He'd simply opened his arms and welcomed death in, but it was true. No sores at all.

"I could still be infected," he said. "It's just – I don't know what it is, but..."

Cate began weeping. Frank looked down and this time Autumn was dead. Just like that. Mid-sentence, Frank carrying on about his own bullshit. She was one he'd wanted to say goodbye to. It wasn't fair.

If he was clean, if he was going to live through this, and see Cate die too – that was beyond unfair. That was cruelty on a cosmic scale. Frank collapsed and sobbed next to Autumn's body. He held and kissed her hand and prayed for the sickness to take him.

#

Another two days passed, and it did not take him. It ignored him, while Cate rolled into a shivering ball and cried. Frank had to bury Autumn by himself.

He lay next to her and said nothing, but he was staring so hard at her that she finally spat, "What?"

"You must hate me," he said, and tears filled his eyes.

He felt her fingers brush against his. "Why?" she asked, her tone soft now.

"Because I'm alive. Because I brought you both here."

"We chose it," she said.

His throat was thick and hard and he pinched his eyes shut. He finally croaked, "I wanted to die here. I wanted to be finished."

He wiped his eyes and looked into hers. "Heroes aren't supposed to walk away while everybody else—" He was crying now and stammered through it in a voice that was barely intelligible. "While everybody else fucking dies. I was supposed to die."

Cate didn't say anything. She let him cry until he was completely drained. Frank pressed his head into the hard ground and drew ragged breaths.

"I'm glad I'm dying," Cate said.

She waited for him to look up, and then went on. "I wouldn't go on without her. I know she'd want me to. I know she thought I was stronger than that. I worked to make her think that...and I could do it...but I don't want to."

She said to Frank, "You must hate me because I'm dying."

"I don't hate you."

"I don't hate you either, and I think you can walk away from this and keep going. I think you will. Even if you hate it. I think that's a hero."

They told stories for a while after that. He told stories about Nan and she told stories about her sister. After a bit she began having trouble remembering. Then she was gone.

#

Frank buried her next to Autumn at nightfall. He sat up to await the sun. In that time he had a long talk with himself. He asked a lot of questions, listened to the silence that followed, and then put the questions away somewhere deep inside.

He broke out in a cold sweat and felt as if another episode was coming on, but it didn't. It wouldn't happen again, he thought. Hell Walks was dead. The last he remembered of her was her jaws locked around his head, her hot breath mingling with his cries. Then he'd awakened in the trench and she was nothing but a pair of broken legs.

When dawn broke, it blazed across a clear sky and enfolded Frank in warmth. He rose to his feet. He stared into the rising sun, his eyes like glowing cinders—

The End